Travellers in the Mediterranean: Linguistic and Cultural Encounters

Emanuela Ettorre, Giuliano Mion (eds.)

Travellers in the Mediterranean: Linguistic and Cultural Encounters

Moving texts/Testi mobili
Vol. 11

PETER LANG

Bruxelles - Berlin - Chennai - Lausanne - New York - Oxford

Library of Congress Cataloging- in- Publication Data
A CIP catalog record for this book has been applied for at the
Library of Congress.

**Bibliographic Information published by the
Deutsche Nationalbibliothek**
The Deutsche Nationalbibliothek lists this publication in the Deutsche
Nationalbibliografie; detailed bibliographic data is available online at
http:// dnb.d- nb.de.

This volume is published with the contribution of the Dipartimento di Lingue,
Letterature e Culture Moderne, Università "G. d'Annunzio" Chieti-Pescara.

ISSN 2033-1274 • ISBN 978-2-8076-1234-1 (Print)
E-ISBN 978-2-8076-1235-8 (ePDF) • E-ISBN 978-2-8076-1236-5 (ePUB)
E-ISBN 978-2-8076-1237-2 (MOBI) • DOI 10.3726/b22216

D/2024/5678/44

© 2024 Peter Lang Group AG, Lausanne
Published by Peter Lang Éditions Scientifiques Internationales - P.I.E.,
Bruxelles, Belgium

info@peterlang.comhttp://www.peterlang.com

Contents

Preface

Charting the Mediterranean: Journeys, Narratives, Cultural Dialogues

Emanuela ETTORRE and Giuliano MION

The multifaceted experience of travel has always fascinated the human imagination. Whether through physical journeys, or through imaginary and literary adventures, the essence of travel inevitably transcends mere physical movement and encompasses a wide range of experiences and intentions. Some travel out of necessity, whether as exiles or for survival, others for exploration or tourism, and still others for trade or religious pilgrimage, or in pursuit of an ideal. The motivations behind travel are as varied and complex as the destinations themselves, often shifting and evolving during the voyage, as the traveller encounters the "other", engages with the unfamiliar, and as a person grows and matures. What begins as a journey for exploration can therefore become a quest for self-discovery, since the foreign lands do not simply represent immersion in unknown landscapes and territories, but also the possibility of uncovering new aspects of one's own identity. Journeys unfold at different paces: some are slow and protracted, thus allowing deep reflections and the sedimentation of discoveries; others are hasty, quick, and driven by the urgency and the thrill of movement or of new experiences.

Amid the vast taxonomy of travel possibilities, this book delves into the experience of travel around, and travel writing about the Mediterranean – a sea steeped in history, rich in culture, and full of diversity. Throughout the centuries, and in the context of literary travels, the Mediterranean has inspired an enormous number of narratives. Intellectuals and writers have long been attracted to and inspired by the ancient ruins, historical sites, and wonders of nature, which together testify to the extraordinary heterogeneity of this space – "an unstable space of variable intensities, alliances and tensions [...] where the continents of Europe, Africa and

Asia meet"[1]. With this in mind, our exploration of the Mediterranean travels takes us on a journey through time and space, across millennia of shared histories and diverse encounters.

We do not need to trouble Fernand Braudel[2] or any other great historian of the Mediterranean to recall the vastness of this small sea; how limited it is in its extent, but how enormous in its richness; how (en)closed it may appear when it is seen on a map, but also how permeable are its shores, peoples, cultures, and civilisations, all often characterised by shifting frontiers. Millennia of shared history and diverse contacts have fostered the development of cultural landscapes of incredible beauty and charm, which have captivated the minds of travellers, sailors, explorers, adventurers, all of whom have sailed the waters of this sea. In the present volume, we can only offer a few examples of how the Mediterranean voyage can be "narrated" within its different forms, models, purposes, and destinations. No collection of essays could ever be exhaustive; it is not possible to do justice to the long history of this sea, with its peoples, conquests, and losses. Thus, whilst our selection may appear fragmentary and partial, its very lack of any claim to completeness serves as a testament to the enduring appeal and the extreme complexity of the Mediterranean travel.

Spanning travels from the nineteenth century to today, the contributions in this volume offer crucial insights into cultural encounters, practices and perceptions as travellers have experienced and still experience them in the Mediterranean regions. Through an investigation of travelogues, diaries, letters, novels, poems, tourist guides, and blogs, the authors of this collection navigate the intricate relationship between Self and Other; they contribute to a wider understanding of travel, and writing about travel, in mediating cultural exchange, while shedding light on the major challenges posed by stereotypes and socio-cultural bias. In terms of its geographical scope, this volume gathers contributions covering a substantial part of the Mediterranean area, with reference to

---

1   Patrick Crowley, Noreen Humble and Silvia Ross, "Introduction: The Mediterranean Turn", in *Mediterranean Travels: Writing Self and Other from the Ancient World to Contemporary Society*, edited by Patrick Crowley, Noreen Humble and Silvia Ross, Abington, Oxon, Modern Humanities Research Association and Routledge, 2011, p. 1.

2   Fernand Braudel, *The Mediterranean and the Mediterranean World in the Age of Philip II*, New York, Collins, 1972–1973 (translated from the French 2nd ed., 1966).

specific regions and countries such as Greece, Sicily, Tunisia, Egypt, Syria and Lebanon. Within the ten chapters of the volume, five contributions (by Emanuela Ettorre, Carlo Martinez, Adrian Tait, Silvia Antosa, Paola Partenza) deal with the British and American travellers who reached the coasts of the Mediterranean from the mid-nineteenth century until the 1970s; one contribution (by Lorella Martinelli) can be ascribed to the French cultural area and the literary genre of poetry. Two other chapters (by Lorenzo Buonvivere and Antonio Gurrieri) set aside hodeporic literature in order to investigate tourist discourse and language practice in the Mediterranean. Two final contributions (by Miriam Al Tawil and Elisa Gugliotta) touch the Arab world more deeply, one dealing with the Middle East in the nineteenth century, and the other with contemporary North Africa. Apart from the final chapter, the predominant point of view offered in this volume is that of the Westerner traveller venturing into exotic lands, discovering "oddities" and new customs. These oddities can indeed be interpreted as manifestations of an orientalist perspective, a phenomenon extensively explored by Edward Said and numerous other scholars since[3].

In the first chapter Emanuela Ettorre investigates the kind of "philhellenic sentiment"[4] that was widespread among British travellers. Her analysis focuses on George Gissing's travel experiences to Greece and their profound impact of his sense of identity and exile. Through an investigation of Gissing's autobiographical writings and of his short novel *Sleeping Fires*, this chapter reveals Gissing's constant oscillation between his idealised view of the Mediterranean, derived from classical literature, and his disillusionment with the realities of industrial modernity. Thus, Ettorre explores how Gissing's experiences in Greece challenged his romanticised notions of the classical world, revealing the ecological consequences of industrialisation and the need to reassess literary portrayals of nature in

---

3   Cf. Edward Said, *Orientalism*, New York, Pantheon Books, 1978. For counter-deductions to the debate, see also, for example, Fred Dallmayr, *Beyond Orientalism: Essays on Cross-Cultural Encounter*, Albany, NY, State University of New York Press, 1996; Karla Mallette, *European Modernity and the Arab Mediterranean: Toward a New Philology and a Counter-Orientalism*, Philadelphia, University of Pennsylvania Press, 2010; Laetitia Nanquette, *Orientalism Versus Occidentalism: Literary and Cultural Imaging Between France and Iran Since the Islamic Revolution*, London and New York, I. B. Tauris, 2013.

4   Richard Stoneman, "Introduction: Travellers in an Antique Land", *A Literary Companion to Travel in Greece*, Harmondsworth, Penguin, 1984, p. 7.

the context of environmental degradation. Interestingly, Gissing's representation of Greece oscillates between admiration of natural wonders and an unambiguous disdain for the backwardness of its social systems and the commonness of its populace. A close reading of Gissing's writings therefore emphasises his ethnocentric biases, and within him, a clear struggle to reconcile his English identity with the foreign territories he encounters. By delving into Gissing's sense of identity, exile, and the illusion of a nostalgic past, this chapter uncovers the intricate layers of his self-divided imagination and the profound impact of his Mediterranean travels on his literary production and psyche.

Chapter II moves us into the Mediterranean in American literature between the mid-nineteenth and early twentieth century. Here, Carlo Martinez analyses the emergence of mass tourism and its transformation into a powerful economic force and a major cultural form itself characteristic of modernity. The Mediterranean has always had a key role in the American imagination for its association with history, culture, and high art. Starting in the nineteenth century, however, it also became a popular tourist destination. Through a discussion of four travelogues (both well known and overlooked) by Nathaniel Parker Willis, Mark Twain, Edith Wharton and Samuel Gamble Bayne, this chapter reconstructs the manifold meanings that the popularised image of the cruise in the Mediterranean played in the American imagination in the second half of the nineteenth and the early years of the twentieth century.

Adrian Tait's contribution, in Chapter III, leads the reader into the Arab culture through the eyes of two British women travellers, Marianne Brocklehurst and Mary Booth or "MBs", and their journey through the Nile. Marianne wrote her own account of the trip she made there in 1873, a diary never intended for publication; by turns picaresque, picturesque, and elegiac, it provides an intimate counterpart to Amelia Edwards's Nile travelogue. Inadvertently, it also reveals the seemingly innocuous way in which British travellers constructed the exotic otherness of the Orient, reducing the intricate realities of a modernising nation to an "Eastern spectacle". For the two travellers, the Arab peoples they encountered were simply "specimens" of this strangeness, and variously "savage", "strange", or "wild"; the scenery was only ever "picturesque" or "pretty"; and Egypt itself was invariably an "Old World", whose antiquities were there to be appropriated by the new, and whose wildlife was there to be shot at and "bagged". As they continued with their journey, however, Marianne's diary suggests a deepening interest in the people they meet and the places they visit, and a growing recognition that trips such as these were not without consequence: even as she negotiated for illicit artefacts, Marianne pronounced it "abominable" that visiting British travellers had carved their names in "temples and tombs". As this chapter discusses, the MB's Nile trip marks the beginning of their deep and life-long enthusiasm for Egypt and its history. In turn, a close reading of Marianne's diary deepens our understanding of these two remarkable travellers, and of Victorian travellers in general, whilst also underlining the way in which Western visitors mapped their own, reductive notions of cultural superiority on to the rich complexity of contemporary life along the Nile.

In reimagining the Mediterranean through the lens of Vita Sackville West's novel *Challenge* (1924), Silvia Antosa explores the intersections of geography and identity in literary narratives. Significantly, and as Chapter IV explains, *Challenge* is set in the fictional Greek city of Herakleion, which is inspired by Monte Carlo, and whose representation reflects the complex dynamics of a cosmopolitan community. The protagonist, Julian Davenport, grapples with his family's colonial legacy and his own identity as he navigates political intrigues and personal relationships. Through Julian's journey, Sackville West challenges stereotypes and taboos about sexuality, gender and power, and offers a subtle exploration of the paradigms of love and desire set against a backdrop of societal expectations and personal struggles. Antosa brilliantly succeeds in examining the complex interplay of travel and subversion in Modernist women's writing, while focusing on Sackville-West's portrayal of the Mediterranean as a realm of possibilities for exploring sexuality and desire. While celebrating the liberating potential of the Mediterranean, Antosa argues that Sackville-West's novel also reflects and reinforces stereotypes related to nationality, class and gender, thus revealing an unresolved tension between subversion and tradition.

In Chapter V, Paola Partenza analyses Patrick Leigh Fermor's book *Mani. Travels in the Southern Peloponnese* (1958), which celebrates the landscape of the Peloponnese region with its mountains, hills, and archaeological sites. *Mani* offers a nuanced portrayal of Greek culture, blending archaeological and ethnographic perspectives to illuminate both the past and the present. The narrative is brought to life through detailed descriptions and insightful commentary, which encompass the people, customs, and landscapes of Greece. Fermor reveals the complexities of Greek society, from social hierarchies to ritual integration, to identify the essence of Greek culture spanning antiquity to modernity. This work not only documents Fermor's journey, but also extends an invitation for readers to explore their own connections to Greek history and culture. The chapter follows Fermor's footsteps, embracing memories, interactions, and first-hand experiences to reconstruct a vivid and accurate portrait of Mani. It emphasises the enduring role of travel as a crossroads of diverse cultures and customs, in line with Foucault's notion that experience offers a gateway to the collective memory of humanity.

In Chapter VI, Lorella Martinelli investigates the portrayal of Italy in the poetry of Tristan Corbière (1845–1875), focusing particularly on his Italian cycle within the collection *Amours jaunes*. By analysing Corbière's ironic collage of Italian clichés, Martinelli identifies the subversion of the traditional iconography of the Grand Tour. Thus, Corbière's poetic journey through Italy is characterised by an ironic and exaggerated depiction of the country, in sharp contrast with the idealised views offered by earlier French travellers. The *Bel Paese* no longer represents a sunny, primitive, and seductive place, and what the selected poems highlight is Corbierè's distinctive and provocative poetic style, a critical engagement with cultural stereotypes, and his exploration of the grotesque, macabre, and comedic aspects of Italian landscapes and characters.

In Chapter VII, Lorenzo Buonvivere offers a completely different perspective by analysing the specialised field of tourism communication, and looking at one of its most recent and relevant forms: ecotourism, defined as a type of sustainable travel to natural areas which preserves the environment and supports local communities. Given the persuasive function of metaphors in general tourism discourse, this chapter seeks to understand whether figurative language employed in the sub-field of ecotourism plays a role in the positive/negative conceptualisation of the relationship between humans and non-humans. It investigates a corpus of nine guides produced within the EU-funded EMbleMatiC Project (2015–2019), a project which led to the creation and advertising of "eco-itineraries" across the mountainous regions of the Mediterranean. The research refers to Conceptual Metaphor Theory in order to select recurrent metaphorical expressions that target nature in the texts. Results show that nature is consistently portrayed figuratively in terms of war, art, guardianship, competition, as well as human body, character and emotion. The analysis suggests that some expressions are peculiar to ecotourism discourse, and indeed participate in the recognition of nature's salience and human dependence on it. However, findings also reveal a consistency with general tourism discourse, so that metaphors in ecotourism texts mainly fulfil a persuasive function to increase the perceived value of the destinations advertised. The chapter concludes by advocating for an exploitation of the educational role of metaphors, which might reconcile the economic character of ecotourism with its ethical objectives.

In Chapter VIII, Antonio Guerrieri also focuses on the topic of tourism, with a specific attention to the tourist guides of Sicily, which have generated and maintained over time a stereotyped image of Sicily, imposing on it a well-defined imagery. A selection of tourist guides portray Sicily as a mythical island at the centre of the Mediterranean, a melting pot of cultures with a paradisiacal climate that French-speaking tourists particularly enjoy. However, some guidebooks attempt to go beyond this generic representation of Sicilian reality. The Mediterranean climate is not always perfect, and one may not always experience a paradise on Earth. What prevails, of course, is a positive representation of the island that aims to persuade and captivate the reader with the promise of unique experiences.

In Chapter IX, Miriam Al Tawil analyses the life and customs of the Bedouin communities as described by European travellers during the nineteenth and twentieth centuries, in Syria, Iraq, Palestine, and Egypt. All the travellers Miriam Al Tawil deals with were not only interested in Arab culture, as would any ethnographer, but they also had some knowledge of the Arabic language – a characteristic that allowed them to merge with the societies they were visiting. Aside from the literary and ethnographic value of these travelogues, one can also uncover linguistic testimonies of the varieties of spoken Arabic used by these Bedouin communities, and compare the features described by the travellers with the studies produced in modern time; these accounts therefore represent a valuable source for the diachronic analysis of poorly documented languages.

However, travelling does not simply mean going to distant places, it may also be intended as a rediscovery of one's own country. In this way, travels become spatially limited and circumscribed, but they inevitably allow for experiences that are no less meaningful and emotionally touching. The last chapter by Elisa Gugliotta is centred on a digital travelogue. Inkwells, pens and papers are abandoned, and the keyboard and screen take over: this is the journey of a young Tunisian blogger, Hiba Boujnah, who is popular among the post-revolution generation of Tunisians. She wishes to rediscover the southern regions of her country, that can be considered as a world apart from the modernity of the capital, as a result of the changes that occurred after the revolution of 2011 and, particularly, after the crisis of tourism of 2014. The travelogue offers intriguing reflections on Tunisia from a Mediterranean point of view, as an intersection of different linguistic layers that have been studied adopting the perspective of Arabic dialectology.

As we journey through these chapters we are reminded of the multifaceted nature of travel and exploration, not only as physical experiences, but also as intellectual and cultural endeavours that allow us to engage with past, present and the future, and with the challenges of different societies and territories. Each chapter invites us to reflect on the way in which travel narratives, cultural representations and linguistic analysis contribute to our understanding of the complex variety of human experiences and interactions across diverse geographical and cultural boundaries.

Navigating Identity and Exile: George Gissing's Voyage to Greece

Emanuela ETTORRE

"I am in the wrong world": Gissing's Mediterranean Escape

In November 1889 George Gissing set off on a longed-for sea voyage to Greece. He had already spent several months in Italy the year before, but his fascination with Mediterranean countries and his burning interest in the classics compelled him to make several other journeys to the South, journeys that are carefully recorded in his diary and letters. Greece was a popular destination for nineteenth-century travellers, many of whom were interested in classical history and archaeology, and were also drawn to the country's natural beauty, with its rugged coastline and picturesque islands. For Gissing, however, travelling to the Mediterranean represented a more profound and multifaceted experience: it was a process of discovery, at once cultural, literary and personal. As John Pemble puts it, his travel books constitute "a personal testament, describing an inward as well as an outward journey"[1]; they represent an act of liberation from the constraints of Victorian society, and an attempt to recover from the corrosive effects of the metropolis, with its commodity culture, disorderly crowds, and debased slum life. Thus, and whilst Gissing is remembered as the writer of the urban modernity, his experiences in Italy and Greece and his subsequent works of travel writing (both autobiographical and

---

1   John Pemble, *The Mediterranean Passion: Victorians and Edwardians in the South*, London, Faber and Faber, 2009, p. 12. As he further notes, "Butler, Gissing, Lawrence, and Douglas signified in their accounts of journeys to the South a hostility towards the values of the modern world and a desire to withdraw from its problems and complexities. They write less as representatives of their society than as its casualties and defeated rebels" (*Ibid.*).

fictional) constitute an essential part of his literary production. His three
voyages to Italy converge in *By The Ionian Sea*, a memorable book published in 1901, two years before his death, and a trip to Greece made
between November and December 1889 provides significant material for
Sleeping Fires[2], a short novel Gissing wrote in 1895 which draws extensively from his diary and the letters written daily during his voyage.

Gissing travelled to the Mediterranean for several reasons: not only
was he looking for relief from his physical ailments, but his trips to Italy
and Greece were also the expression of his sense of permanent exile and
restlessness[3]. "Unclassed and itinerant"[4], Gissing never felt at home in
England, and like some of the characters that populate his narratives,
he expressed his discontent through a nomadic life – a life of travels and
displacements, escapes, quests and returns. As he wrote to his mother
while heading towards the harbour at Piraeus in 1899: "Ah! It does
me good, this travel. […] I think I shall never spend another winter in
England. […] Here life is worth living; I am well & hopeful – whereas
in England I am neither"[5]. On a similar note, and having returned to
England a few months later, he wrote to his friend Eduard Bertz:

> I shall never be able to make myself at home again in England. The days are
> infinitely wearisome to me, & I work only in the hope of getting away very
> soon. […] Bad weather; scarcely to be called summer. That helps to depress
> me. But the worst of all is that *I am in the wrong world*. Heaven be thanked,
> the time draws near when I shall be able to flee from this provincial air.

2   George Gissing, *Sleeping Fires*, edited by Pierre Coustillas, Hassocks, The Harvester
    Press, 1974. All quotations are from this edition, with the page number in brack-
    ets preceded by SF. For this paper I have also referred to the Italian edition of the
    novel: George Gissing, *Il fuoco sotto la cenere*, traduzione, introduzione e cura di
    Maria Teresa Chialant, Roma, Aracne Editrice, 2014. For a detailed analysis of this
    novel, and of Gissing's experience in Greece see also Maria Teresa Chialant, "George
    Gissing, Greece and the Mediterranean Passion", *Literary Geographies*, 3, no. 2, 2017,
    pp. 153–168.
3   As David Grylls observes: "Another symptom of exile which was also a cause was
    perennial restlessness. Convinced he was mouldering in 'the wrong world' ", Gissing
    continually switched his address in search of his ideal niche. […] (*The Paradox of
    Gissing*, London, Allen & Unwin, 1986, p. 122).
4   *Ibid.*, p. 122.
5   *The Collected Letters of George Gissing: Volume IV 1889–1891*, edited by Paul
    F. Mattheisen, Arthur C. Young, and Pierre Coustillas, Athens (Ohio), Ohio
    University Press, 1993, p. 145.

Roberts urges me to live abroad altogether, & I believe he is right. I cannot make friends, – not even acquaintances, – in England; & the small success of my books embitters me against the country. Yes, I shall move about on the Continent [...] I am so much more myself, when abroad. In the society of people here I am stiff & awkward & contemptuous[6].

Evidently, England represented a hindrance to Gissing's personality and to his career. Yet it is also true that during his travels to Greece he never abandons the perspective and the stance of a "true" Englishman, with all the values, rules and demureness this implies. It is through the lens of a Victorian Briton, in fact, that he often observes the regions of the Mediterranean, and attempts to reconstruct their literary geography. For example, on the 6th of December 1889, in a letter to William Henry Hudson written while he is in Athens, Gissing cannot refrain from comparing his native land to the Mediterranean country he is visiting:

[...] there is much to be said for England, as one always discovers when one has been for a short time in these countries of *sunlight & evil smells*. England is the land of *comfort* & *decency*, of *warm* homes, of civic *order*, – of old-standing *peace*. One pays dearly, in the South, for glorious light & air. Here in Greece I feel the discomforts more than in Italy. Partly because I find the people far less sympathetic. As far as I am able to judge the Greeks, I don't like them. In appearance they are – in the mass – singularly ignoble, & their manners lack both vivacity & suavity. What can one expect, after ages of varied slavery? Well, they are now trying to join in the industrial race, & civilize themselves on the approved pattern[7].

In this passage, Gissing establishes a dichotomy wherein a flattering portrayal of England is contrasted with a Greece seen in terms of the perceived vulgarity of its (unprincipled) inhabitants. Here, Gissing assumes an evaluative and critical perspective rooted in a distinct paradigm of civilization epitomized by England and the English, which he suggests should serve as a blueprint for emulation. By adopting such a stance, he aligns himself with a specific set of cultural and societal values associated with what David Cannadine defines as a "strident imperial self-consciousness"[8].

---

6   *Ibid.*, p. 226, italics mine.

7   *The Collected Letters of George Gissing: Volume IV 1889–1891*, cit., p. 159.

8   David Cannadine, *Victorious Century: The United Kingdom, 1800–1906*, New York, Viking, 2017, p. 441.

This discriminating and also discriminatory stance suggests a hierar-chical notion; it implies a preference for certain socio-cultural standards, and the imposition of a particular worldview as normative. Moreover, this passage highlights Gissing's divergent and often paradoxical stand-points, which mirror the complexities found in both his life and literary works: British proletarians evoke in him a blend of disdain and compas-sion; the upper classes provoke a profound envy combined with scorn; and Gissing's conflicting notions regarding Greece and the Greeks simi-larly extend to matters of social classes and propriety, ultimately serving to validate his perceived intellectual superiority over the general popu-lace. Thus, for Gissing the Mediterranean countries represent both an ideal refuge from the squalors of an industrialized society, and an under-developed place that is grappling with the challenges of industrial moder-nity in its own struggle to become more civilized.

Against that background, the aim of this paper is to explore Gissing's autobiographical writings and his short narrative *Sleeping Fires* to see how the Greek countries he crossed, visited, and vividly portrayed give us deeper insights into his complex personality, and to identify in the intense experience of travelling his feelings of being exiled and dispos-sessed. They are, as I suggest in this paper, the expression of an anguished and self-divided imagination.

Greece and the Illusion of a Nostalgic Arcadia

Gissing is often critical towards the Greeks and the Italians, partic-ularly when the reality he confronts deviates from the idealised notions he has long cherished. Evidently, Gissing was an enthusiast of the clas-sics, and once he had the opportunity to travel to the Mediterranean, he visited the places he had read about in his books, places engraved in his mind since childhood. In his endeavour to rediscover traces of the past, however, Gissing's experiences in Greece diverged from historical and literary narratives: "[t]he age of mythology was past"[9], observes Pierre Coustillas in his biography of the Victorian writer. Indeed, the entries in Gissing's diary, and the numerous letters he sent during his journey, register a persistent oscillation between recollections of the bygone era

---

9   Pierre Coustillas, *The Heroic Life of George Gissing, Part II: 1888–1897*, London, Pickering & Chatto, 2012, p. 76.

described in books, and the remarkable transformations effected by industrial modernity: "Piraeus is growing to be a very large and busy town", we read in his dairy. "Already some dozen high mill-chimneys are belching black fumes"[10]. During his visit to the Aeropagus, and the rocky recess that is the Eumenides' well of Aeschylus's play, what he finds instead is "a vast public ordure-ground, [...] a centre of pest"[11]. Both examples embody Gissing's reflection on the relentless objectification of the environment in Greece, as well as his reaction to the clash between an idealised literary representation of the past and the stark reality of modern age – an age that subverts idyllic and pastoral imagery. The Piraeus, in fact, has now the appearance of an industrial hub, and a mythical site such as the Eumenides' well has become a public waste ground, further emphasising the degradation of natural spaces. Indeed, such an observant account of his Greek journey points to the ecological consequences of industrial modernity, and the need to re-evaluate portrayals of nature in literature in the context of environmental transformation. Perhaps in response to modern-day degradation, Gissing often romanticised the legendary territories of the classical world, and, as David Grylls observes, he viewed Italy and Greece as "Arcadian constructs", primarily representing "idealised lands of serenity and culture". For him "[t]he classical world was a cherished ideal *because* it was irrecoverable"[12]. Such a sentiment is similarly expressed in a heartfelt letter that Gissing's last wife Gabrielle Fleury wrote to H. G. Wells in 1901, in which she highlighted her husband's elusive quest for an ideal space, and pondered his struggle to find happiness in "unchanging circumstances and surroundings": "Discontent is in his nature, I repeat it; paradise is always for him where he is not – *I mean settled*"[13]. Clearly Gissing's dissatisfaction is strictly connected to

---

10 *London and the Life of Literature in Late Victorian England: The Diary of George Gissing, Novelist*, edited by Pierre Coustillas, Hassocks, The Harvester Press, 1978, p. 179.

11 *Ibid.*, p. 189. This same description is found in a letter to Eduard Bertz (14th December 1889, *The Collected Letters of George Gissing: Volume IV 1889–1891*, pp. 165–166), and in *Sleeping Fires* where Louis who describes the mill-chimneys at the Piraeus as an "abomination" (SF, p. 67); for him this is an inevitable result of the new era in which even the Greeks have to adapt to the laws of industrial modernity, which means that "they have their lives to live. They can't feed on the past" (*Ibid.*).

12 David Grylls, *op. cit.*, pp. 110, 123.

13 *George Gissing and H. G. Wells: Their Friendship and Correspondence*, edited by Royal A. Gettmann, Urbana, University of Illinois Press, 1961 (italics mine).

his inability to remain rooted in place, or rather, to his inability to find relief and tranquillity in the world. While engaging with the different spaces and places he crossed or inhabited[14], he seemed to lack what David Matless defines as the "geographical self"[15], that is, the capacity to create one's own subjectivity through landscape. Notwithstanding Gissing's attempt to escape from the known geography of his own country in search of "a retreat into an unchanging mythic past"[16], even in the territories of the Mediterranean countries he ultimately experiences what E. C. Relph calls "outsideness"[17], a term that implies "uninvolvement, an alienation from people and places, homelessness, a sense of the unreality of the world, and of not belonging"[18].

Thus, whilst Gissing is fascinated by the idea of the classical world, he finds it difficult to engage fully with the multifaceted reality of Greece. He never truly endeavours to assimilate into the locales he visits; he is often and profoundly destabilized by the contradictions he discovers in the country – a country of natural beauties and great artistic heritage, but also one still entrapped by what he saw as the backwardness of its social systems and the "commonness" of its population.

Moreover, the great paradox of Gissing's sense of place is that his attempt to appreciate the distinctive identity of this Mediterranean country is filtered through the critical lens of its (impossible) resemblance to his motherland, and to a compliance with certain socio-cultural standards. Greece is often referred to as "Oriental" in a manner that would seem quite derogatory, echoing Edward Said's famous observation that puts "the Westerner in a whole series of possible relationships with the Orient without ever losing him the relative upper hand"[19]. As Gissing writes to his brother Algernon: "It will be very long before Greece gets

14 George Gissing spent most of his life in England; however, as a young man, and amidst difficult circumstances, he sojourned in Boston and Chicago; he made three long journeys to Italy, a trip to Greece, and he spent the last phase of his existence in the South of France, where he died in 1903.
15 David Matless, *Landscape and Englishness*, Second Expanded Edition, London, Reaktion Books, 2016, p. 31.
16 This is one of the definitions Terry Gifford gives to Arcadia, in *Pastoral*, London and New York, Routledge, 2010, p. 43.
17 Edward C. Relph, *Place and Placelessness*, London, Pion, 1976, p. 51.
18 *Ibid.*
19 Edward W. Said, *Orientalism*, London, Penguin Books, 2003, p. 7.

rid of its orientalism. All the quick & easy traffic is with Constantinople & Asia Minor. The public markets are called Bazaars. The extraordinary costumes worn by the lower classes suggest *Oriental barbarism*"[20]. In his portrayal of Greece, Gissing often succumbs to certain stereotypical views that reinforce his ambivalence: he experiences a sense of alienation in his own country from which he desires to escape, yet at the same time, he recognizes its superiority over the places where he seeks "refuge". Even in a long and honest letter to Eduard Bertz, Gissing describes Athens as a town full of "dirt", completely enveloped in "a cloud of dust". He feels surrounded by a pervasive "Oriental atmosphere" towards which he often expresses estrangement and disappointment:

> The Greeks [...] are all bent on money-making, & are, on the whole, *grossly uneducated – if not unintelligent.* [...]
>
> Excepting the *dirt*, Athens is not like an Italian town; the houses are low; & there is an *absence of colour. The character of the people does not appeal to me.* I see *very little liveliness* [...] *Politeness is the exception.* The *voices are very harsh*, & modern Greek sounds disagreeable. [...]
>
> Life is v. strange in these countries that have been the battlefields of age after age of civilization & *barbarism*. Save in the small tracts of land which are built upon or cultivated, you are absolutely *in the desert* [...] you are soon *lost in utter wilderness* [...]
>
> The Athenians *do not interest me.* They are *impolite & have no pleasant live-liness* in demeanour. [...] The town swarms with *soldiers* [...] *They are short, thin, badly shaped; their faces are small, bony, ignoble, of dirty complexion.* [...] As for their *intelligence,* it must be of the *most elementary kind*[21].

The language used in these fragments of letters highlights Gissing's ethnocentric biases, which are expressed in his evaluation of the Greeks against Western standards. Lexical choices such as "impolite", "short", "thin", "badly shaped", "ignoble", "dirty complexion" and "unintelligent", contribute to the construction of power relations as they place the speaker in a position of superiority, while perpetuating a blunt and racist categorization of what appears to him as a "foreign" population. In line with Teun van Dijk's analysis of discursive practices as a reproduction of domination, Gissing's depiction of Greek's inhabitants thereby engages with power dynamics, as it oscillates between "the emphasis on exotic

20 *The Collected Letters of George Gissing: Volume IV 1889–1891*, cit., p. 146, italics mine.
21 *Ibid.*, cit., pp. 149, 152, 157, 158. All italics are mine.

difference, on the one hand, and supremacist derogation stressing the Other's intellectual, moral and biological inferiority, on the other"[22].

Yet, in Gissing's contradictory imagination, Greece is also a land of natural wonders, with its glowing twilights, azure sea, delightful islands, and magnificent mountains. On 18 November 1889, during his journey from Genova to Greece, and as he approached Mount Taygetos on the Peloponnese peninsula, he wrote in his diary: "Such a view is not of this earth, as *we* understand it; [...] This is indeed the land of Apollo"[23]. Later, while standing on a hill on the west side of the Acropolis, he is spellbound by the rays of the setting sun, by the wonderful wide plain that stretches to Piraeus, and by the rose and purple colours of the clouds on the summit of Pentelicon that seem "to conceal the abode of the gods on the unattainable height". It is a feast of images and colours that he can only regard "with awe and worship"[24], a magnificent feast for the eyes which finally offers him the reward of Greece as an unreal place, as a work of art, composed of forms that "are so marvellous that one does not seem to be gazing at earthly objects"[25]. This dreamlike space, far removed from the reality of the present, and completely decontextualized from its cultural and social structures, embodies the difficulties of a travel writer who struggles "to navigate between the inchoate impression on the one hand and the commonplace cliché on the other"[26]; to negotiate between the striking beauty of nature (for him the sole custodian of an ancient and venerable history), and the backwardness of an uncivilized country. Moreover, the Greek spaces are often identified with terms such as "scenery", "landscape", "picturesqueness"[27]. Unlike places, landscapes refer to "a portion of the earth's surface that can be viewed from one spot"[28], from the outside; even the word "scenery" implies the overall view of

---

22 Teun A. van Dijk, *Discourse and Power*, Basingstoke and New York, Palgrave Macmillan, 2008, pp. 96–97.

23 *London and the Life of Literature in Late Victorian England: The Diary of George Gissing, Novelist*, cit., p. 174. Italics in the text.

24 *The Collected Letters of George Gissing: Volume IV 1889–1891*, cit., p. 156.

25 *Ibid.*, p. 160.

26 Brian H. Murray, "Introduction: Forms of Travel, Modes of Transport", in *Travel Writing, Visual Culture, and Form, 1760–1900*, edited by Mary Henes and Brian H. Murray, Basingstoke, Palgrave Macmillan, 2016, p. 8.

27 *The Collected Letters of George Gissing: Volume IV 1889–1891*, cit., pp. 160, 156, 159, 147.

28 Tim Cresswell, *Place: A Short Introduction*, Oxford, Blackwell Publishing, 2004, p. 10.

a place from a distance that somehow objectifies what is seen; and by "picturesque", we mean an "aestheticization of landscape to extreme", since it is the spectator who aesthetically and mentally produces "a work of art where before there had been a work of nature"[29]. Thus, Gissing's lexical choices often establish an appreciation of the landscape which is more influenced by the perspective of the observer than by the inherent characteristics of the scene. In this process of reification, nature and its beauties are the ultimate way to fulfil his aesthetic sensibility and to recreate his fictional space, his "country of the mind".

"This is mere fairyland": *Sleeping Fires* and the Fictional Representation of Greece

In February 1895 George Gissing writes his fifteenth novel: *Sleeping Fires*. He has reached his maturity and is now working on several shorter narratives that he himself defines as "a frothy trifle for a popular series"[30], but which mark his detachment from the stylistical and structural conventions of the triple-decker.

In *Sleeping Fires* Gissing crafts a narrative that partially unfolds within the geographical and cultural confines of Greece, in fact seven of the fourteen chapters are set in Athens. However, the portrayal of Greece is filtered through the perspectives of English characters who, lying somewhere between tourists and exiles, seek to reconstruct their own identities or to rebuild their own lives. The novel focuses on a man in his mid-forties, Edmund Langley, a fervent enthusiast of the classics. He goes to Greece to escape the recollections of a troubled past, and there he encounters Worboys, an old friend from college in Cambridge, who is equally fascinated by the classics as well as by archaeology. Worboys is accompanying Louis Reed, a boy entrusted to him by his guardian Lady Revill (formerly Agnes Forrest); they have travelled to Greece to distance Louis from the influence of Mrs. Tresilian, a London lady of liberal ideas. Langley's encounter with Louis in Athens brings out a peculiar

---

29 Alison Byerly, "The Uses of Landscape", in *The Ecocriticism Reader: Landmarks in Literary Ecology*, edited by Cheryll Glotfelty and Harold Fromm, Athens and London, University of Georgia Press, 1996, p. 55.

30 *The Collected Letters of George Gissing: Volume VI 1895–1897*, edited by Paul. F. Mattheisen, Arthur C. Young, and Pierre Coustillas, Athens (Ohio), 1995, p. 29. Here Gissing is referring also to "The Paying Guest".

resemblance between the two; at the same time, it rekindles memories of Langley's failure to woo Agnes Forrest – a courtship that ended when Langley revealed to Agnes's father that he had a son with a woman (Eliza) who then left him to marry another man. Now Agnes is a widow. On Langley's return to London, she reveals to him that Louis is the son he had with Eliza. Tragedy strikes in Greece: Louis dies. His death forces Langley and Agnes/Lady Revill to confront their shared histories. Langley recognizes his enduring love for Agnes, but she refuses his proposal once again as a form of atonement, for keeping the identity of his son a secret for so long. In a final twist, Agnes accepts Langley's love, bringing closure to their tumultuous past.

The troubled love story between Langley and Agnes, together with the tragic destiny of young Louis, seems to be connected to bad life choices, which place the protagonist in a constant confrontation with his difficult past. Langley is clearly ensnared by his own history: anguished by regrets and remorse for having abandoned his son, he travels to Greece to exorcize pain and melancholy, and to fight against the "tormenting memory" of his "turbulent youth" (SF, pp. 37–38). But the great paradox of the story (which is somehow distinctive of Gissing's cynical and contradictory imagination) is that after his failed relationship with both the mother of his son and with Agnes, Langley's voyage to Greece neither alleviates his sadness, nor exorcizes his pain, because it is exactly in Athens that he confronts himself with what he was trying to elude. Hence his unexpected encounter with the son he had never met, and his consequent return to England to meet Lady Revill once more.

Sleeping Fires orchestrates a dynamic interplay between two dimensions: the geographical-topological (Greece and England), and the temporal (past and present), with the latter encompassing not only the lives of the characters, but also the reality of the locales themselves. Greece is a place that celebrates and revolves around its glorious past in terms of art, literature, and history. Through the experience and the perspective of the characters, however, we learn that it is necessary to move away from the past, as the final paragraphs of the novel underline: writing a letter to Agnes, and anticipating his own return to England, Langley hints at the prospect of a shared future, one attainable only by disengaging from the bygone days; "Yes, let the past be past. To you and me, the day that is still granted us" (SF, p. 230). Langley – whose melancholic temperament, restlessness, and enthusiasm for the classics seem to be based on the character of Gissing himself – is captivated by the allure of ancient times, before then realizing that it is difficult to find a correspondence between past and present. Moreover, Greece is also and often depicted as a dream world, an imaginary realm from which one must awaken to keep on living:

> [...] this is *mere fairyland*; to us of the north, *an escape* for rest amid scenes we *hardly believe to be real*. The Acropolis, rock and ruins all tawny gold, the work of art inseparable from that of nature, and *neither seeming to have bodily existence*; the gorgeous purples of Hymettus; that cloud on Pentelikon, with its melting splendours which seemed to veil the abode of gods – what part has all this in our actual life? [...] Worboys is right; living in the past, he forgets the present altogether. I, whose life is now to begin, must shake off *this sorcery of Athens*, and remember it only as *a delightful dream*. *Mere fairyland*; and our Louis has become part of it – to be remembered by me as calmly, yet as tenderly, as this last sunset (SF, pp. 229–230, italics mine).

The lexical items of this final passage (as well as other descriptions in the novel and in Gissing's autobiographical writings) substantiate the representation of Greece as a magical space which offers an overwhelming experience to the visitor: to the eyes of the "northern" traveller in fact, the landscapes are so far removed from reality that they become immaterial[31]. The fictional reconstruction of Greece seems to entrap the writer in "essentialist anthropological categories romanticised in the aesthetic cliché of the "beautiful land""[32], wherein spaces resonate with an enchanted atmosphere:

> His eyes wandered over the vast scene, where natural beauty and historic interest vied for the beholder's enthusiasm. Plain and mountain; city and solitude; harbour and wild shore; craggy islands and the far expanse of sea: a

---

31 The perceived sacredness of the territory he is visiting is so vivid and palpable in the text (as well a in the letters Gissing writes during his trip) that H. G Wells wrote about *Sleeping Fires*: "the possibility of a gospel of Greek delight from this minute and melancholy observer of the lower-middle class fills us with anything but agreeable anticipations" (H. G. Wells, *Saturday Review*, LXXX, 11 January 1896, p. 49, in *Gissing: The Critical Heritage*, edited by Pierre Coustillas and Colin Partridge, London and Boston, Routledge & Kegan Paul, 1972, pp. 260–261).

32 Serenella Iovino, Enrico Cesaretti, and Elena Past (eds.), "Introduction" to *Italy and the Environmental Humanities: Landscapes, Natures, Ecologies*, Charlottesville and London, University of Virginia Press, 2018, p. 6. Even if this quote applies to the representation of Italy and not of Greece, we can fairly admit that a consideration of Greece within environmental humanities would be relevant for "its significant literary and artistic heritage, its importance in shaping the Western construction, appreciation, and aesthetics of nature and landscape" (*Ibid.*, p. 4).

miracle of lights and hues, changing ever as cloudlets floated athwart the
sun [...].

"Look at the white breakers on the shore of Salamis. – *It's all so real* to me
now; and yet I never saw anything like these Greek landscapes for suggesting
unreality. I felt something of that in Italy, but this is more wonderful. [...]
*It's the landscape you pick out of the clouds, at home in England. Again and
again I have had to remind myself that these are real mountains and coasts*" (SF,
pp. 65–66, italics mine).

Greece is the land of excesses and contradictions, of heterogeneity
and variety; here nature is enduring, yet dynamic and sublime; it stirs the
imagination of the Victorian traveller just as it reinforces a certain distaste
for urban industrial environments. Surrounded by the natural wonders
of this territory, Langley experiences a "sense of mirage" (SF, p. 66): he is
dominated by a feeling of abstraction from reality as the country appears
somehow illusory to his eyes. When travelling by train along the coast
of the Peloponnesus towards Patras, the protagonist is overwhelmed
by the beauties of the "Attic soil", with its "enchanted shore" (SF, p. 98),
the olive plantations, the currant fields and the torrents that flow from
the Achæan mountains. And amidst these "visions", experienced as he is
turning his gaze to the sea, he perceives "*as in a magic mirror those forms
which appear to be bodied forth by the imagination rather than viewed with
common sight*" (SF, p. 99, italics mine). Again, what his mind's eye can see
appears far removed from the actual reality; it is instead the product of
a sophisticated literary imagination, a territory of the mind. This incorporeal quality of the Greek landscape reinforces the figurative level of
language with its similes, metaphors, antitheses and powerful synesthetic
effects[33].

But from a journey one must return, and it is also necessary to be free
of the spell of Greek's ancient narrations, as the fascination of the ancient
past would entrap the protagonist in a desperate and futile attempt to
reconnect with a world that does not exist any more. At the end of the
story, Langley's words make it clear that one has to move away from the
sins and mistakes of the past. This is the sole way to be granted a future

---

33 Most significantly, the description of Greece often encompasses occurrences of
   antithesis: "vast yet incorporeal" (SF, p. 99); of metaphors: "a miracle of lights and
   hues"; of synaesthesia: "Parnassus, glimmering on the liquid heaven with its rosy
   wreath" (*Ibid.*); and of personifications: "Megara, its white houses clustered over the
   two round hills; silent, sleepy, ignorant of its immortal fame" (SF, p. 98).

which, in this narrative, is symbolized by marriage. Yet, the much anticipated prospect of marriage, whilst ensuring a happy ending through a reconnection with the beloved, inevitably signifies the denial of the dream represented by Greece, as it brings the protagonist back to the challenges of the quotidian that in Gissing's life and works are invariably arduous. With a sense of growing expectation for the days to come, Langley will leave the "unspeakably glorious" (SF, p. 229) sunsets of Greece as any other traveller of his time would do, well aware that the journey has come to an end, that the land of the Greeks will soon dissolve into a memory, and that it will be necessary to depart from this enchantment to return to everyday life.

As this discussion highlights, Langley does not want to identify himself with a tourist, who is in his opinion an inferior kind of traveller. He wants to be more than that. Thus, it is through this fictional narrative that Gissing tries to expose the stereotypical tourist who "moves towards the security of pure cliché", setting it against the figure of the traveller, who instead seeks "that which has been discovered by the mind working in history"[34]. In *Sleeping Fires*, the figure of Langley embodies the passionate traveller who has an ample knowledge of the classics and who prefers to stay in a hotel "unknown to his touring countrymen" (SF, p. 8), who eats local food, tries to speak Greek, and can easily recognize a tourist amidst the chaos of the modern Athens:

> Looking dreamily before him, Langley saw a man who drew near – a man with a book under one arm, an umbrella under the other, and an open volume in his hands – *a tourist*, of course, and probably an Englishman, for his garb such as no native of a civilised country would exhibit among his own people (SF, pp. 11–12).

Here Gissing warns against the deleterious effects of tourism. What the narrator denounces when describing Patras is in fact "A clamour of porters hotel-touts; a drive through chocking dust; dinner table where he heard all languages save Greek. [...] But it was the modern world; he could now give little thought to Homer or to Thucydides. In the last glimpse of Parnassus he had bidden farewell to the old dreams" (SF, pp. 99–100). The chaos of modern Athens serves as a stark contrast to the serene beauty of the ancient world, and what Gissing suggests is that the

---

34 Paul Fussell, *Abroad: British Literary Traveling Between the Wars*, Oxford and New York, Oxford University Press, 1982, p. 39.

allure of modern conveniences and commercialism inevitably distracts the visitor from the profound significance of historical sites. Moreover, he urges readers to reconsider their approach to travel and recognize the importance of genuine cultural exploration. However, in Gissing's imagination, even the most sensitive and enthusiastic travellers ultimately experience frustration and disillusionment: they go to Greece as exiles, and once they are there, they find themselves equally isolated and adrift amongst people with whom they do not engage (and feel they cannot). What they experience is a dual sense of exile: they are estranged both from their native England and from the place in which they have sought solace.

Conclusion

As this chapter has argued, the Mediterranean provided Gissing with an important inspiration for his work, an inspiration that reflected his own contradictory investment in it. In turn, his feelings about the Mediterranean – which directly inform his writings about or inspired by Greece – make it impossible for him to view it dispassionately, without bias. Thus, Gissing's rendering of Greece betrays but also illustrates the dividedness of his personality, and the confusions of his poetic imaginary, as he see-saws between his poetic (re)creation of a hallowed past, and his rejection of a filthy, inconvenient, degraded present. Apart from the natural beauties of land and sea, to him, the towns of Greece and Italy are no more acceptable than those one might find in his own country, because they are simply reproducing the conditions of industrial modernity that Britain has pioneered. To the contrary, that filth and squalor is itself a reason why he constantly seeks an escape from his own shores. Still, once abroad, Gissing is compromised not only by a burgeoning modernity modelled on the very thing he is trying to flee; he is trapped by his own identity, his own sense of self as an English gentleman. A well-educated Englishman, who was raised on the classics, but is constantly defeated by modernity's onward movement, by its erasure of what has gone before. He simply cannot see – or bear to see – Greece and Italy for the places they have become and are becoming, or see their people for what they are, and not for the heroes and heroines of the mythological narratives in which he is steeped.

However, this is not the sum of his distorting Englishness. An exile from his own class – his own, middle-class – Gissing looks down on the proletariat as might the most snobbish of the gentry; yet he resents the upper classes, in part because he is so obviously not one of them. This feeling of alienation from social ranks – of a simultaneous inferiority and superiority – is almost stereotypically English, but in Gissing it reaches a new level, amplified by his own artistic creativity, which has itself become a source of profound frustration to him. Gissing would never achieve the success he felt he was owed; in fleeing England, he is also fleeing his own sense of relative professional failure. But where does that leave him? Consigning those whom he encounters in Greece or Italy to the "othered" identities of exotic Orientals, crude peasantry, or degraded products of modernity, and never once extending any kind of imaginative sympathy towards them, he somehow fails to understand the peopled world through which he travels, instead imposing on those around him the crude markers of his own English snobbishness and bias. In these transactions – in these failed transactions – Gissing emerges in a decidedly unfavourable light.

Yet he sometimes escapes from his own divided self, reflecting on the scenes that he encounters with an imaginative warmth and inspiration that gives his autobiographical writings and fictional extrapolations real worth. Ultimately, whilst these works may tell us very little about the countries Gissing visits, they disclose a great deal about the kind of man he was, the milieu he inhabited, and the broader social dynamic of the Englishman abroad. In glimpses of brilliance such as these, they also demonstrate the immense power of imagination to transform the world around us.

"The pleasure of travel is in the fancy": Cruising the Mediterranean in the American Imagination, 1853–1909

Carlo MARTINEZ

The image of the Mediterranean figures prominently in American history, culture, society and imagination ever since the very beginnings of the US. Leaving aside the ties with the early European explorers of Mediterranean origins, it is worth remembering that the newly born country fought its first war abroad in the Mediterranean, the "barbary" war from 1801 to 1805. The Mediterranean area was also a main point of departure for numberless immigrants to the US. "The Mediterranean", historian Ronald Steel writes in a volume about the relationships between the Mediterranean and the US, "is a critical part of the American cultural mosaic"[1]. Whether we want to consider it as such or not, it is certainly true that the Mediterranean has been a key reference and has played an important role for the US in historical, geographical, social, and cultural terms.

During the nineteenth century, with technological developments fostering the so-called "transportation revolution", the Mediterranean also became a chief destination for American travelers desiring to see with their own eyes the Old World. The slow democratization of travel made it affordable to increasing numbers of Americans, eager, on the backdrop of the Grand Tour tradition, to experience classic art and culture, and to acquire social and cultural capital through a first-hand knowledge of the places. First, packet lines, then, in the 1840's, the introductions of steamships brought torrents of American tourists to the Mediterranean shores.

---

1   Ronald Steel, "America's Mediterranean Coast", in *America and the Mediterranean*, edited by Massimo Bacigalupo and Pietrangelo Castagneto, Torino, Otto editore, 2003, pp. 19–22, 19.

This work intends to focus on a specific facet of the development of tourism in the US during the nineteenth and early twentieth centuries: the cruise in the Mediterranean taken by Americans over that period of time. Cruising is a special kind of touristic travel, which reached its heyday after World War II, but became gradually popular with Americans during the nineteenth century. Even before the advent of steamships, some cruise reports were enormously well-known. I will consider four instances of such reports signaling the importance of the cruise in the touristic and cultural American imagination[2].

The earliest text is Nathaniel Parker Willis' *Summer Cruise in the Mediterranean*, recounting a sea voyage accomplished in 1833, but pieced together and published as an autonomous volume twenty years later, in 1853, from Willis' very well-known European travelogue *Penciling by the Way*[3]. The second, quite obviously, is Mark Twain's celebrated *Innocents Abroad*: the story of his Atlantic crossing and cruise through the Mediterranean he accomplished on board the steamship Quaker City in 1867 and published in book form in 1869[4]. According to many critics, this text signals the definitive rise of mass tourism in the western world[5]. The third work is the recently discovered text by Edith Wharton *The Cruise of the Vanadis*, published posthumously in 1991, but written as early as 1888, when she actually did the voyage and before her first fictional attempts[6]. Although she revealed to a friend "that she would give anything in the world to make a cruise in the Mediterranean"[7], she never intended to publish the account of that much desired cruise, which

---

2   On the US and the Mediterranean, see also Waldemar Zacharasiewicz, "Perspectives on the Mediterranean: Americans as Transatlantic Sojourners", in Id., *Imagology Revisited*, Leiden, BRILL, 2010, pp. 489–502; Pau Obrador Pons, Mike Crang and Penny Travlou, eds., *Cultures of Mass Tourism: Doing the Mediterranean in the Age of Banal Mobilities*, Farnham, Ashgate, 2009.

3   Nathaniel Parker Willis, *Summer Cruise in the Mediterranean* (1853), Miami, Hard Press, 2019 (reprint).

4   Mark Twain, *The Innocents Abroad* (1869), with an Introduction by Tom Quirk and Notes by Guy Cardwell, New York, Penguin, 2002.

5   See Jeffrey Alan Melton, *Mark Twain, Travel Books and Tourism: The Tide of a Great Popular Movement*, Tuscaloosa, The University of Alabama Press, 2002.

6   Edith Wharton, *The Cruise of the Vanadis* (1888), London, Bloomsbury, 2004.

7   Edith Wharton, *A Backward Glance* (1933–4), in Id., *Novellas and Other Writings*, edited by Cynthia Griffin Wolff, New York, The Library of America, 1990, pp. 767–1064, 857.

was accidentally retraced and brought to light by the French scholar Claudine Lesage, while she was researching on other topics in the local library of Hyères, in the French Riviera. The fourth text is *A Fantasy of Mediterranean Travel*, which Samuel Gamble Bayne published in 1909, in New York, by Harper. The author, an interesting Irish-born business-man who went to the US in search of fortune in 1869, authored books of disparate subjects, some of which were travelogues[8].

What the four texts have in common, and what makes them symp-tomatic of the emergence of a new touristic cultural logic, is their tak-ing the Mediterranean as a setting in which to display American vogues, experiences, dramas, and reflections. This is the case of Willis, Twain, Wharton and Bayne alike, although each with his or her own peculiar-ities, sensibilities and cultural background. However, what makes these travelogues peculiar are not only the locations visited or the sights seen, but the experiences lived through the means of transport, the ship on board of which they cruise the Mediterranean.

Crusading on a Warship

Nowadays an all but forgotten figure, Nathaniel Parker Willis, or N. P. Willis as he liked to sign himself, was a prominent protagonist of the antebellum literary scene. An eclectic and very prolific author, Willis wrote poetry, drama, fiction and travelogues, in addition to being maga-zine editor and newspaper columnist. And yet, as Sandra Tomc has noted in one of the few contemporary critical discussions on him, Willis was a paradoxical, controversial figure even in his heydays[9]. While, his biog-rapher Henry A. Beers stated, "he lived very much in the world's eye"[10], his social manners and style of writing attracted much criticism. In his memoir, his contemporary Samuel Griswold Goodrich recorded: "One

---

8   Samuel Gamble Bayne, *A Fantasy of Mediterranean Travel*, New York, Harper, 1909. His other travelogues include *On an Irish Jaunting Car* (1902) and *Quicksteps through Scandinavia* (1908).

9   In "An Idle Industry: Nathaniel Parker Willis and the Workings of Literary Leisure Author(s)" (*American Quarterly*, 49, no. 4, 1997, pp. 780–805), Tomc comments on the "strange interdependence of Willis's success and failure" (792) arguing that Willis created his authorship through a quaint combination of fashionable idleness and tough grind.

10 Henry A. Beers, *Nathaniel Parker Willis*, Boston, Houghton Mifflin and Company, 1890, p. vii.

thing is certain – everybody thought Willis worth criticising. He has been, I suspect, more written about than any other literary man in our history"[11].

Oddly enough, in his days he was very popular and at the same time very disparaged. Thus, he is in many ways illustrative of the emergence of a clash between being very much read and gaining admittance to the canon of consecrated authors. It is not a chance, then, that he was also "unique among his contemporaries for being able to earn a decent living with his magazine publications alone"[12]. In promoting his own journalistic career, at the beginning of the 1830s Willis moved from Boston to New York, where, together with Theodore S. Fay and others he established the weekly *New York Mirror*. He also convinced his partners to sponsor him as a correspondent from Europe, where he intended to go for a two-year stay, eventually extended to almost five years, from November 1831 to May 1836. Willis had contracted to write articles for the *Mirror*, which were very favorably received by the American readership. He later collected his pieces in a volume titled *Pencillings by the Way*, which came out in London in 1835 and the following year in the US. The book sold extremely well on both sides of the Atlantic and decisively contributed to establish him as a renowned author, as well as a social celebrity, endowed with significant symbolic capital coming solely from his pen; as Sandra Tomc notes: "Almost from the moment his correspondence from abroad appeared in print, Willis was famous as a social climber"[13]. Travel writing was extremely popular and Willis skillfully took advantage of it to make a name for himself in the literary and social scene. "Indeed", Tomc adds, "the power of Willis's writing, its immense popularity, resides to a great extent in the fact that Willis actually lived the life he seemed to promise to his readers"[14].

A noteworthy part of this promise is represented by the volume Willis extracted from the successful *Pencillings by the Way* and published some twenty years later, in 1853: *Summer Cruise in the Mediterranean*, which recounts his 1833 pleasure trip of six months on board the American

11 Samuel Griswold Goodrich, *Recollections of a Lifetime*, vol. II, New York and Auburn, Miller, Orton & Mulligan, 1856, pp. 265–6.
12 Sandra Tomc, "An Idle Industry: Nathaniel Parker Willis and the Workings of Literary Leisure", *American Quarterly*, 49, no. 4, 1997, pp. 780–805, 796.
13 *Ibid.*, p. 786.
14 *Ibid.*

frigate United States. Set along the Italian and eastern Mediterranean shores, the text operated a critical symbolic move in that it turned a sailing warship into a sort of cruise liner, thus associating the idea of travel no longer to a war-imaginary of suffering, grief and deprivation, but to a pleasurable travel experience. Indeed, the text is indicative of a major change that was taking place in the American social scene for the affluent few who could afford it: transatlantic tourism. This substitution opened up sea travels to an entirely new experience, based on a mix of enjoyable idleness on board, exciting and pleasurable new experiences during the visits to the sights, in an atmosphere of exotic glamour. Thus, what in the past had been an unavoidably dangerous and uncomfortable means of transportation to reach a desired destination, now was planned to coincide with the end of the travel itself.

In presenting the volume to the public, the author enveloped his account in a fairytale aura, partly stemming from memory, partly from travel itself: "Even at the time it was written, the author felt its experiences to be a dream [...] but, now, after an interval of many years, it seems indeed like a dream, and one so full of unmitigated pleasure"[15]. This dreamlike quality confers a fictional character to the account, reminiscent almost of the Hawthornian notion of romance: "It is with a mingled sense of the real and the unreal, therefore, that the book it offered, in a new shape, to the Public" (p. v). Willis, in other words, is inviting readers to read his travel account not simply in a strict matter-of-fact way, but also in a symbolic and fictional one. As these short quotations make clear, Willis is writing for a readership made of potential travelers, as well as for armchair tourists, thriving on the popularity of travelogues in that period and the popularity of the Mediterranean in US imagination.

At a first sight, Willis's travelogue follows the pattern of travel accounts, with the usual mix of noteworthy places and sightseeing, personal anecdotes, and descriptions of local manners and customs. Composed of forty-seven letters to the readers, the book opens with the author receiving an invitation to board a US frigate for a six-month sailing in the Mediterranean. Right after departing, the author visits Naples and the nearby area, giving voice to his enthusiastic comments: "What an extraordinary succession of objects were embraced in the fifty miles

---

15 Nathaniel Parker Willis, *Summer Cruise*, cit. v. Subsequent references quoted parenthetically in the text.

between! – Paestum, Pompeii, Vesuvius, Herculaneum! – and, added to these, the thousand classic associations of the lovely coast along Sorrento!" (58). He then concludes by exalting the virtues of travel: "The value of life deepens incalculably with the privileges of travel" (p. 58). Shortly afterward, Willis shifts his attention from the scenery in front of him, to the pleasures of cruising itself in a description which is worth citing in full:

> I do not know that a mere scene like this, without incident, will interest a reader, but it was so delightful to myself, that I have described it for the mere pleasure of dwelling on it. The desert stillness and loneliness of the sea, the silent motion of the ship, and the delightful music swelling beyond the bulwarks and dying upon the wind, were such singularly combined circumstances! It was a moving paradise in the waste of the ocean (p. 59).

Repeatedly, Willis underscores how it is the act of cruising that gives him pleasure and is indeed pleasurable – even a "moving paradise". Cruising itself becomes a scene, or an attraction worth of "dwelling on", as he says. Further on, he reiterates this concept when he defines his cruising as "the poetry of sailing" (p. 97) and observes that his experience is for him "a paradise. I am glad to escape from the contact, the dust, the trials of temper, the noon-day sultriness, and the midnight chill, the fatigue, and privation, and vexation, which beset the traveller on shore", adding as a concluding remark: "I shall return to it [land] no doubt willingly after a while, but for the present, it is rest, it is relief, refreshment, to be at sea [...] the Utopia of enjoyment" (p. 97). These passages seem a prefiguration of the cruise advertising we are familiar with nowadays. But Willis points out how the value of his cruise does not consist of rest and pleasure only, but also instruction: "The cruise, thus far, has been one of continually mingled pleasure and instruction, and the best of, by every association of our early days, is to come" (p. 163).

Thus, Willis shows a keen awareness of the implications of cruising within the rise of tourism when he states that a "summer cruise in the Mediterranean is certainly the perfection of sight-seeing" (p. 248). He sees cruising as a most desirable tourist experience. At the same time, he seems also aware of the possible negative sides of an unsustainable and destructive development of touristic practices, such as that of collecting souvenirs from ancient artifacts: "For my own part, I cannot conceive the motive for carrying away a fragment of a statue or a column. I should as soon think of drawing a tooth as a specimen of some beautiful woman I had seen in my travels. And how one dare show such a theft to any person of taste, is quite as singular" (p. 213). The concluding remark raises an issue which by then had already become a staple of touristic discourse: that of a discrepancy between refinement, culture, and "taste" on one hand, and improper, irresponsible tourist behaviour on the other. Through a narrative which provides amusement and a kind of useful knowledge to readers, Willis is careful to present himself as a respectful, responsible, and mindful tourist, making the best of the opportunity offered to him in personal as well as social terms. At the same time, the author never claims to be an expert of European culture, an art connoisseur, as his visit to a mosaic copy of da Vinci's *Last Supper*, nearby Vienna, displays

> On the lower floor of the entrance-hall in the former palace, lies the copy, in mosaic, of Leonardo da Vinci's 'Last Supper,' done at Napoleon's order. Though supposed to be the finest piece of mosaic in the world, it is so large that they have never found a place for it. A temporary balcony has been erected on one side of the room, and the spectator mounts nearly to the ceiling to get a fair position for looking down upon it. That unrivalled picture, now going to decay in the convent at Milan, will probably depend upon this copy for its name with posterity (p. 125).

The passage seems a foreboding of Mark Twain's well-known description of the visit to "the mournful wreck of the most celebrated painting in the world" he pays during his cruise in the Mediterranean in 1867 on board the steamship Quaker City[16].

"A picnic on a gigantic scale"

For Willis, the opportunity to make a cruise came from an invitation to join the crew of the "United States" frigate, which was patrolling the Mediterranean upon orders of the US navy. Mark Twain's cruise in the Mediterranean, instead, had a different origin: the travel was widely advertised among well-off Americans, with the promise of a trip combining the lure of the exotic with that of an exclusive and unique experience. Twain's ironic travelogue repeatedly makes fun of the high-class pull through which the cruise was marketed. Contrary to the organisers' expectations, though, the cruise did not sell well and several well-known figures who were expected to be "of the party" in the end decided not to go, so that, as Twain writes, there remained "never a celebrity left" (p. 11) except himself.

---

16 Mark Twain, *Innocents Abroad*, cit. p. 135. Subsequent references quoted parenthetically in the text.

And yet, the journey itself and the fictional account Twain made out of it were enormously successful, to the point that both became major landmarks of the rise of modern mass tourism. Although it is at the heart of the journey itself, the Mediterranean in this case does not seem to be the protagonist of Twain's narrative, which appears to be more a middle-class version of the old, aristocratic grand tour, now rapidly turning into a commodified experience, as described by the author who, in subscribing for the cruise finds himself "drifting with the tide of a great popular movement. Every body was going to the famous Paris Exposition – I, too, was going to the Paris Exposition" (p. 13). The shores of the Mediterranean, nevertheless, constitute the route of Twain's journey, a trip to the heart of classic history and art. What makes Twain's travelogue unique, though, are not so much the places he visits, nor the works of art he pays homage to, as the caustic comments and scathing wit of his writing targeting his fellow travelers, whom he portrays as "venerable fossils" (p. 492), as well as his experiences in Paris where, "From earliest infancy it had been a cherished ambition of [the author] to be shaved some day in a palatial barber-shop of Paris" (p. 78). When he finally got the chance, Twain experienced something quite different from what he had anticipated – "The first rake of his razor loosened the very hide from my face and lifted me out of the chair" – so that he "never, never, never desired to dream of palatial Parisian barber-shops any more" (p. 79). Through his travelogue, Twain lampoons travel guides, hotel staff, and many renowned attractions. His visit to Venice, for example, is thus portrayed: "This the famed gondola and this the gorgeous gondolier! – the one an inky, rusty old canoe with a sable hearse-body clapped on to the middle of it, and the other a mangy barefooted guttersnipe with a portion of his raiment on apparition which should have been sacred from public scrutiny" (p. 155).

In this way, Twain subverts and undermines traditional *topoi* and stylistic features of the travelogue genre, remaining true, however, to its overall motives and narrative logic. Thus, readers have the weird sensation of experiencing something recognizable and familiar, but, at the same time, also new and unsettling, very much like a touristic travel experience itself. Accordingly, the Mediterranean is cast in a new light, for it no longer appears only as a prefabricated and stereotyped image, the sacred cradle of Western civilization, but as a place where potentially everybody can go and experience it first-hand. Emblematic of this change in the travelogue rhetoric is Twain's description of his visit to da Vinci's *Last Supper*: "I recognized the old picture in a moment [...]. The world seems to have become settled in the belief, long ago, that it is not possible for human genius to outdo this creation of Da Vinci's. I suppose painters will go on copying it as long as any of the original is left visible to the eye" (p. 135). Then, Twain writes a passage which has become exemplary of the logic of modern mass tourism:

> [...] as usual, I could not help noticing how superior the copies were to the original, that is, to my inexperienced eye. [...] People come here from all parts of the world, and glorify this masterpiece. They stand entranced before it with bated breath and parted lips, and when they speak, it is only in the catchy ejaculations of rapture [...] I only envy these people [...] How can they see what is not visible? [...] I am willing to believe that the eye of the practiced artist can rest upon the Last Supper and renew a lustre where only a hint of it is left, supply a tint that has faded away, restore an expression that is gone [...]. But I can not work this miracle. Can those other uninspired visitors do it, or do they only happily imagine they do? (pp. 135–137)

Several key indicators of the popularization of the new tourist discourse are at stake in this passage. Similarly to what happens today with the touristic visit to *Mona Lisa* at the Louvre, Twain goes to see the *Last Supper* not because he likes the painting, or can particularly appreciate its artistic value, technique, or significance, but because it is a "must-do", a marker of Renaissance high culture. However, differently from his travel companions, from seeing the masterpiece he does not try to derive any sort of cultural legitimacy, any social capital to be spent once back home; rather, Twain seems to seek a form of cultural recognition through his debunking the popular touristic logic and from his shift of attention from the masterpiece itself (which to him appears as barely discernible and noticeable) to the social scene around it and the tourist practices through which it is enjoyed.

Surprisingly enough, this well-known passage does not appear in the reports Twain wrote to the newspapers during the cruise[17], but only in the revised, narrative version he published two years afterward. This is indicative of a change in the style of travel accounts. While Willis' narrative was firmly grounded on a powerfully romantic notion of selfhood, occupying the central stage of the account, Twain's narrative in *The Innocents Abroad* is centered upon the unconventional tourist gaze

---

17 See *Traveling with the Innocents Abroad: Mark Twain's Original Reports from Europe and the Holy Land*, edited by Daniel Morley McKeithan, Norman, The University of Oklahoma Press, 2012, pp. 57–8.

cast by an unorthodox self. Emblematic is Twain's shift of attention from the fresco to its copyists: they supersede it as the real focus of Twain's touristic attention. In this way, Twain makes the touristic experience virtually available to ordinary people to a degree unimaginable before, and contributes in a substantial manner to the rise of more realistic styles of narration. A narration at the center of which there is not simply "the most celebrated painting in the world", the exceptional and inimitable work of art, but also the scene of reproduction of the mediatic effects generated by the masterpiece as a mass touristic attraction. While paving the way to new representative modes and narrative styles, Twain's text yet also retains, a traditional appeal to readers, functioning as a transitional connector between a by-then past romantic narrative tradition and new, more realistic prose forms.

"The cruise, from first to last, was a success": Edith Wharton and *The Cruise of the Vanadis*

At the end of the trip on board the Quaker City, Twain apparently felt so exasperated that in the last report written for the *New York Herald* he defined the cruise "a funeral excursion without a corpse" (p. 492)[18]. However, upon reconsidering the travel one year later, while revising the text for volume publication, he came to view his experience in a decidedly more optimistic light: "Travel is fatal to prejudice, bigotry, and narrow-mindedness [...]. Broad, wholesome, charitable views of men and things cannot be acquired by vegetating in one little corner of the earth all one's life" (p. 498). Such vision seems to underpin also Edith Wharton's conception of travel. In her times, travel writing was often considered a kind of apprenticeship, preparatory to nobler narrative forms. Like in the case of her friend, Henry James, Wharton's travel experiences date from her earliest infancy, when, at the age of four, her parents took her to Europe for a stay of six years. Since then, travel had been a lifetime habit for Wharton who, in 1911, decided to take up residence in France, visiting

---

18 In the same letter Twain reports that "perhaps [the cruise] was a pleasure excursion, but it did not look like one" (p. 491). For the thirty-two-year-old writer, the average age of Twain's fellow travelers was a major motive of disappointment: "Three fourths of the Quaker City's passengers were between forty and seventy years of age. [...] Is any man insane enough to imagine that this picnic of patriarchs sang, made love, danced, laughed, told anecdotes, dealt in ungodly levity?" (p. 491).

the US only sporadically afterward. The daughter of an affluent family, Wharton could afford travelling in style. And yet, as I hope to show, her earliest travelogue about a cruise in the Mediterranean clearly exhibits signs of an advancing mass-tourism logic Twain had inaugurated with his popular masterpiece.

Wharton's cruise in the Mediterranean took place in 1888, when she was twenty-six and had been married three years. While Twain had opened his travel account in a half bantering tone, describing his excitement at "being 'select'" (p. 10), being part of a fortunate few, Wharton was aware from the beginning that she belonged to a privileged class, as revealed by her memories of how the idea of a three-month cruise in the Mediterranean had first come up: "One day I happened to say to our old friend James Van Allen: 'I would give everything I own to make a cruise in the Mediterranean'"[19]. Challenging as it is, the remark has been read as also possibly masking her disappointment with her married life.[20] Whatever the reasons behind it, Wharton's expression in the optative mood graphically signals her investment in the desired travel. Her exclamation calls attention, more than to the destination, to the means of the travel: she wants to see the Mediterranean through a cruise; it is the cruise the real object of her desire. Her emphasis on the mode of voyage is symptomatic of broader transformations in travel trends, as her report records.

Without hesitation, Whartons' friend chartered a luxurious steam-yacht, the Vanadis, with sixteen crewmen, a maid and a valet. The Whartons insisted on sharing the expenses, even when they found out that the cost of the trip would match a year's income for them. Despite some grievances from Edith's family, the couple "promptly decided to do [it]!"[21]

Fortuitously retrieved in 1991, in the local library of Hyères (in the French riviera, where in 1927 Wharton bought a house in which she would spend winters and springs for the rest of her life), the manuscript is among her earliest narrative attempts. What first strikes the reader is that the text consists of a day-by-day (sometimes hour-by-hour) record of the trip. In this sense, Wharton's writing is a travel-log much more than

---

19 Edith Wharton, *A Backward Glance*, cit. p. 857.
20 Sarah Bird, *Edith Wharton's Travel Writings*, cit., p. 13.
21 Edith Wharton, *A Backward Glance*, cit. p. 858.

a travelogue, a chronicle rather than a narrative account. And yet, her style is unmistakable. While carefully registering sights, places, people, attractions and sceneries, she impresses on them the stamp of her individuality. Her persona dominates the text and makes her two male companions almost disappear. Despite the comfort of the yacht, the account bears witness to an intense journey, during which Wharton did not spare herself and went the extra mile whenever she had an opportunity to gain new experiences and see new places. The distinctive tone of her account is well expressed by the following passage, describing her visit to Syracuse:

> After luncheon we went ashore and down to the Greek theatre. It stands on a slope below Epipolae, looking over Ortygia, the bay, and the intervening stretch of olive and orange orchards; a far lovelier view than met the eyes of the Greek audiences who had the crowded house-roofs of Neapolis as a background to their stage [...] but far more interesting to me was the carpet of wild flowers which overspread the whole hill-side[22].

The author presents herself as a very well read, educated person, familiar with classic culture and history who, nevertheless, seems to find "wild flowers" much more "interesting" than the "Greek theatre" and "Ortygia". This combination of traditional traits and inventive attitude makes Wharton a tourist of a kind. As a traditional tourist, she is definitely in search of the picturesque in her travel along Mediterranean shores and suffers from the typical sense of disillusionment experienced by tourists: she comments that the "streets of Palermo are [...] uninteresting from a picturesque point of view" (p. 65), even though Sicily on the whole is for her a "most picturesque country" (p. 70). Likewise, the "Cathedral of Monreale", which "had been the chief object of [her] pilgrimage", gives her "a feeling of disappointment when [she] found [herself] face to face with it" (p. 65).

However, Wharton also wants to distance herself from ordinary tourists and to assert her individuality: she criticises tourist guides ("*The Mediterranean Hand Book* proved as untrustworthy as usual" [p. 104]) and claims her right to her own perspective on the sights she sees: "I know that in saying this I am running counter to the opinion of the highest authorities; but this Journal is written not to record other people's opinions, but to note as exactly as possible the impression which I myself received"

---

22 Edith Wharton, *Cruise of the Vanadis*, cit. p. 54. Subsequent references quoted parenthetically in the text.

(p. 67). This last statement is symptomatic of Wharton's viewpoint. In voicing her own subjective identity, Wharton transforms a pleasure travel, the privileged experience of a cruise to traditional and less known tourist destinations, into an affirmation of individual agency, freedom, and personal choice. In this sense, as Sarah Bird Wright states, *The Cruise of the Vanadis*, "anticipates the connoisseurship that will be the hallmark of her later travel writing"[23]. More than that, it also foreshadows Wharton's later authorial stance. Building on the opposition between travel and tourism, Wharton reiterates in new terms a traditional vision of the Mediterranean as "the location for the origin of culture"[24]. Yet, what makes this text revealing is precisely its peculiar pattern of what, following Dean MacCannell's landmark work, one may term touristic rhetoric of anti-tourism[25]. In other words, Wharton's log is a carefully crafted record of a journey to both typical touristic destinations and off the beaten-track sites. Like that of a modern tourist, Wharton's journey is characterised by a constant emphasis on time and the lack thereof. As it progresses, a growing earnestness marks the cruise, till it seems to end in a hurry. "The cruise", Wharton declares in the concluding lines of the travel record, "from first to last, was a success" (p. 221). The fashionable combination of sightseeing, taste and cultural capital she displays registers the rising social status of the cruise as an exclusive and luxury form of tourism, giving access to travel as an experience of privilege, comfort, and leisure.

Cruising the Mediterranean between Imagination and Consumption

Samuel Gamble Bayne is a fairly unknown figure. Born in Ireland in 1844, he emigrated to the US right after the Civil War, in 1869, to seek fortune. A successful businessman, Bayne is the author of several travelogues, among which *A Fantasy of Mediterranean Travel*, published

---

23 Sarah Bird Wright, *Edith Wharton's Travel Writings: The Making of a Connoisseur*, New York, St. Martin's Press, 1997, p. 14. On Wharton in Europe, see Katherine Joslin and Alan Price (eds.), *Wretched Exotic: Essays on Edith Wharton in Europe*, New York, Peter Lang, 1993.

24 Robert Burden, *Travel, Modernism and Modernity*, Farnham, England, Ashgate, 2015, p. 201.

25 See the classic study of Dean MacCannell, *The Tourist: A New Theory of the Leisure Class* (1976), Berkeley, University of California Press, 1999.

in New York in 1909 and detailing his travels in Southern Europe, North
Africa and the Near East which, according to what he records in his autobiography, took place in the winter of 1903/4[26]. Although with little
literary ambitions, the work is highly indicative of the success of this kind
of travelogues at the time. Also, as several echoes make clear, *A Fantasy*
bespeaks of the popularity of Twain's travelogue which Bayne seems to
take as model for his narrative, as an explicit reference suggests[27]. As the
author states in the opening page of his text, he "started to scribble [...]
following the fantastic idea" [...] arising during a "spasmodic dream [he]
had one evening in a steamer chair, of what [he] imagined was to happen
on [their] coming voyage"[28]. Right from the start, the cruise is enveloped
in a dream-like, imaginary atmosphere, which seems to clash with the
matter-of-fact, business-like approach of the author. Presenting himself
as a practical man, Bayne is nevertheless hooked by the flair and glamour
that the idea of a Mediterranean cruise had attained by then. Beside the
planned tourist destinations, it is the cruise itself that piqued the curiosity of Bayne, pushing him to embark on the journey.

Immediately after introducing the cruise, Bayne provides a lengthy
description of his fellow passengers, focusing on the peculiar traits of
many of them. He dwells on the "most picturesque and amusing man
on board... a Mexican rubber planter from Guadalajara, known on the
ship's list as Senor Cyrano de Bergerac" who "looked like the leader of a
Wild West show", and appeared to the other travelers as "a contradiction
in terms" (p. 9). This portrait is representative of the ironic and apparently detached perspective that Bayne adopts towards the enterprise; a
perspective typical of the disenchanted, savvy, and yet ordinary traveler
he wants to embody. In a vein similar to Twain's, he comments on various fellow travelers of the "seven hundred" who took part in the cruise.
The sheer size is revealing of the mass dimension of the voyage: while
Twain was making fun of the alleged "select" character of his journey,
Bayne is inescapably aware that he is joining in an experience still passed
off as exclusive but actually part of mass culture. Emblematic of this are
Bayne's words about one of his travelling companions: "It is impossible

---

26 See his *Derricks of Destiny*, New York, Brentano, 1924, pp. 172, 187.

27 When visiting Granada, Bayne writes that he had "transmitted Mark Twain's name of
    'Billfinger'" to their guide, who recognises the allusion and "was very much pleased
    by this notable mark of distinction", Bayne, *A Fantasy*, cit. p. 23.

28 Samuel Gamble Bayne, *A Fantasy*, cit. p. 1. Subsequent references quoted parenthet-
    ically in the text.

for any large body of travelers to escape the man who by every device tries to impress his fellows with the idea that he is a Mungo Park on his travels" (p. 6) and who ends up giving "the impression of being a mammoth comique on his annual holiday" (p. 7). The definitive evidence is, for the author, provided by "the post-card mania", which he defines "the most pernicious disease that has ever seized humanity since the days of the Garden of Eden, and in no better place can it be seen at its worst that on a steamer calling at foreign ports" (p. 11). Bayne talks at length about the postcard which he defines a "veritable Frankenstein", for it is "harder to break away from this habit than from poker, gossiping, strong drink, tobacco [...]" (p. 11).

Postcards, first produced around 1870, were in their heyday at the time Bayne undertook his Mediterranean cruise. In many ways, the illustrations that accompany Bayne's text appear to recall the postcard: many of them portray famous tourist destinations or typical local color scenes, and have captions explaining the pictures. This resemblance has led Monica Cure, in the only critical discussion of Bayne's *Fantasy* I could find, to claim Bayne's "complicity with the postcard, mania" (p. 64), reading his illustrated travelogue as a form of *extended* postcard[29]. However, Bayne's words seem quite undisputable, especially in his final considerations on the matter, when he states that the "ultimate fate of the post-card mania is as yet undecided. [...] In any case its foundations are laid in vanity and egotism, and that will eventually prove its undoing" (p. 13). Rather than a postcard replica, Bayne's illustrations seem an authentication of his experiences recorded in the travelogue, as well as a way to involve the readership into that experience. Bayne seems to oppose the mass anonymity and vacuity of the postcard which ends being "quietly dropped in the waste-basket" (p. 12), to the illustrations of his book, which instead provide the reader with a vivid visual testimony of the well-known tourist destinations he discusses in his narrative account. Fully acknowledging his partaking in mass tourism, Bayne strives to distance his work from the disposable quality of postcards while ascribing to it some form of longevity and persistence.

---

29 According to Cure, "far from being in competition with the postcard, Bayne's narrative incorporates it. The view Bayne is offering is also for sale, in the form of his book, and it is a bargain". Monica Cure, *Picturing the Postcard: A New Media Crisis at the Turn of the Century*, Minneapolis, University of Minnesota Press, 2018, p. 65.

Thus, Bayne's cruise in the Mediterranean can be read as an attempt to add a personal note on a by then largely prepackaged and commercialised mass travel experience, as this passage emblematises:

> Seville has one of the largest, finest and richest Gothic Cathedrals in existence; it has absolutely everything that can in reason be demanded of a cathedral, with or without price, including in part a full line of old masters, headed by Murillo and Velasquez (who were born here); bones of the good dead ones – and some bad ones – silver gilt organs, a court of orange trees in full bloom, the Columbian library (established by Fernando, Columbus' son), containing nothing but books, books, books! Then again there are *acres* – I was going to say – of stained glass windows, but perhaps I had better stick to the simple truth and say innumerable windows, showing every variation of the rainbow in their brilliant, deftly interwoven tints (p. 20).

This apparently ironic account is indicative of the kind of work Bayne is attempting to produce, that is, impressing a personal stamp on his beaten-track itinerary, while, at the same time, reaching out to the common readership of the day.

A considerable part of his narrative is devoted to his stay in Egypt which, again, is described in a curious way. Exemplary is a passage about pharaoh Ramses II, who is portrayed almost as a contemporary celebrity, as an alluring picture for the contemporary, average-culture reader:

> Rameses II. was the greatest advertiser of any age or time. He erected rows of colossal statues to himself all over Egypt, and for fear some one would not notice a *single* figure, he would place half a dozen side by side. He was usually represented in his Sunday clothes, with a pleasing smile, and a granite goatee on his chin as big as a narrow-gauge freight car. (See photograph.) "Ram" was the most celebrated of the Pharaohs (p. 73).

At the end of his cruise, in Liverpool, on his way to cross the Atlantic back home, Bayne makes some interesting final considerations on the cruise and the experiences he has just lived:

> Then we took a new steamer to New York, and the cruise of the *Cork* was a thing of the past.

> Retrospectively I might add that we suffered from a kind of artistic and historical dyspepsia, brought about by our inability to digest the immensity of the things we had seen and their variety. After leaving Madeira the stopping places came so fast that our sightseeing was indeed hard work, each new place blotting out the one that had preceded it. Undoubtedly we would after a while remember the scenes and places visited, and we would surely do so if we read the standard writers on these subjects (p. 103).

One more time, Bayne makes clear his full awareness of cruising the Mediterranean as a mass experience, which was then becoming available to larger numbers of people. He also makes no pretense he is a traveler of the old days, but wholly accepts his condition as a modern tourist. In fact, in a somewhat similar guise to Wharton, and very much like a contemporary tourist figure, he regrets the speed with which he visited the various sites, with the sights notched up as fast as possible. In reaffirming the perspective of the practical, well-off businessman, who wants to get value out of his money, he is also aiming at enhancing his social, more than cultural, capital. By concluding on the "standard writers", the author bluntly declares his unsuitableness to be ranked among them. He is satisfied with having written the record of his cruise, bearing his own, personal stamp on it.

Conclusion

As we have seen, the image of cruising the Mediterranean plays a notable role in the American literary imaginary over the course of the nineteenth and early twentieth centuries. But, over time, it also radically changed, following the new social and cultural patterns that were developing. Certainly not an experience available to everyone, cruising the Mediterranean, between the 1830s and the first decade of the twentieth century was never only a pleasure trip, but also, and especially, a voyage into history as well as art. In different ways and varying degrees, Willis's, Twain's, Wharton's, and Bayne's works voice the authors' expectations to derive cultural and social prestige from the cruise, and not simply because they went to and visited the Mediterranean, but because they did so in a cruise. Taken together, these texts bespeak of the enduring popularity of the Mediterranean as a travel destination for Americans, from the early transatlantic packet lines to the rise of modern mass tourism. At the same time, though, they also reveal the manifold meanings that the popularised image of the cruise in the Mediterranean may have: from Willis' shrewd use of his visit to enhance his social prestige, to Twain's evident contrast between an old world and an America which was in the aftermath of a devastating civil war and desperately needed to rebuild a sense of identity; from Wharton's elite experience and subtle ability to cast light on off-the-beaten-track sites, customs, and aspects of the Mediterranean thanks to the breath of her culture and refinement of her education, to Bayne's businessman's attitude, who relishes in the pleasures and entertainment of the cruise as much as in the renowned tourist sites he is able to afford visiting in person. Despite the different approaches exemplified in these texts, however, they all share a deep fascination for the aura that, despite the passing of time and the growing commodification of travel, still lingers, for the American imagination, on the fantasy of a Mediterranean cruise.

Victorian Travellers on the Nile: Marianne Brocklehurst, Mary Booth, and Egypt's "Eastern spectacle"

Adrian Tait

Late in 1873, the novelist Amelia B. Edwards set off on a long and adventurous journey up the Nile. Eschewing the tourist steamboats that were by then plying the great river, she chose the more leisurely option, travelling aboard a traditional, sail-powered dahabeeyah (or barge) called the *Philae*. The *Philae* did not, however, set sail alone: as Edwards recorded, "[c]lose behind" came "the 'Bagstones,' – a neat little dahabeeyah in the occupation of two English ladies who chanced to cross with us [...] from Brindisi, and of whom we have seen so much ever since that we regard them by this time as quite old friends in a strange land. I will call them the M.B.'s"[1].

The "M.B.'s" in question were Marianne Brocklehurst (1832–1898) (hereafter M.B.) and Mary Isabella Booth (1830–1912) (hereafter M.I.B.), for both of whom this was to be the first of several trips to Egypt[2]. As it would later transpire, M.B. kept her own account of the trip, in a diary that was bequeathed to the museum in her home town of Macclesfield, and eventually published in 2004. Entertaining and engaging, M.B.'s brisk account of her experiences provides a fascinating and informal counterpoint to Amelia's Nile travelogue. Inadvertently, it also reveals the "highly ethnocentric" way in which British travellers

---

1   Amelia B. Edwards, *A Thousand Miles Up the Nile*, London, George Routledge & Sons, 1890, pp. 35–6. Originally published 1877.

2   For a brief illustrated overview of this and their later trips, see Margaret Serpico and Heba Abd el Gawad, *Beyond Beauty: Transforming the Body in Ancient Egypt*, London, Two Temple Place, 2016, pp. 69–73.

recapitulated and reinforced an image of the exotic otherness of the Orient[3]. As a consequence, M.B.'s narrative reduces the intricate realities of a modernizing nation to an "Eastern spectacle"[4]. For M.B., the Arab peoples she encountered were "specimens" of this strangeness, and variously "savage", "strange", or "wild"; the scenery was "picturesque" or "pretty"; and Egypt itself was an "Old World", an "old Egypt" (p. 105), whose ancient history was more commanding than its complex and compromised present.

At the same time, however, M.B.'s record of their trip also reveals their own indomitability, as energetic explorers and budding Egyptologists who were in no way daunted by the challenges of their trip, and in no way held back by the domestic ideology that defined their roles as women in polite Victorian society. To the contrary, the M.B.'s plunged headlong into their encounters with Egypt, both old and new, sacking their dragoman (or guide and translator), and taking full control of their trip – and of their dahabeeyah. As Edwards records of their time in "Minieh" (Minya), "[t]he M.B.'s, who had no dragoman and did their own marketing, were very busy here, laying in stores of fresh provision, bargaining fluently in Arabic, and escorted by a bodyguard of sailors"[5].

In spite, therefore, of the "racial differentiation from [and superiority to] 'foreign others'" which M.B.'s diary so often assumes, it also captures something of the way "in which peoples geographically and historically separated come into contact with each other and establish ongoing relations"[6]. In these "contact zones" – in these "interactive, improvisational" encounters – M.B. also sees "the relations among colonisers and colonised, or travellers and 'travellees,' not in terms of separateness, but in terms of co-presence, [and] interaction"[7].

---

3   Carl Thompson, "Nineteenth-Century Travel Writing", in *The Cambridge History of Travel Writing*, edited by Nandini Das and Tim Youngs, Cambridge, Cambridge University Press, 2019, pp. 108–124, 117.

4   Marianne Brocklehurst, *Miss Brocklehurst on the Nile: Diary of a Victorian Traveller in Egypt*, Disley, Millrace, 2004, p. 18. Hereafter all references to M.B.'s diary will be found in parenthesis in the text.

5   Amelia B. Edwards, *op. cit.*, p. 84.

6   Mary Louise Pratt, *Imperial Eyes: Travel Writing and Transculturation*, 2nd ed., London, Routledge, 2007, p. 119. Janice Schroeder, "Strangers in Every Port: Stereotypes of Victorian Women Travellers", *Victorian Review*, 24, no. 2, 1998, pp. 118–129, 8.

7   Mary Louise Pratt, *op. cit.*, p. 8.

Thus, and whilst M.B.'s narrative reproduces Orientalist constructions of the east, it also resists and sometimes rejects outright the domestic ideology of Victorian society; in turn, it reflects her own first-hand
exposure to the rich complexity of contemporary life along the Nile, and
her own, deepening interest in it.

Travel and tourism expanded enormously over the course of the nineteenth century, as well-to-do Britons took advantage of new forms of
transport such as steam-ship and steam-train to expand their horizons.
For Victorians, travelling the Mediterranean was, as John Pemble argues,
a particular passion, since the Mediterranean was associated with both
Biblical and classical Greek and Roman history[8]. Italy was an obvious
focus, and the Levant and Holy Land – accessed through Cairo – another.
Increasingly, however, travellers took an interest in Egypt for its own
sake. Where once travellers simply paused to spend a day looking over
the historical highlights of Cairo, they now began to embark on lengthy
trips up the Nile to see newly discovered and newly excavated antiquities.
Frequently they left with mementos of their trip, which would later find
their way into private collections and public museums. These travellers
also generated a steady stream of letters, memoirs and diaries, a stream
that quickly rose into a torrent: writing in 1849, Robert Curzon observed
that the public was "already overwhelmed with little volumes about palm-
trees and camels, and reflections on the Pyramids"[9]. Increasingly, travellers read about the country before they left home, "took libraries of travel
literature with them", and "retraced familiar routes and tropes – now,
not only those of the classical sources and the Bible, but also those of
fellow tourists, travel writers, and guidebooks"[10]. The M.B.'s, for example
took with them both a copy of Murray's *Hand-book for Travellers in Egypt*
(1847) and Lucie (Lady) Duff-Gordon's *Letters from Egypt, 1863–1865*
(1865). As Pemble observes, "[i]t says much for its peculiar allure that
the Mediterranean continued to inspire travel books in the age of the
guidebook"[11].

---

8   John Pemble, *The Mediterranean Passion: Victorian and Edwardian Travellers in the
    South*, Oxford, Oxford University Press, 1988.

9   Robert Curzon, *Visits to Monasteries in the Levant*, London, John Murray, 1849, p. iii.

10 Rebecca Jones, "African Travel Writing", in *The Cambridge History of Travel Writing*,
    edited by Nandini Das and Tim Youngs, Cambridge, Cambridge University Press,
    2019, pp. 283–297, 288.

11 John Pemble, *op. cit.*, p. 7.

As the example of Amelia and the M.B.'s itself underlines, a growing number of well-to-do Victorian women also chose to travel to Egypt by themselves, sometimes taking advantage of the improved lines of communication opened up by mass tourism: whilst the M.B.'s eschewed a Cook's steamboat for a dahabeeyah once in Eygpt, they too took the "P&O Boat" (p. 8) from Brindisi to Alexandria. For women travellers and would-be travel writers, however, there were further challenges to negotiate. As Janice Schroeder argues, women found themselves precariously positioned "within England's imperialist, patriarchal political order", at the problematic intersection of two hegemonic discourses[12]. On the one hand, they found themselves caught up in a "colonial discourse" with its roots in the Orientalist constructions identified by Edward W. Said, a body of knowledge which assumed European superiority and non-European, eastern inferiority[13]. As Said explained in his ground-breaking book, first published in 1978, the west defined the Orient in terms of "its sensuality, its tendency to despotism, its aberrant mentality, its habits of inaccuracy, its backwardness", unchanging characteristics that positioned (and marginalised) eastern societies along "with all other peoples variously designated as backward, uncivilised, and retarded"[14]. On the other, women travellers had to contend with their own gendered status, as women in the context of "nineteenth-century gendered ideologies of 'natural' domesticity, the civilizing mission, and separate spheres"[15]. It was one thing for married women to travel accompanied by their husbands, Schroeder points out; they could be (re)presented as "an example of ideal domestic womanhood" whose role was simply an extension of women's "civilizing mission"[16]. Unmarried women were something quite else; "redundant, [and] anomalous", they were stereotyped as "The Spinster Abroad", "eccentric, improper, [and] mildly embarrassing"[17].

For the Victorian woman traveller, therefore, travel did not "necessarily signify an unqualified, emancipatory escape"; it entailed a further set of boundaries to negotiate[18]. At the same time, however, these

---

12 Janice Schroeder, *op. cit.*, p. 125.

13 Carl Thompson, *Travel Writing*, London, Routledge, 2011, pp. 136, 135.

14 Edward W. Said, *Orientalism: Twenty-Fifth Anniversary Edition*. New York, Vintage, 2003, pp. 205, 207.

15 Janice Schroeder, *op. cit.*, p. 119.

16 *Ibid.*, pp. 122, 119.

17 *Ibid.*, pp. 123, 118, 122.

18 *Ibid.*, pp. 123, 118, 123.

stereotypes offered women travellers an identity within which to work. In other words, Shroeder argues, these stereotypes "do the work of 'allowing' women to be known as travellers without disturbing Victorian gender ideologies which do not permit women to travel, at least not alone"[19].

This dynamic also influenced the way in which women chose to write about their experiences. One approach was simply to write as men wrote, echoing "male-dominated modes of writings" by referencing the past and thereby demonstrating their own scholarly erudition[20]. Sometimes, they too adopted the "imperial eye/I of the supposedly detached, omniscient observer", a trope closely linked to male travel writing[21]. A second approach lay in recapitulating the domestic ideology of the separate spheres, and creating a kind of travel writing that was less concerned with larger questions of politics and power, more concerned with the realities of domestic, day-to-day life, and characterised by a "strong emphasis on the personal"[22]. As Sara Mills has argued, these limitations were nevertheless productive, in that they enabled "a form of writing whose contours both disclose the nature of the dominant discourses and constitute a critique from its margins"[23]. Precisely "because of their position within the discourse of the 'feminine'", argues Mills, and "[t]hrough elements such as humour, self-deprecation, statements of affiliation, and descriptions of relationships [...] these texts constitute counter-hegemonic voices within colonial discourse"[24]. A third, more radical approach was suggested by the conditions that the act of travelling independently itself created: that, free from societal expectation, women could set about creating an entirely different and much freer form of travel writing, perhaps openly resistant to the hegemonic constructions of women and to the racial structuration implicit in Orientalist discourse, or disruptive of their homogenising

---

19 *Ibid.*, p. 126.

20 Efterpi Mitsi, "'Roving Englishwomen': Greece in Women's Travel Writing", *Mosaic: An Interdisciplinary Critical Journal*, 35, no. 2, 2002, pp. 129–144, 135.

21 Muireann O'Cinneide, "Oriental Interests, Interesting Orients: Class, Authority, and the Reception of Knowledge in Victorian Women's Travel Writing", *Critical Survey*, 21, no. 1, 2009, pp. 4–23, 7.

22 Susan Bassnett, "Travel Writing and Gender", *The Cambridge Companion to Travel Writing*, edited by Peter Hulme and Tim Youngs, Cambridge, Cambridge University Press, 2002, pp. 225–241, 231.

23 Sara Mills, *Discourses of Difference: An Analysis of Women's Travel Writing and Colonialism*, London, Routledge, 1991, p. 23.

24 *Ibid.*, p. 22.

assumptions simply because (argues Billie Melman) their work emphasised "differences and heterogeneity"[25]. As Susan Bassnett notes, some
women travel writers chose to write "in full knowledge of the absence of
a tradition into which they could insert themselves with any degree of
comfort or familiarity", and took full advantage of that absence[26]. "One
of the effects of this breaking-through can be discerned in the clarity of
some of the voices that speak from women's texts"[27].

This brings us to M.B. herself, whose own voice as a writer is so distinctive, and whose diaries were not, it seems, written with any other intention than that of providing a family record. M.B. was, it seems, writing
without the conscious need to meet the expectations of Victorian readers
or subscribe to the terms of the discursive regimes whose constraints she
was challenging through the very act of travelling as she did. How, then,
does M.B. describe her encounters on the Nile? How, more specifically,
does she negotiate the domestic stereotype of herself as a woman traveller
and, in describing her experiences on the Nile, the Orientalist stereotypes
of exoticised peoples and places, stereotypes according to which the (per-
ishable and fast-fading) past was majestic and splendid and worthy of
admiration, but the present was "uncouth, disorderly, and dirty"[28]?

The scene is set when M.B. lands at Alexandria, and beholds "the
Egyptians – first impressions, never to be forgotten of the crowds in
the streets, the strange and many coloured dresses, the dark faces and
white turbans, the stately men and veiled and mysterious women. It is
almost a shock to plunge so suddenly into the Old World and its fash-
ions which have not yet passed away" (p. 12). This is the Egypt of which
she approves, an Egypt that most closely fits the image (and her ideal)
of the still-living past: "the avenues of 'Eastern' trees, the strings of camels, the picturesque people, the little mosks [mosques], the weirdy burial
grounds, the bright bazaars and the dahabeeiahs [dahabeeyahs]" (p. 12).
As she declares when, eleven days later, she witnesses "the procession of
pilgrims starting for Mecca", "we were altogether greatly satisfied with
this Eastern spectacle" (p. 18).

---

25 Billie Melman, "Under the Western Historian's Eyes: Eileen Power and the Early
    Feminist Encounter with Colonialism", *History Workshop Journal*, 42, no. 1, 1996,
    pp. 147–168, 149.

26 Susan Bassnett, *op. cit.,* p. 231.

27 *Ibid.*

28 Janice Schroeder, *op. cit.,* p. 124.

As her journey continues, her diary continues to stress these kinds of encounter, constructing them in a way that corresponds to and confirms an Orientalist construction, such as the moment when she sees "the Kedive [Khedive] in his carriage", accompanied by "his wives promiscuous in very thin veils (some are great beauties from Circassia)" (p. 17). In fact, the then Khedive or viceroy, Isma'il Pasha, was intent on modernizing and Europeanizing the country, a programme that (somewhat ironically) left it so indebted to the European powers that they had then had an excuse to intervene in its rule. By contrast, M.B. unexpectedly finds that the Ottoman Consul at Luxor, one "Mustapha Agha is [...] very polite and pleasant for an old Turk" (p. 32) (he is, after all, supposed to be a sensual and arbitrary despot). Fortunately, the Egyptian sailors aboard the dahabeeyah share her view of the Ottomans as corrupted and corruptible figures. As she records one evening, the Egyptian "[s]ailors sing and dance and do fantasia, one acting a Governor. Very comic performance. All his judgements duly given to the biggest bribe [...]" (p. 26).

Entertaining as she finds her crew (p. 20), and whilst she clearly enjoys their mockery of the Ottomans, she does not have a high opinion of the Egyptians people themselves. In her view, they are often simply a more primitive version of their Ottoman rulers, an opinion suggested by this aside, as she describes how, one night, the M.B.'s "smuggled [a] papyrus away in the sleeve of a thick Inverness coat [...] a very hot night too and if Arabs had brains, which they haven't, it might have struck some one as an odd thing to wear on such occasion" (p. 112). The local people, she writes, may be "doughty" but they are also often "dirty" (p. 40), untrustworthy and unreliable; the "Sheikh of the Cataract" has been asked to provide manpower to haul Bagstones (p. 38), she observes at one point, but none appear (p. 39). "Specimens of Christian monks who swim across and board us for backsheesh [charitable largesse] not prepossessing" (p. 27), she observes at another.

Contemporary Egyptians are most satisfactory when they resemble their ancient ancestors, or when they conform to her own view of what a savage, primitive people should be. "[H]ere we first find the genuine Nubian lady, who smells of castor oil and has her hair in little plaits like the old Egyptian hieroglyphics, each little plait glittering with oil" (p. 42); these women are nevertheless, she writes, "utterly savage and strange" (p. 42). This too is satisfactory. Setting out to "bazaar" (p. 57) with a "caravan [...] arrived from Soudan" (p. 56) she finds nothing for which she can shop, although she is offered "a very tall savage" for sale (the price "was considered rather too dear") (p. 57). "[W]ith a fire [...] and a tent, and wild looking fellows all round", the caravan is (that favourite phrase) "very picturesque" (p. 54).

Conversely, she is dismayed when Egyptians aspire to modernity, as when "that fine Ethopian, Marmoor", changes into European clothes (with "white French boots") (p. 78). However, and as her diary also records, many of the Egyptians she meets are neither savage, strange, exotic, nor modern, but simply impoverished. "[S]qualid inhabitants" (p. 25), she writes; "wretched Arabs in one-sided erections of straw or rough covering, not to be called tents" (p. 23). "Our two attendant sailors", she records, "kept off a portion of the population, the crawling dirty children and filthy women being the most objectionable part" (pp. 25–26). "Pretty place", she observes at one point, "horrible looking people" (p. 34).

M.B. is being perfectly logical, therefore, when she chooses to concentrate on the scenery, and overlook the inhabitants of it; as we shall also see, the same effect can also be achieved by shifting the narrative emphasis towards the past, and the relics of it. Thus, villages can be declared picturesque when they are seen at a distance (p. 61). Similarly, the scenery is at its most entrancing when it is unpeopled, as when she waxes lyrical about "a very beautiful and very strange wild view of the desert [...] like a sea of sand, the hills beyond like islands, bare rocks of a lovely colour and all sorts of shapes, pyramids, sugar loafs and inverted pie-dishes" (p. 59), or when she declares that "[n]either pen nor pencil could paint the warm golden soft shapely waves of sand, the beautiful forms of hills and rocks that push out from beneath, the lovely bends of river where the purple cliffs come down almost perpendicular and the blue hills melt away in the distance [...]" (pp. 44–45). Alternatively, M.B. focuses on the antiquities that line the Nile: with its often extended descriptions of the visits she makes to them, her narrative underlines a prevalent Eurocentric view that the past was simply grander and more important than the shabby present; that, in fact, the past should take precedence. For example, she calmly notes how "an Arab village [has been] cleared away" to allow for "Mariette Bey" – the French archaeologist, Auguste Mariette – to dig for antiquities (p. 82).

This sense of the primacy of the past has two consequences. The first is that it recapitulates and reinforces her low opinion of contemporary Egyptians. In so doing, and secondly, it justifies her in her own efforts to rescue the antiquities which she encounters. If the past is everywhere falling victim to the present, she has an obligation to rescue its remnants. This creates a jarring clash of perspectives within the text. On the one hand, she is appalled by the damage that has been and continues to be done to the antiquities along the Nile. For example, she decries a "party of American missionaries" (p. 90) for adding to the "promiscuous autographs" left on a tomb (p. 91), and considers it "abominable to disfigure the tombs and temples"; she is "grieved to see [the] great name of [John] Murray [from whose guidebook series she quotes on several occasions] itself confronting us [...] as first you enter the Temple of Abou Simbel" (p. 55).

More seriously, and as she notes, everywhere "the mummy has been unearthed" and removed (p. 84). "Persians, Romans, Greeks, all the successive conquerors of Egypt are to blame for this, and if they had not done it, the British Museum would, but not for greed!" (p. 84). Yet she does not register her own compromised and anomalous position, as a traveller without any mandate or authority to collect antiquities, who is nevertheless intent on making off with whatever relics she encounters. Chancing across "a nice little head of Cleopatra" (p. 81), she duly appropriates it, or as she puts it, "rescued [it] from further destruction" (p. 81). This is a few lines after she describes a "most picturesque ruin" "built by Ptolemy somebody and finished by a somebody Caesar" (p. 81). Moreover, she is as determined on securing a mummy as Alfred (her nephew) is on returning home with the carcass of a crocodile; typically, however, she is successful where is not.

The story of her success is sufficiently important for M.B. to write a separate account of it (pp. 107–116), an account that is in itself deeply revealing, since she is negotiating the sale of an artefact whose export is, in fact, illegal. If that account is (somewhat perversely) a testament to her intrepid nature, ingenuity, and determination, it also offers further insights into the Eurocentric norms of the moment. As she notes – and as Amelia's account confirms – she is not the only European trying to abscond with a mummy[29]. Some, however, have a more official role than others. As M.B. points out, she is not simply competing with her fellow travellers, but also with Auguste Mariette, who had been named the official "Conservator of the Antiquities of Egypt" (p. 111). "Mariette Bey", she records, "is said to be very stern and cruel with [...] contrabandists if he catches them, even if it is also whispered that [...] he manages to do

---

29 See Amelia B. Edwards, *op. cit.*, pp. 450–1.

a little that way on his own account, and that not a few little things find themselves in the Paris Museum" (p. 111)[30].

Through a combination of bribery and good fortune (p. 115), the M.B.'s contrive to get these relics aboard a steamer (p. 115), by which stage the mummy itself (as opposed to its case) has been "buried by night with great secrecy and left in his native land" (p. 114). Amelia's account of its fate is rather different: "unable to endure the perfume of their ancient Egyptian, [the M.B.'s] drowned the dear departed at the end of a week"[31].

As M.B.'s anecdote underlines, there is little that seems to daunt her during her travels. She is rather the quiet mistress of all she surveys; and there is a strong sense in which her narrative echoes the "monarch-of-all-I-survey" trope so characteristic of male travel writing of the period[32]. This sense of ownership and appropriation can also be detected in her responses to the Egyptians with whom she does engage. As a woman in Victorian society, she may be the inferior, but in Egypt, she is the equal of any man; by extension, she is also superior to the women she meets, and her diary reflects her sense of that superiority, as when she visits the home of one her crew, and encounters his "marah (wife)": "[she] peeped out of the door shyly enough. She had handsome gold ornaments and was a nice clean looking woman, a very good specimen of the kind [...]" (p. 93). M.B. is not inclined to defer to the Egyptian men she meets; like the "old hunter" she encounters – himself "a fine old specimen" (p. 56) – she sees her own position in relation to the Egyptians as that of their superior. In moments like this, there is no question that M.B. sees these foreign "others" as equals; to the contrary, her diary insists on their status as objects, passively available as specimens for inspection. M.B.'s

---

30 M.B. understates the extent of Mariette's appropriations. Mariette was engaged in a complex struggle to beat competitors to discoveries, ensure that a substantial proportion of those discoveries made their way to France, and direct the rest to Egyptian museums, whilst keeping the Ottoman ruler of Egypt from appropriating those finds as treasure, and simultaneously excluding other Europeans (and especially the English) and "indigenous would-be Egyptologists" from the new antiquities service; Donald M. Reid, "Indigenous Egyptology: The Decolonization of a Profession?", *Journal of the American Oriental Society*, 105, no. 2, 1985, pp. 233–246, 234. As Donald Reid adds, "[i]t is well to recall that Egyptology and modern Western imperialism grew up together"; Reid, "Indigenous Egyptology", p. 234. The glee with which M.B. records her success in eluding Mariette's control suggests that nationality was also a factor in shaping her narrative.

31 Amelia B. Edwards, *op. cit.,* p. 451.

32 Mary Louise Pratt, *op. cit.,* p. 197.

account simply "reproduces the monopoly on knowledge and interpretation that the imperial enterprise sought"[33]. Even her own, obvious emerging interest in Egyptology – an interest that would become a life-long
concern – is refracted through the imperialist lens.

The question, nevertheless, is whether her assumption of racial superiority is in any way tempered or conditioned by her status as a woman,
or whether she draws on the very qualities that supposedly define her
as subordinate in Victorian society – her femininity – to construct an
alternative, oppositional point of view. As these examples (above) suggest, subordinate is not a word that immediately springs to mind in
describing M.B. She is rather a forceful, even dominant personality, who
takes for granted her right to go where she pleases. Class is itself a factor
in this sense of confident entitlement. This is not simply a question of
wealth, but of the leisure that accompanies it. She has a low opinion of
"[Thomas] Cooks' excursionists", to whom the temples are (a somewhat
ironic choice of word) "prey" (p. 75), but they are on a budget and a
timetable. The M.B.'s, by contrast, take a leisurely four months over their
trip, drinking punch (p. 28) and travelling with a manservant and a large
crew, often as part of a large and companionable flotilla of like-minded
and similarly well-to-do Victorians. "This is society on the Nile", she
declares (p. 44). "The mutual dinner parties given and champagne that
flowed need not to be mentioned here" (p. 21).

Nor does her narrative leave any real sense of a writer straightforwardly
defined or confined by the gendered role given to her by society. For
example – and the example is a complex one – M.B. writes about the "poor
young dragoman" (p. 39) on another of the dahabeeyah. He has an abscess
on his knee, and she mentions him several times, draws his picture, and
is clearly solicitous for his welfare (p. 39, p. 44, pp. 49–50). It is difficult
to imagine "the bold adventuring hero of male travel texts" acting in this
way[34]. M.B., however, is writing from within a dominant construction of
femininity that emphasises a woman's role as "nurse/doctor, […] the angel
in the house and […] caring mother"[35]. This kind of interest is allowed to
her. What is interesting, however, is that M.B. does not live up to that role.
Her concern clearly has its limits; there is no question that (for example)

---

33 *Ibid.*, p. 7.
34 Sara Mills, *op. cit.*, cit., p. 22.
35 *Ibid.*, p. 22.

she might offer herself up as his care-giver or nurse. Instead, she (gently) ridicules the dragoman for his own remedy to the problem, noting that "he has himself bled at nearly every town and thinks that if this and fasting and a row of amulets round his neck with bits of the Koran in them won't cure him, it is Allah's will that he should die" (p. 50).

Thus, and whilst M.B.'s interaction with the dragoman is clearly influenced by Orientalist constructions, there is no compensatory sense in which it reflects her given role as a woman in this miniature, floating version of Victorian society. If there is an oppositional voice at work in her narrative, it is not quietly encoded in M.B.'s willingness to present herself as a lady-traveller, suitably chaperoned by her nephew, who then draws on constructions of femininity to counter-point the limitations of an Orientalist perspective that (as Said argued) "encouraged a peculiarly (not to say invidiously) male conception of the world"[36]. As we have seen, M.B.'s diary continuously recapitulates dominant colonialist constructions of the East: that is the point. Those constructions assume a position of authority and superiority, and it is that position of (male) authority that M.B. everywhere usurps.

There is almost nothing, it seems, that M.B. cannot, will not, and does not do. Thus, she exploits her supposedly marginal role as a woman to impose her personality on the dahabeeyah and exert her (matronly or matriarchal) authority over the crew – "our own little chaps" (p. 49) – whom she patronises as one might a child (or, more exactly, as a westerner). It is not long before she and the equally indomitable Mary are marching off into "Esneh" (the modern city of Esna) to provision the entire floating household, returning with "geese, chickens, eggs, sheep, all in odd quantities and up very odd streets" (p. 34).

Nor does she defer to the European men with whom she travels. Her nephew, Alfred, is part of her party, but she is most certainly not a (subordinate) part of his. She is, to the contrary, a witty commentator on his foibles – he "shoots a fox and thinks more of it than the temples, naturally" (p. 33) – and frequent failings. Indeed, she often writes very wryly at the expense of the men: "Mr MacCallum waxing wrath takes to sketching by way of cooling himself" (p. 39). And whilst she may prefer to observe Alfred as he pursues crocodiles, she nevertheless acts as his spotter, and elsewhere goes hunting, variously shooting sand grouse, plovers (p. 27), pigeon (p. 29), and quail (p. 61).

36 Edward W. Said, *op. cit.*, p. 207.

Indeed, her diaries are at their most fulsome and engaged when she is herself at risk or taking risks. There is, for example, this description – in breathless present tense – of the descent of a Cataract:

> We see before us a narrow passage between high granite rocks where the water is regularly roaring [...] and with a sudden rush and a bound we are in for it. The great boat gathers fresh impetus every moment, the very Arabs forget to scream for some moments, and just at the last, when we see to be tearing straight upon the wall of rocks before us, the steersman (four of them) give us a good twist and we turn sharp to the left and escape with our lives (p. 76).

Her account of "How We Got Our Mummy" (pp. 107–116) is itself a tale of derring-do tale, involving secret meetings, midnight exchanges, skulduggery and subterfuge: "entangled" with an Arab "whom we had reason [...] to suspect of treachery, [and of] informing against us", she propitiates him with "a present of champagne and cognac" (p. 110).

The figure who emerges from the diary is, therefore, an adventurous and indomitable one, who refuses to conform to the expectations imposed upon her (except, perhaps, in relation to clothing; her own illustrations show the M.B.'s in full skirts and dresses, even when they are spotting crocodiles for Alfred whilst crouching in a felucca, which, quite naturally, M.B. has been steering (pp. 64–65)). Furthermore, and whilst her views of the Egyptians and Ottomans are undeniably coloured by Orientalism – an Orientalism then so dominant that it constituted "a system of truths" amongst Europeans – her narrative does give the reader glimpses into life along the Nile[37]. There are, for example, brief accounts of her various dealings with officials, asides about bazaars, comments about the crew's interpersonal dynamic, and observations on local customs. These include speculations about funeral rites (pp. 48–49) and a lively description of the sailors' music-making (p. 35), which M.B. also depicts (p. 36). Indeed, the most revealing aspect of M.B.'s diary are these thumbnail pen-and-ink illustrations – and occasional, exquisite, fully worked up water-colours – many of which depict everyday life. By contrast, her written narrative sometimes fails the inquisitive reader by virtue of its brevity, perhaps because it was only ever intended as an aide memoire, shorthand for memories which M.B. assumed she and M.I.B. would always share. Had she developed this into an exhaustive account like Amelia's, how might

---

37 *Ibid.*, p. 204.

it read? Finally, and whilst her attitudes towards the antiquities are, in so many respects, typical of the Eurocentric norm, there is no denying her obvious excitement and delight at some of the sites she comes across; describing the reliefs in one temple, she writes that "[w]e were immensely impressed and think it is the finest thing we have seen in the world. I suppose there is no temple so old or so grand anywhere" (p. 51).

As M.B.'s narrative unfolds, therefore, and as its discursive hybridity and complexity becomes more evident, so she herself emerges as something rather more than the product of dominant discursive regimes; instead, she figures as another in a "series" of what Said identified as "fiercely individualistic Victorian travellers in the east"[38]. With apparently inexhaustible energy, M.B. negotiates and often contradicts the domestic ideology of her day, while pursuing her own wide interests and her own developing curiosity about the world that she was encountering, a curiosity that was in its own margins beginning to escape the centrifugal force of Orientalist assumptions. Increasingly, her encounters with Arab peoples generated a kind of narrative surplus, not easily reconciled with Orientalist constructions: ultimately, M.B. is writing with genuine affection for and growing insight into the lives of those with whom she comes into contact.

In spite, however, of her apparently indomitable sense of self, M.B. does not in the end present herself as remarkable or her experiences as exceptional. Had she seen herself in these terms, she might (like Amelia) have prepared her diary for publication. Perhaps she saw her adventure in terms of the other women with whom she travelled, all of whom were pushing back the boundaries of Victorian expectations, and saw that the "theory of the exceptional woman" could just as easily be used to marginalise her achievements and theirs[39]. As Bassnett underlines, scholarship today tends to emphasise the diversity and complexity of women's travel writing[40]. M.B.'s narrative is a fascinating example of this complex particularity, variously "inflected by gender, class, and nationality"[41].

---

38 *Ibid.*, pp. 194–5.

39 Bassnett, *op. cit.*, p. 228.

40 *Ibid.*

41 Billie Melman, "The Middle East/Arabia: 'the cradle of Islam'", in *The Cambridge Companion to Travel Writing*, edited by Peter Hulme and Tim Youngs, Cambridge, Cambridge University Press, 2002, pp. 105–121, 106–7.

Re-Imagining the Mediterranean: Vita Sackville West's Fictional Excursions in *Challenge* (1924)

Silvia Antosa

Imagining Geographies, Re-imagining Identities

Historically, for British travellers and writers, the South has been identified as a space with shifting and unstable borders, open to multiple forms of representation and reconfiguration. As Nelson Moe has discussed, the very notion of what constituted the South for early British and European explorers is crucial in order to understand the wide range of their experiences[1]. Mediterranean areas like Southern Italy were not usually included in the Grand Tour, even though from the second half of the eighteenth century onwards, British and European artists and intellectuals began to travel in those less explored areas and to write about them, thus producing a growing body of books which could be used by those who could not (or did not) travel abroad.

In Western narratives, the South (like the Orient) was connected to the possibility of observing and experiencing new forms of encounter with other people. These encounters sometimes defied and deconstructed the Western normative sociocultural frame and subverted notions of gender identity and heterosexual desire. In discussing the reasons given by English travellers for embarking on a journey to Southern European and Mediterranean countries, John Pemble has identified at least three main factors: pilgrimages, cultural interests and health. However, as he notes, these motivations were often pretexts which concealed unofficial, less-socially acceptable reasons[2]. In his view, these "cover" strategies were

---

1   Nelson J. Moe, *The View from Vesuvius: Italian Culture and the Southern Question*, Berkeley, University of California Press, 2002.

2   John Pemble, *The Mediterranean Passion: Victorians and Edwardians in the South*, Oxford, Clarendon Press, 1987 (part 2: "Motives", pp. 53–109).

adopted because leaving England without a specific reason was reputed to be, in the British imaginary, a subversive act against one's own country and its established set of values. Furthermore, travelling to the South was particularly suspicious, because it was seen as a space which was less constrained by conventions and rules, and, therefore, given over to vice and corruption.

Representations of the South have provided an incredibly rich variety of literary inspiration for narrative texts, especially from eighteenth-century Gothic fiction onwards, as the ideal setting where transgressive, excessive and taboo passions and desires could be represented. Southern, Mediterranean locations symbolised the foreign "other" which allowed British and European authors to express, in Fred Botting's words, strong "anxiet[ies] over cultural limits and boundaries" by producing "ambivalent emotions"[3]. Moreover, these works also undermined traditional values such as the sacrality of the nuclear, bourgeois family and what Adrienne Rich would define as the compulsory heterosexuality of interpersonal relations[4].

In *The Seduction of the Mediterranean: Writing, Art and Homosexual Fantasy* (1993), Robert Aldrich has further emphasised the connection between travel and illicit sex in relation to male (homo)sexual passions and desires[5]. Similarly, Ian Littlewood has explored the complex network of relations between travel and sex since the Grand Tour and has written that "travel itself was a form of sexual expression"[6], which allowed and encouraged different forms of liberation from the moral constraints that dominated in the home country. From this perspective, travelling helped to construct a new perception of the self and challenged inherited values. This conception favoured the view of the Mediterranean (and of the Orient) as "immoral" sites, where any form of sexual experience was available.

---

3   Fred Botting, *Gothic: The New Critical Idiom*, London and New York, Routledge, 1996, p. 2.

4   See Adrienne Rich, "Compulsory Heterosexuality and Lesbian Existence", *Signs*, 5, no. 4, *Women: Sex and Sexuality*, Summer, 1980, pp. 631–660.

5   Robert Aldrich, *The Seduction of the Mediterranean: Writing, Art and Homosexual Fantasy*, London and New York, Routledge, 1993.

6   Ian Littlewood, *Sultry Climates: Travel and Sex since the Grand Tour*, London, John Murray, 2001, p. 20.

Both Aldrich and Littlewood have explored "the interplay of sex, travel and subversion" in relation to the sociocultural construction of Western masculinity and male homosexual relations[7]. Fewer works have studied this kind of interplay in work by women travellers, especially at the beginning of the twentieth century. As is well known, British women travelled in the Mediterranean, especially from the eighteenth century onwards. They left valuable accounts, which have often suffered from forms of diminishment and censorship due to the predominance of works on travel, conquest and discovery authored by their male counterparts[8]. Notions of "difference" and "alterity" have functioned at various levels in their work and experiences: unlike other women, they ventured abroad risking the comfort of their homes; unlike men, they were relegated to the margins of dominant sociocultural discourses and had to contend with gendered constraints[9]. In addition, they did not have a literary tradition with which they could engage. In a sense, each woman traveller had to forge her own text in relation to her experience, literacy and status. In Joyce Kelley's words,

> Travel to remote regions was especially transgressive for many Western women of the nineteenth and early twentieth centuries who sought both *escape* and *pleasure* abroad. These women, themselves 'Other' to masculine concepts of biology, thought, emotion, and sexuality, *found the authority* they were denied at home by becoming experts of an exotic area. The Otherness they found served as a vehicle for inscribing something new, even something unspoken about themselves. Writing about foreign bodies in a strange land compelled a woman writer to consider the position of her own body as a foreign object and to make choices about the presentation of that body on paper[10].

---

7 *Ibid.*, 129.

8 Dea Birkett, *Spinsters Abroad: Victorian Lady Explorers*, Basil Blackwell, Oxford-New York, 1989; Alison Blunt and Gillian Rose (eds.), *Writing Women and Space: Colonial and Postcolonial Geographies*, The Guilford Press, New York, 1994; and Mary Russell, *The Blessings of a Good Thick Skirt: Women Travellers and Their World*, Collins, London, 1988.

9 Sarah Mills, *Discourses of Difference: An Analysis of Women's Travel Writing and Colonialism*, London, Routledge, 1991; Susan Bassnett, "Travel Writing and Gender", in *The Cambridge Companion to Travel Writing*, edited by Peter Hulme and Tim Youngs, Cambridge, Cambridge University Press, 2002, pp. 225–241.

10 Joyce Kelley, "Increasingly 'Imaginative Geographies': Excursions into Otherness, Fantasy, and Modernism in Early Twentieth-Century Women's Travel Writing", *Journal of Narrative Theory*, 35, no. 3, Fall, 2005, p. 357, my emphasis.

In embracing their own status as different and "other" from the dominant gender, class, sexual and sociocultural models of their own society, women writers of the late nineteenth and early twentieth centuries tended to open up the focus of their own explorations and writing. On the one hand, they followed what Manfred Pfister has defined as "the textual and material traces" left by previous generations of travellers: they actively contributed to the construction of the "archives of cultural memory" through the production of a "web of intertextual references and allusions"[11] in their own accounts. In this way, to varying degrees, their texts contributed to the consolidation of collective sociocultural stereotypes on Mediterranean countries and populations.

On the other hand, while searching for "pleasure" and "escape" from their home country, some women travellers found a self-conscious, liberating "authority" within themselves and their own identity in the exotic and distant space of the Mediterranean. In other words, in their work the Mediterranean becomes a transformative and performative space in which they could find and redefine their selves and empower their own narrative voices. If historically women's travel writing has been consistently defined as more "confessional"[12] and "subjective"[13], early twentieth-century women travellers and writers redefine the intimate nature of their writing by reshaping the very form(s) they used.

In *Orientalism*, Edward Said emphasises the importance of individual, subjective perspectives in the descriptions of foreign places. In his words, "space acquires emotional and even rational sense by a kind of poetic process, whereby the vacant or anonymous reaches of distance are converted into meaning for us here"[14]. He calls this conversion of

---

11 See Manfred Pfister, "Travellers and Traces: The Quest for One's Self in Eighteenth-to Twentieth-Century Travel Writing", in *Life Writing: Autobiography, Biography and Travel Writing in Contemporary Literature. Proceedings of a Symposium Held by the Department of American Culture and Literature, Haliç University, Istanbul, 19–21 April 2006*, edited by Koray Melikoğlu, Stuttgart, Ibidem Verlag, 2012, p. 2.

12 Shirley Foster, *Across New Worlds: Nineteenth-Century Women Travelers and Their Writings*, London, Harvester, 1990, p. 19.

13 Cheryl McEwan, *Gender, Geography, and Empire: Victorian Women Travelers in West Africa*, Burlington, VT, Ashgate, 2000, p. 87.

14 Edward W. Said, 1985 [1978], *Orientalism: Western Representations of the Orient*, Penguin, Harmondsworth, p. 55.

meaning "imaginative geography"[15]. According to Said, imaginative geographies tend to familiarise what is distant and difficult to imagine or experience for readers at home. The process of imagining geographies can also affect the adoption and subversion of different textual forms of representation. Travel writing and fiction have always overlapped and the boundaries between them have frequently been blurred[16]. The fictional effort of narrativising one's own experience concerns any travel account to varying degrees; this is especially true of Modernist texts, as pointed out by Kelley: "[Women's] wandering and inward excursions, during a period when these attributes were being explored in fiction, gives them an intriguingly strategic position in the development of modernist writing"[17].

Thus, the connection between travel, sex and "immorality" in women's writings went alongside the formal experimentation that I have discussed above. This connection is crucial to understand the work by Modernist women writers, whose awareness of a changed relationship between identity and sexuality is at the core of their own texts. By re-imagining the Mediterranean as a space in which they could be freer to investigate their own sexuality and desires, they also produced alternative narrative spaces by conflating existing textual forms in order to give a discursive shape to disruptive forms of identity.

This interlacing, complex network of thematic and formal connections and re-imaginations can be found in the work by Modernist writer Vita Sackville-West (1892–1962). This essay analyses her second novel, *Challenge* (1924), which re-imagines the Mediterranean as a space full of possibilities where, to use Carla Locatelli's words, "the discrepancies, gaps, and silences of one's own story of coming to a representable/readable

---

15 On imaginative geography as a specialised mode of representation, see also Edward W. Said, "Orientalism Reconsidered", in *Reflections on Exile and Other Literary and Cultural Essays*, London, Granta Books, 2001, pp. 198–215; and Edward W. Said, "Representing the Colonised: Anthropology's Interlocutors", in *Reflections on Exile and Other Literary and Cultural Essays*, London, Granta Books, 2001, pp. 293–316.

16 See also Silvia Antosa, 2008, "Formal and Thematic Influence of Travel Writing on the Novel: From the Pilgrims' Accounts to Gothic Fiction", *Fogli di Anglistica*, 2, nos. 3–4, pp. 55–66.

17 Joyce Kelley, "Increasingly 'Imaginative Geographies'", cit., p. 358.

identity"[18] can be articulated. As in Gothic fiction, the Southern spaces in which events are set, the fictional Greek city Herakleion and the smaller island of Aphros in the nearby archipelago, enable a subtle and powerful "interplay of sex, travel and subversion" mentioned by Littlewood[19], as they give voice to alternative subjectivities embodying conflicting and tabooed political, identititarian and sexual feelings which could not be so easily expressed at home. However, as I discuss, while Sackville-West searches for "pleasure" and "escape" in her fictional representation of the Mediterranean, which is largely based on her own travels and experiences, she also consolidates a number of stereotypes about Southern populations along the lines of nationality, class and gender identity. Thus, the novel is characterised by a tension between subversiveness and tradition which, ultimately, reveals Sackville-West's own ambiguous positionings towards a wide range of issues, from gender identity to sexuality, from colonialism to class disparity.

Challenging Rules

Written between May 1918 and November 1919, *Challenge* was Sackville-West's second novel. It was first published in the United States in 1924 and came out in England only in 1976. It was composed while she was living her intense love affair with Violet Trefusis (née Keppel). Sackville-West had been married to Harold Nicolson since October 1913; both had extramarital affairs with people of their own sex even before their marriage. However, unlike her past and future relationships, Vita's affair with Violet Trefusis ran the risk of undermining her marriage as both women eloped to Europe (Paris, Avignon and Monte Carlo) from late November 1918 until late March 1919. They were eventually obliged to return to England after numerous, strenuous requests from their families[20]. As Louise DeSalvo has pointed out, it was in foreign, European cities that Sackville-West felt able to live and express her love relationships

---

18 Carla Locatelli, "Figures of Displacement and Displacements of Figures: The Play of Autobiography in *Moments of Being*", in *La tipografia nel salotto: saggi su Virginia Woolf*, edited by Oriana Palusci, Turin, Tirrenia, 1999, p. 20.

19 Ian Littlewood, *Sultry Climates*, cit., p. 129.

20 Victoria Glendinning, *Vita: The Life of Vita Sackville-West*, London, Weidenfeld & Nicolson, 1998, pp. 92–101.

with women more openly[21]. For many British women at the onset of the twentieth century southern European locations were a queer elsewhere, an alternative space in which rules could be overcome and inhibited, censored passions enacted more freely.

Suzanne Raitt has claimed that for Sackville-West, as for many Modernist women writers and artists such as Violet Trefusis and Virginia Woolf, "lesbianism was not disruptive of marriage"[22], even though the sociocultural and scientific background had changed since the previous century. Scholars such as Carroll Smith-Rosenberg and Lillian Faderman have discussed how in the nineteenth century relationships between (married) women could be defined as "romantic friendships": "Emotionally and cognitively, their heterosocial and their homosocial worlds were complementary"[23]. According to these scholars, erotic friendships between women were thus tolerated and did not affect their married lives. However, with the publication and diffusion of sexological work by Richard von Krafft-Ebing[24] and Havelock Ellis[25], as well as the psychological writings by Sigmund Freud[26], a new perspective on female same-sex relations came out at the turn of the twentieth century. While the former posited the figure of the lesbian as an identifiable type of person, the invert, the second exposed it as a stereotype. The sexological theory of sexual inversion stated that one's sex represented the bodily exterior and another sex the interior soul; therefore, a man could be trapped in

---

21 See Louise A. DeSalvo, "Every Woman Is an Island: Vita Sackville-West, the Image of the City, and the Pastoral Idyll", in *Women Writers and the City: Essays in Feminist Literary Criticism*, edited by Susan Merrill Squier, Knoxville, University of Tennessee Press, 1984, p. 102.

22 Suzanne Raitt, *Vita and Virginia: The Work and Friendship of V. Sackville-West and Virginia Woolf*, Oxford, Clarendon Press, 1993, p. 5.

23 Carroll Smith-Rosenberg, "The Female World of Love and Ritual: Relations between Women in Nineteenth Century America", in *Feminism and History*, edited by Joan Wallach Scott, Oxford, Oxford University Press, 1996, p. 373. See also Lillian Faderman, *Surpassing the Love of Men: Romantic Friendship and Love between Women from the Renaissance to the Present*, London, Virago, 1997.

24 Richard von Krafft-Ebing, *Psychopathia Sexualis: Contrary Sexual Instinct. A Medico-Legal Study*, London, F.J. Rebman, 1894 [1886].

25 Havelock Ellis, *Sexual Inversion: Studies in the Psychology of Sex,* 6 vols, Philadelphia, F.A. Davis Company, 1901 [1897].

26 Sigmund Freud, "The Psychogenesis of a Case of Homosexuality in A Woman (1920)", in *That Obscure Subject of Desire: Freud's Female Homosexual Revisited*, edited by Ronnie C. Lesser and Erica Schoenberg, London, Routledge, 1999, pp. 13–33.

a female body and vice versa. Heterosexuality and sexual inversion were classified in a range which went from "normality" to degenerate depravity[27]. According to Esther Newton, at the turn of the century, the "cross-gender figure [of the mannish lesbian] because of her behaviour or dress became the public symbol of the new social/sexual category 'lesbian' "[28].

However, this new typology of subjectivity – exemplified by the well-known case of the British trial and censorship of Radclyffe Hall's novel *The Well of Loneliness*, 1928, which portrayed a mannish lesbian as its protagonist[29] – was not the only existing type. There were many women who lived what Raitt has defined "the apparent paradox of the married lesbian"[30], who conceived their relationships with other women "as an intermittent sexual or emotional orientation, [which] could flourish happily in the interstices of heterosexual existence, hardly threatening it at all"[31]. Sackville-West's affairs went along her married life. Her love story with Violet Trefusis was the only notable exception to this state, and it posed a serious threat to the apparent stability of her marriage. *Challenge* was written while both women were in France, and it seems that Trefusis largely contributed to its composition[32].

The novel developed from their own love story, and the two protagonists do explicitly represent both of them. However, the lesbian element of the novel is completely drawn out from the text, which is about a heterosexual love affair. In other words, the two women are turned into a straight couple. In making the account of their relationship as

---

27 See Michel Foucault, *The History of Sexuality. Vol. 1: The Will to Knowledge*, New York, Pantheon Books, 1978. Lucy Bland and Laura Doan have pointed the fixation of theorists of sexual inversion fixation with the subjects of pathology and abnormality (*Sexology Uncensored: The Documents of Sexual Science*, Chicago, Illinois, University of Chicago Press, 1998, pp. 1–7).

28 Esther Newton, "The Mythic Mannish Lesbian: Radclyffe Hall and the New Woman", *Signs*, 9, no. 4, Summer 1984, p. 560.

29 *The Well of Loneliness* was not banned because it portrayed explicit sexual scenes, but because it posited the very existence of lesbian identities, which in itself was judged obscene. See Bonnie Kime Scott, *Refiguring Modernism: The Women of 1928*, Bloomington, The University of Indiana Press, 1995, pp. 242–252, and Adam Park, *Modernism and the Theatre of Censorship*, New York, Oxford University Press, 1996, Chapter 4.

30 Suzanne Raitt, cit., p. ix.

31 *Ibid.*, p. 7.

32 Cf. Victoria Glendinning, cit., Suzanne Raitt, cit.

heterosexual, Sackville-West attempted to render the disruptive and threatening potential of the lesbian subjectivities "readable" and acceptable, and very much in line with contemporary theories of sexual inversion as posited by Ellis and Krafft-Ebing. In addition, the displacement of the homosexual into the heterosexual in the novel is inspired by real events, as during their stay in France, Sackville-West often cross-dressed and passed as a man, Julian, thus performing the "mannish lesbian" model identified by sexologists[33]. Trefusis frequently called her Julian in their correspondence[34]. The homological relation between the two lovers (Vita and Violet) and the protagonist and his lover in the novel, together with a plot that is deeply inspired by real life events occurring to both of them at the time of the writing, has led critics to define this novel a piece of autobiographical work – albeit fictionalised[35].

As Georgia Johnston has emphasized, contemporary understandings of sexuality and psychology were deeply pervasive, and many autobiographies or autobiographical texts authored by women who loved other women were not always recognizable as such. These generic transgressions went alongside the crucial question "of how autobiographers can represent lesbianism in societies that regulate and censor direct representation

---

33 See Nigel Nicolson, *Portrait of a Marriage*, London, Phoenix, 1973, pp. 111–112.

34 See *Violet to Vita: The Letters of Violet Trefusis to Vita Sackville-West, 1910–21*, edited by Mitchell A. Leaska and John N. Phillips, London, Methuen, 1989. The novel was first dedicated by Sackville-West to Trefusis. Later, the epigraph was changed with an inscription in Romani language ("This book is thine, honoured witch"). On the adoption of Romani language and the indirect reference to the Gypsy community as a marker of lesbianism, Kirstie Blair writes: "Claiming kinship with gypsies, [...] provided one means for women engaged in same-sex relationships to play with gender roles, particularly by emphasizing their femininity while also consciously representing femininity as a masquerade" (Kirstie Blair, "Gypsies and Lesbian Desire: Vita Sackville-West, Violet Trefusis, and Virginia Woolf", *Twentieth Century Literature*, 50, no. 2, Summer, 2004, p. 143). This reference confirms the construction of Sackville West's and Trefusis' gender roles constructed around the masculine *vs* feminine dichotomy.

35 Sackville-West's affair with Trefusis was scandalous at the time, and there were serious concerns that readers would easily understand the "real" gender identity of the protagonists. For this reason, upon the insisting request of her family, the author decided to withdraw the novel from publication in England (the manuscript had been accepted by the publisher Collins). It came out a few years later only in the States.

of lesbian relationships and sexuality"[36]. To put it differently, the representation of the erotic and affective life between women had to be "defined through attempts to deny its existence"[37], and had to manipulate existing generic forms in order to be expressed. Sackville-West's transposal of herself into a fictional male figure is one of the strategies with which a socially perceived deviant desire is conveyed in narrative form, and the only way to represent it in a positive way. In her literary autobiography, *Portrait of a Marriage*, Sackville-West presents her love affair with Trefusis by validating Ellis' theory of inversion as she discusses herself as two different people, one lesbian and one heterosexual. In offering her life as a case study, she shows the damaging effects that pathologizing discourses about her "perverted" identity had on her. The heterosexual transposition of the lesbian relationship in *Challenge* instead offers the possibility of articulating, albeit in a problematically oblique way, the stigmatised side of her identity[38].

Stereotypes and Taboos

The setting of the novel is the fictional version of the Greek city of Herakleion, which is inspired by Monte Carlo, where Sackville-West spent several months together with Trefusis at the time of her writing. However, many other Mediterranean cities and locations where Sackville-West had been on a number of occasions, such as France and Italy, contributed to its representation. The lengthy depictions of the subtle dynamics of the diplomatic, international community of Herakleion are also influenced by Sackville-West's stay in Constantinople, where she spent six months as the newly wedded wife of Nicolson, who at the time was the Third Secretary of the British Embassy. Her insider knowledge of life in a foreign embassy can be found in the vivid portrayals of a large number of international characters that animate the political scene of the novel. It is in this varied and cosmopolitan environment that the character of Julian Davenport is introduced.

---

36   Georgia Johnston, *The Formation of 20th-century Queer Autobiography: Reading Vita Sackville- West, Virginia Woolf, Hilda Doolittle, and Gertrude Stein*, Basingstoke, Palgrave Macmillan, 2007, p. 14.

37   *Ibid.*, p. 3.

38   See Nigel Nicolson, *Portrait of a Marriage*, cit.

Julian is the young descendant of a British aristocratic, colonial family, which has long held economic and political power in the Greek cities of Herakleion and Aphros:

> He knew that his family for three generations had been the wealthiest in the little state, wealthier than the Greek banking-houses, and he knew that no move of the local politics was entirely free from the influence of his relations. [...] He supposed that one day he would inherit his father's share in the concern, and would become one of the heads of the immense family which had spread like water over various districts of the Mediterranean coasts[39].

The Davenports have become one of the most widespread and rich families in Greece, by colonising and exploiting its natural and economic sources. Julian is to inherit their enormous power and wealth. For this reason, while still in England, he is "trained" by his uncle to embody the ethos and the spirit of British colonialism: " 'You don't belong there, boy; [...] You're English. Bend the riches of that country to your own purpose [...] Impose yourself. Make them adopt your methods. That's the strength of English colonisation' "[40]. Julian is raised with the notion of his own racial and economic superiority to the colonised, subaltern Greek "others".

However, as soon as Julian arrives in Herakleion from Oxford, where has finished his studies, he finds himself in a different situation from the one he expected. He soon understands that the political scenario on the islands where his family has power is unstable, as the locals want independence from the mainland state of Herakleion. Moreover, he quickly infers from several conversations with Embassy delegates and Ministers that his family is disliked and mistrusted by everyone:

> 'I hear', he said, 'that there is fresh trouble in the Islands'. 'We can leave it to the Davenants', said Christopoulos with an unpleasant smile. 'But that is exactly what I have always urged you not to do', said the French minister, drawing the little Greek into a corner. 'You know the proverbial reputation of the English: you do not see them coming, but they insinuate themselves until one day you open your eyes to the fact that they are there. You will be making a very great mistake, my dear friend, if you allow the Davenants to settle disputes in the Islands. Have you forgotten that in the last generation a Davenant caused himself to be elected president?' [...] 'The Davenants are

---

39 Vita Sackville-West, *Challenge*, London, Virago, 2012, p. 26.
40 *Challenge*, cit., p. 27.

sly; they keep apart; they mix with us, but they do not mingle. They are like oil upon water [...]'[41].

This brief exchange unveils the widely held negative view about the Davenants, who are reputed to be insinuating, sly and untrustworthy. They are isolated in the diplomatic community of the Greek city, thanks to their "proverbial reputation". Significantly, the dichotomy us *vs* them which was so poignantly asserted by Julian's uncle, who embodies the British colonial perspective embraced by the Davenants, is somehow paradoxically turned against them due to their exploitative and arrogant attitude, which has led to them being isolated and despised. In addition, another ominous event contributes to the Davenants' poor reputation: Julian's grandfather had roused the islanders against the Greek government for his own purposes. This past event also prefigures the unfolding of the plot, as Julian will lead the revolution among the islanders against Herakleion by proclaiming himself their leader.

From the outset, Julian is described as shy and reserved within the cosmopolitan context where he finds himself. Significantly, he encounters two women who represent different worlds: Madame Kato, a singer who has worked as a performer in France[42] and who supports the revolutionary ideas of the islanders, and his cousin Eve, whom he initially dismisses as being too young and childish. While the former becomes a reference for Julian's radical political views, which disrupt his father's own conservative, colonial agenda, the latter instead will be his lover. Julian's first visit to Aphros is the moment in which he acknowledges the situation of exploitation and subalternity experienced by the islanders, who ask him to free them from the dominance of Herakleion and its colonial exploitation. Julian promptly responds to the request by promising to liberate them; however, this revolutionary act also condemns him to spend two years in exile.

---

41 *Challenge*, cit., pp. 8–9.

42 France, and Paris in particular, is frequently referred to in the novel as the space of elaboration of a revolutionary counterculture. It is no accident that in the quotation mentioned above the character who clearly expresses his view on the English's untrustworthiness is the French minister.

Gender Roles and Sexual Rebellions

Upon his return, Julian acts on his idealistic revolutionary ideals to support the Islanders against the oppression of the main government and his own family. It is in this second phase that his relationship with Eve begins. As mentioned above, the taboo element of homosexuality is here turned into a heterosexual liaison; however, Julian and Eve are cousins, and this render their passionate affair incestuous and illicit. The threatening homosexual element is thus transformed into a different form of taboo. It is crucial to emphasise that the political drive which animates Julian's actions develops alongside his love for Eve. Indeed, it is only when he moves to the Southern islands to lead the revolution of the local people against the government that he and Eve become intimate. In other words, the revolutionary space of the islands provides the ideal background for their incestuous, passionate love story.

The space of the Mediterranean island is crucial in this novel. It is the place where a violent struggle for liberation takes place both at a political and at an individual level. To put it differently, Julian's political commitment to the islanders' revolutionary cause goes hand in hand with his growing, illicit passion for his cousin Eve, even though she doesn't share his idealistic views. One of the earliest descriptions of the islands seems to anticipate its intrinsic connection to Eve:

> Herakleion was hidden from sight, on the other hand, by the curve of the hill, but the islands were visible opposite, and, caring only for them, he gazed as he had done many times, but now their meaning and purport crystallised in his mind as never before. There was something symbolical in their detachment from the mainland – in their clean remoteness, their isolation; all the difference between the unfettered ideal and the tethered reality. An island! land that had slipped the leash of continents, forsworn solidarity, cut adrift from security and prudence! One could readily believe that they made part of the divine, the universal discontent, that rare element, dynamic, life-giving, that here and there was to be met about the world, always fragmentary, yet always full and illuminating, even as the fragments of beauty[43].

The geographical "remoteness" and "isolation" of the islands symbolises the secretive and self-contained nature of the love affair between them. Moreover, their symbolic separation from "security" and "prudence" speaks volumes about the precarious, and somehow revolutionary

---

43 *Challenge*, cit., p. 57.

choice of the two cousins to love each other. In addition, as Raitt has pointed out: "The islands represent seclusion and glamour [...] The lovers' withdrawal to the island, like that of Sackville-West and Trefusis to France, symbolises a rejection of rules and traditional sexual institutions [...] At the same time it is a retreat, a carving out of an enclosed space for a sexual and political rebellion [...] The islands are an area of sexual and political energy which asks simply to be left alone"[44].

The close association which is drawn between Eve and the islands also unveils the highly gendered and colonial dynamics in place in the novel. Even if Julian ostensibly revolts against the traditional colonial order established by his family, he ends up embodying a similar form of colonial and masculine control over the island/female lover. His uncle's lessons in domination over the colonised "other" have taken hold and developed in new ways. Julian apparently rebels against his father, but eventually develops similar strategies of control over the Southern "others", as his idealistic, revolutionary views gradually take a more conservative shape. Julian is praised as a virile, Byronic and solitary hero, who holds his power thanks to his strength. His male virtues are foregrounded in opposition to Eve's threatening feminine allure. Eve is portrayed as a stereotypical *femme fatale*, who holds a sensual and dangerous power on all those around her:

> Eve was, of course, very charming, though not beautiful. She could not be called beautiful, her mouth was too large and too red. It was almost improper to have so red a mouth; not quite *comme il faut* in so young a girl. Still, she was undeniably successful. Men liked to be amused, and Eve, when she was not sulky, could be very amusing. [...] Nothing was sacred to her, not even things which were really beautiful and touching – patriotism, or moonlight, or air – even Greek art [...] Love was the most beautiful, the most sacred thing upon earth, yet Eve – a child, a chit – had no veneration either for love in the abstract or for its devotees in the flesh. She wasted the love that was offered her. She could have no heart, no temperament.

Eve's "dangerous" nature is signalled by her large, red lips, which are deemed "improper", especially for a young girl. She is not conventionally beautiful, but nonetheless exercises a successful charm on men. Moreover, Eve disdains all things that the protagonist deems sacred – including love. It is precisely her lack of interest in anything which makes her simultaneously distant and impenetrable but also charming and alluring. Julian's

---

44 Suzanne Raitt, cit., p. 95.

efforts to become the leader and master of the revolutionary islanders thus goes alongside his attempt to conquer and dominate his detached but incredibly fascinating cousin, who eventually decides to accompany him to the islands.

Eventually, Julian symbolically possesses her when he becomes the leader of Aphros: "He shut his eyes for a second as he realised that she could be, if he chose, his own *possession*, she the elusive and unattainable; he might claim the redemption of all her infinite promise; might *discover* her in the role for which she was so obviously created; might *violate* the sanctuary and tear the veils from the wealth of treasure hitherto denied to all; might *exact* him for himself the first secrets of her unplundered passion"[45]. The highly gendered dynamics between the two characters, with its association with colonial images of masculine dominance, violence and rape against the female colonised land and female subjectivity, somehow also reflects/gives a vivid transposition of the sexologists' theories on the dual gendered dynamics which characterised same-sex relationships by literally representing the virile masculinity of the mannish lesbian in opposition to her female partner[46].

Significantly, Julian's self-proclaimed role of dominance over both the islands and Eve is doomed to fail. The signs of the imminent end of his idealistic albeit self-referential political project can be found precisely in Eve. It is Eve, who has never embraced or shared his political project, who betrays him and consigns him to the government forces in Heraklion. However, the end of Julian's political dream also marks the end of his role as a rebel against his own family and the political and sexual conventions that they represent. In addition, it also marks the end of his subversive, illicit love for Eve, which is immediately reinscribed along conventional lines, as he invites her to escape to Athens with him and marry him:

'[…] We can marry in Athens to-morrow'. 'Marry?' she repeated. 'Naturally. What else did you suppose? That I should leave you? now? Put up your clothes. Should I help you? Come!' 'But – marry, Julian?' 'Clearly: marry,' he replied […] 'but we had nothing to do with marriage', she whispered. […] 'No, we had to do only with love – love and rebellion! And both have failed me. Now, instead of love, we must have marriage; and instead of rebellion,

---

45 *Challenge*, cit., p. 85, my emphasis.

46 Sackville-West and her lover Trefusis perceived their own gender roles in a very traditional way in their relationship, as it emerges from their letters. See, for instance, *Violet to Vita*, cit., p. 207.

law. I shall help on authority, instead of opposing it'. [...] 'You no longer love me' she said slowly[47].

The rebellious, transgressive love between Julian and Eve can only take place in the boundless space of the Mediterranean islands of Aphros. As soon as Julian understands that Eve betrayed him to the authorities in Herakleion and that his mission of revolutionary leadership has failed, he proposes that she should marry him and abide by the law, thus sanctioning the end of their passionate, illicit love. Eve cannot accept it. The novel concludes with Julian who flees on a boat at night with a group of faithful rebels who take him to Athens, while Eve runs after him and, while seeing the boat moving away from the coast, decides to commit suicide by immerging herself in the cold waters of the Mediterranean.

Conclusion

I argue that in reinscribing her own love affair with Trefusis in heterosexual terms, Sackville-West writes what Johnston has defined a "palimpsestic autobiographical fiction"[48] in order to give a more socially acceptable representation of her experience, albeit transposed in heterosexual terms. At the same time, she validates Ellis' theories of gender inversion by creating two highly gendered characters along traditional lines. The relationship between the two characters is subversive and taboo as they are cousins. It can thus only take place in the open space of the Mediterranean islands, where rules are subverted by the islanders' rebellion led by Julian.

Julian is the Byronic hero who asserts his own masculinity by taking decisions and trying to gain control and mastery over the people he claims he wants to save and the woman he professes to love. His highly improbable political choices[49] nonetheless unveil his adherence to traditional gender and colonial stereotypes. As soon as his political and sexual dream of dominance is over, he almost immediately goes back to abiding by social rules and norms. The escape to the South is for him temporary, and he eventually returns to the life that his uncle had set out for him. Significantly, his return to "normality" coincides with his coming of age.

---

47 *Challenge*, cit., p. 280.
48 Georgia Johnston, cit., p. 23.
49 See Nigel Nicolson's "Foreword" to the 1974 Collins edition, in *Challenge*, cit., p. xvi.

Eve instead is portrayed as the heartless manoeuvring *femme fatale*, who needs somehow to be dominated and controlled in order not to undermine Julian's masculine power. Paradoxically, even though she does not adhere to Julian's utopian political dream, eventually she is the one pays the highest price for the end of their illicit love affair. The ending of the story thus confirms gender stereotypes: Julian is an idealistic, young man who is due to inherit a vast colonial settlement. After experiencing his moment of rebellion, he seems to be ready to get back into the system as a mature man. Somehow, his rebellious phase ends up leading him to adhere to the normativity that he initially did not want to embody. Instead, Eve is a portrayed as a woman who lacks her own political views and is not capable of readjusting herself after the end of her passionate love story. Her final suicide might also symbolise the impossibility of experiencing disruptive forms of love and relationships outside traditional social and sexual rules. In other words, it seems that the "challenge" of the love that binds the two protagonists is doomed to fail from the beginning: this reading of the novel also somehow applies to the end of Sackville-West and Trefusis's love affair, which was eventually reinscribed within the lines of sociocultural heteronormative rules. Therefore, the palimpsestic character of this autobiographical fiction is both transgressively escapist and resigned to the reimposition of the heterosexual matrix.

Patrick Leigh Fermor's *Mani. Travels in the Southern Peloponnese*: The Earthly Frontier of the Modern Imagination

Paola PARTENZA

Introduction

Lord Palmerston, in his foreign policy speech of 1827, declared: "Greece is an emotional word"[1]. Echoing Palmerston's evocative image, for Patrick Leigh Fermor Greece was the country that best represented the link between identity and place, the place of memory, of suggestive imagery, where reality and imagination blurred in a suspended dimension of time. In his introduction to *Mani. Travels in the Southern Peloponnese*, Michael Gorra observes: "In Leigh Fermor's pages any account of the present begins a thousand years back, and to read him is to enter a mind that delights in bounding from moment to moment and century to century, a mind in which all times appear to exist at once"[2]. Published in 1958, *Mani* is not an open window on the author's life story; the point of view is that of a man who

> never take[s] us [...] into Leigh Fermor himself. His eyes look out, not in. We know him by the pace of his sentences, his fondness for lists, his expertly mixed cocktails of metaphor. We know him by his passions, his taste in books and in buildings. We know him by his friends. Yet there's little here

---

1   Kenneth Bourne, *Palmerston: The Early Years 1784–1841*, London, 1982, p. 387, qtd. in Robert Holland, and Diana Markides, *The British and the Hellenes: Struggles for Mastery in the Eastern Mediterranean 1850–1960*, Oxford, Oxford University Press, 2006, p. 1.

2   Michael Gorra, "Introduction to *Mani*", in Patrick Leigh Fermor, *Mani. Travels in the Southern Peloponnese*, New York, The New York Review of Books, 2006, p. 5. All in-text references to *Mani* (hereafter *M.*) are to this edition.

about his private life – just the Christian name of his traveling companion, and eventual wife, Joan Eyres Monsell[3].

The author delves into the deep history of Greece, taking into account the landscape, the mountains and hills of the region (Peloponnese), the archaeological sites and the unknown places. The approach is necessarily amphibian: it is part archaeological and part ethnographic; it speaks of the past and of the present. These characteristics make *Mani* a representative work of Greek culture written by an English traveller in the first half of the twentieth century. Specifically, his work involves a type of narrative that has been variously described as structural: the way in which places, events or people are described. Fermor's travelogue is no mere invention, although, as Carl Thompson notes, [all] examples of travel writing are by definition textual artefacts constructed by their writers and publishers"[4]. His descriptions and commentaries include people and houses, communities and landscapes, myths, and prominent historical figures. Fermor's aim is to portray people from the past, habits and behaviours, in order to bring them back to life and to include them rather than exclude them. In a similar vein, Mary Louise Pratt argues that: "To revive indigenous history and culture as archaeology is to revive it *as dead*. The gesture simultaneously rescues them from European forgetfulness and reassigns them to a departed age"[5]. Inevitably, the link between memory and human society is at the heart of both this inclusion and the combination of past and present: "Leigh Fermor explains many of these things, but his references do tend toward the allusive, as though reminding us of what we already know" (*M.*, p. 14). In *Mani*, the history of Greece seems clear and complete. It is an attempt to reveal a very complex culture that reaches deep into antiquity. By returning to earlier times, to people's lifestyles, social hierarchies, patterns of political and ritual integration and sociality already discussed in other travel accounts, the author focuses on the characteristics or "essentials" of Greek culture. Undoubtedly, his books "do more than record where he went and what he saw, for in the very play of their references they also extend an invitation for explorations of our own" (*Ibidem*).

---

3   Ivi, p. 11.
4   Carl Thompson, *Travel Writing*, London and New York, Routledge, 2011, p. 27.
5   Mary Louise Pratt, *Imperial Eyes: Travel Writing and Transculturation*, London and New York, Routledge, 1992, p. 134.

Mani is both the centre and the periphery of Fermor's reflections. Although his travel experience marks the distance and cultural separation from his place – as his point of origin – "it is Greece to which he has most often returned for a subject [...]" (*M.*, p. 13). As the author states in the *Preface*: "I HAD MEANT *Mani*, before I began writing it, to be a single chapter among many, each of them describing the stages and halts, the encounters, the background and the conclusions of a leisurely journey – a kind of recapitulation of many former journeys – through continental Greece and the islands" (*Preface*, p. 21). He undertakes a sort of double journey. On the one hand, he travels physically to the place where Western culture originated, "[...] setting out from Constantinople which seemed to be the logical point of departure historically, if not politically, for a study of the modern Greek world" (*Ibidem*). On the other hand, he embarks on a historiographical journey through the myths, the legends, the rituals, and the superstitions of Greece.

The author's aim is twofold. First, he wants to give the reader an idea of what Greece is like: "All of Greece is absorbing and rewarding. There is hardly a rock or a stream without a battle or a myth, a miracle or a peasant anecdote or a superstition; and talk and incident, nearly all of it odd or memorable, thicken round the traveller's path at every step" (*Preface*, p. 23). He describes and draws the main features of the historical imagination, almost archetypes, that still exist today and, as he says, "to transmit these things to the reader is one of the two aims of this book". While "the second aim, [...] is to situate and describe present-day Greeks of the mountains and the islands in relationship to their habitat and their history; to seek them out in those regions where bad communications and remoteness have left this ancient relationship, comparatively speaking, undisturbed" (*Preface*, pp. 24–25). By placing so much emphasis on tradition, history and legend, Fermor fulfils T. S. Eliot's principle of the "historical sense", which

> [I]nvolves a perception, not only of the pastness of the past, but of its presence; the historical sense compels a man to write not merely with his own generation in his bones, but with a feeling that the whole of the literature of Europe from Homer and within it the whole of the literature of his own country has a simultaneous existence and composes a simultaneous order. This *historical sense*, which is a sense of the timeless as well as of the temporal and of the timeless and of the temporal together, is what makes a writer traditional. And it is at the same time what makes a writer most acutely conscious of his place in time, of his contemporaneity[6] (my emphasis).

---

6   T.S. Eliot, "Tradition and the Individual Talent", in *The Sacred Wood*, London, Faber and Faber, 1997, pp. 40–41.

In keeping with the aim of the author's work, the purpose of this essay is to follow Fermor's journey in order to reconstruct a picture of the Mani through memories, contacts and direct experience with the people of Greece. This is a country that has always helped, both in the past and in the present, to bring together people of different cultures and customs, creating a favourable climate for transcultural relations and experiences. As Michel Foucault points out: "Experience is [...] the rediscovery of time, it is as if the whole history of mankind, going back to its origins, were accessible in a kind of immediate knowledge"[7].

Empty Peaks Full of History

ON THE map the southern part of the Peloponnese looks like a misshapen tooth fresh torn from its gum with three peninsulas jutting southward in jagged and carious roots. The central prong is formed by the Taygetus mountains, which, from their northern foothills in the heart of the Morea to their storm-beaten southern point, Cape Matapan, are roughly a hundred miles long. About half their length – seventy-five miles on their western and forty-five on their eastern flank and measuring fifty miles across – projects tapering into the sea. This is the Mani (*M.*, p. 54).

The author's description of the place – of its physical characteristics – immediately shows the influence it had on his writings and accounts. His perception, however, creates a strange atmosphere of suspension. It is still seen as a region deeply rooted in Western *imagination*[8] and *culture*. The Mani, Fermor writes, is the place of myth and history, the place where the "blank Mediterranean [...] lies between this spike of rock and the African sands" (*M.*, p. 55). His journey is a gradual process, with each chapter moving from a description of the landscape and wildlife to superstition and traditional beliefs, allowing new thoughts, emotions, and sensations to emerge for both the author and the reader. In this way, the ancient world emerges and intersects with Fermor's experience of the present,

---

7   Michel Foucault and Jay Miskowiec, "Of Other Spaces", *Diacritics*, 16, no. 1, Spring, 1986, pp. 22–27, 26.

8   As Maria Koundoura notes, "Caught between myth and history, Greece has long haunted the Western imagination. [...] Countless visitors, determined to get ocular proof of the spirit of Greece, [...]". "Real Selves and Fictional Nobodies: Women's Travel Writing and the Production of Identities", in *Women Writing Greece Essays on Hellenism, Orientalism and Travel*, edited by Vassiliki Kolocotroni and Efterpi Mitsi, Amsterdam and New York, Rodopi, 2008, p. 77.

and he seems to travel across generations and cultures, past and present, either when he recalls Homeric descriptions ("[The] empty peaks, according to Homer, were the haunt of Artemis and of three goat-footed nymphs who would engage lonely travellers in a country dance and lead them unsuspectingly to the precipice where they tripped them up and sent them spinning down the gulf [...]. "*M.*, pp. 59–60). Or when he happens to meet "two small figures", Anastasia and Antiope with their goats. To his eyes, they appear "delicate, fine-boned and solemn, they could have been nothing but Greek; not so much the Greeks of the pagan world as the spiritual etiolation that gazes from the walls of Saint Sophia and Ravenna: the bewildering combination of aloofness and devouring intensity that radiates from the eye-sockets of eastern Madonnas and Empresses" (*M.*, p. 64). Travel, it could be argued, enables the writer to see places and people differently, to develop a highly refined ear and eye. As Carl Thomson notes, it can be seen as "a confrontation with, or, more optimistically, a negotiation of, what is sometimes termed alterity. [...] [T]ravel requires us to negotiate a complex and sometimes unsettling interplay between alterity *and* identity, difference, *and* similarity"[9].

Leigh Fermor notices how the elements of local culture and tradition contribute both to the preservation of the environment and to a harmonious way of life for the inhabitants of the area. They represent the distillate of long experience and popular wisdom.

An example of this is when Yorgo, Fermor's guide, warns him by saying:

> 'You shouldn't go to sleep under a fig tree,' he said, observing our falling eyelids. "Why not?" "The shadow is heavy." I had heard this before, especially in Crete. There is never an explanation of this heaviness, except that it is alleged to bring on vertigo and bad dreams; it is as odd as the Caribbean superstition that sleeping under the bells of a datura tree in flower drives the sleeper mad. I shifted a few inches out of politeness, though I have never felt the ill effects. Yorgo lay with his head on a stone (*M.*, p. 63).

Leigh Fermor's passionate and constantly evolving journey, both historical and personal, takes him to Kampos and then on to the Gulf of Messenia. Here he travels through time and space, reconstructing and recording the background of a profound history that goes beyond the age when "the last emperor – Constantine XI Palaeologus Vatatses – died

---

9   Carl Thompson, *op. cit.*, p. 9.

fighting in the breach on the day the imperial city was captured by Mohammed II" (*M.,*p. 88). Fermor seems to have preferred the *visual documentation* of his journey through his words; his descriptions are the result of a rich cultural, historical, and literary heritage that has enriched his reconstruction of times and places[10]. Aspects that have had a profound effect on the people of the region, making them reflect on the meaning of their history and, above all, on what came before; as when the author later notes what John Morrit of Rokeby[11] wrote about the Maniots and their land: "if I see any danger of not getting out (of the Mani)", he writes, "it is not from banditti, but from the hospitality and goodness of the Maniots. The mountains were poor in antiquities, but the Ancients survive here in a bolder manner, since certainly these people retain the spirits and character of Grecians, more than we had ever seen" (*M.,* p. 376).

Names are another essential feature Fermor recorded. Names seem to indicate either *"paratsoúklia"*, or nicknames, or multicultural contact. As the author points out, they derive from Greek culture – linked to the folklore and customs of local traditions – and from contact with other peoples of different civilisations. For example, "Michael, whose name of Troupakis is now augmented by Mourtzinos, another nickname, the *dialect diminutive* of mourgos, a bulldog; the complete name now meaning, roughly, Bullpup-in-the-Hole" (*M.,* p. 92, my emphasis). He notes that this is not an isolated fact but, as he points out,

> [...] the same phenomenon occurs elsewhere in Greece. e.g., Byzantine names in Crete, like Skordyli and Kallergi (the followers of Nicephorus Phocas), or Venetian ones, like Morosini, Cornaro or Dandolo, survive in large numbers; but many of their bearers have allowed them to be replaced, even in recent generations, by nicknames which have stuck. There is the same random survival and erasure of great Frankish feudal names – i.e., of the Ghisi, the Giustiniani and the Sanudo, names which appear over shops – in the Cyclades (Fermor's footnote n. 4, *M.* p. 116).

---

10 Martha Klironomos notes, "Through recent strides in archaeological recovery and the analysis of ritual and myth espoused by Edward B. Tylor, George Frazer, Henri Bergson and Sigmund Freud, Harrison went on to ground residual traces of archaic religious practice in modern forms of expression: to argue the case for continuity of shared collective experience across the ages", "British Women Travellers to Greece, 1880–1930", in Vassiliki Kolocotroni and Efterpi Mitsi, cit., p. 138.

11 "Whig squire aged twenty-one" who first journeyed through Greece between 1794 and 1796. Cf. *Mani*, cit., p. 375.

This cultural *hybridity* is thus a significant result of the encounter between different ethnolinguistic groups[12]. It is also emblematic of the changes in the socio-cultural environment in which Greece has been immersed over the course of time. Fermor's travel experience also proves Edward Said's point that "cultures are hybrid and heterogeneous and [...] cultures and civilization are [...] interrelated and interdependent [...]"[13]. In a context in which different voices "frame" habits, customs and traditions, Leigh Fermor, as *author* and *narrator*, acts as a "translator" and interpreter of these voices and experiences. On the one hand, the number of voices is multiplied by the expressive narration of the characters he meets, who tell him the history of the land. On the other hand, the author's voice – immersed in the same context as the characters' narration – comments on the different local cultures, creating and recreating places of memory. His work traces a "story" that the author has to write in order to explain it to an audience unfamiliar with the *language* and *culture* of the Mani. It is a region inhabited by people (the Maniots) who are convinced that they are descended, "in part from the ancient Spartans and in part from the Byzantines of the Peloponnese, both of them having sought refuge from their respective conquerors in these inexpugnable mountains; in the same way that many of the Byzantine families of Athens sought asylum in the isle of Aegina" (*M.*, p. 89).

Significantly, people's beliefs and convictions have roots in the past. They are embedded in historical stories of expansion and migration. People of the past appear as living ancestors. They are revived through the narratives of the Maniots. In this specific context, Fermor emphasises the pride of the Greeks in defining themselves by recalling their historical formation; he points out, for example, how the Cretans's "sense of hierarchy and equality of birth" ("*Ebenbürtigkeit*" equality of birth) plays an essential role in defining their cultural identity, despite the numerous *contaminations* they have suffered in different ages:

> In Crete, nevertheless, in spite of these changes, their descendants have an unrationalized but very definite awareness of their august origins, and in one

---

12 As Peter Burke points out "Although processes of hybridization may be found in the economic, social, and political spheres, [...] cultural trends, defin[e] the term 'culture' in a reasonably broad sense to include attitudes, mentalities and values and their expression, embodiment or symbolization in artefacts, practices, and representations", *Cultural Hybridity*, Cambridge, Polity Press, 2009, p. 5.

13 Edward Said, *Orientalism*, London, Penguin, 1977, pp. 349–350.

or two of the large mountain villages where traditions are strongest – Lakkoi
in the White Mountains, for instance, and Anoyeia on the slopes of Mt.
Ida – the mountaineers, though they may have only half a dozen goats to
their name, possess a tribal pride and a knowledge of the part played by each
family in Crete's innumerable rebellions against the Turks and a feeling of
hierarchy and *Ebenbürtigkeit* [equality of birth] among themselves which is
almost Proustian in its intensity (Fermor's footnote n. 4, *M.,* pp. 116,117).

What the author describes has a lasting and widespread reputation.
Fermor's historical reconstruction of the place has its origins in the story
of Michael Troupakis Mourtzinos, who "was the Bey of the Mani (a virtually independent prince, that is) from 1779 until 1782 when the Sultan
beheaded him" (*M.,* p. 89). It is an example of the inheritance of the
past, in which genealogy – "the traditional genealogy of the Troupakis-
Mourtzinos family" (*M.,* p. 91) – becomes a critical element through
which the author attempts to map the history of the country. On the
one hand, Fermor traces the founding dynasties in order to clarify the
lineage of the Palaeologi. On the other hand, he demonstrates how
the intertwining of history and myth[14] is crucial to an understanding of
the cultural identity by creating images that have an emotional impact, as
when he says: "After the Frankish conquest of Greece, the Mani became a
turbulent feudal oligarchy of powerful families. [...] the Mavromichalis
clan" (*M.,* p. 144) whose origins date back to the middle of the four-
teenth century, to 1340 to be precise, when, according to tradition, they
fled to Mani when "the Turks first crossed the Hellespont" (M., p. 144).
Intertwined with tradition, the figure of George Mavromichalis is the
result of a combination of history and myth, as Fermor notes: "There is a
deep-rooted *legend* that their [a Thracian family called Gregorianos] great
physical beauty springs from the marriage of a George Mavromichalis to
a mermaid"[15] (*M.,* p. 144, my emphasis). Through these narratives, the

---

14 As Ahmet Davutoğlu points out "For Greeks, [...] it was almost impossible to make
    a categorical differentiation between mythology and history. Greeks resorted to
    mythology in explaining the natural order and justifying the socio-political order".
    "The Formative Parameters of Civilization", in *Civilizations and World Order,* edited
    by Fred Dallmayr, M. Akif Kayapınar, and İsmail Yaylacı, Lexington Books, Lanham,
    Boulder, New York, Toronto, Plymouth, 2014, p. 84.

15 It is worth recalling the legend to which the author refers: "Nereids – the word used in
    the account of this legend – in modern Greek superstition are beautiful pale wraiths
    who haunt inland streams and springs. But this one is expressly stated to have been a
    salt-water dweller. The nereid, as opposed to the salt-water 'gorgon', is shaped like a

author preserves the cultural identity, meaning and ethos of the Maniots. If the narrative becomes a necessary tool to help the reader understand the world of the Maniots, how each of them defends their beliefs and their way of life, then the author's accounts also serve to activate his readers' knowledge of an unfamiliar tradition. Travelling becomes a way of learning about oneself. As Lipski observes:

> The *shaping of* and the *exploration of* identity are, then, the two *topoi* that, in my view, best render the eponymous juxtaposition of travel and identity. They are based on the patterns of linearity and circularity, respectively. When the self is being shaped on the road, there is no coming back, strictly speaking; the returned self is a new man[16].

Popular Poetry and Dirges, Myths, and Legends

If history allowed Fermor to discuss the process of cultural transformation of modern Greece, it probably began before 1844, when "a military revolution in Athens forced King Otto to grant a constitution in 1843, and in 1844 Greece had the first general elections in all its long history" (*M.*, p. 255). Literature, he acknowledges, has played an essential role. It has given a specific and solid identity to a country whose mythological tradition has left its mark on Western culture. As already mentioned, Fermor's research is entirely devoted to the knowledge of history, landscape, language and literature, and *Mani* is an account of his thoughts and reflections on an exciting region unknown to many. For example, "The City of Mars (Areopolis)" is described as having an architecture mixed, intertwined, and integrated with the elements and nature, where "each olive tree, motionless in the still air, was turned by the insects into a gigantic rattle, a whirling canister of iron filings" (*M.*, p. 124), and where the wind, the *Meltemi*, seems to be the soul of the place, imprinted in the air. It is a place where the author's perception has led him to describe how "the blue cloud uneasy with electricity had

---

human. The latter, the Gorgona that haunts the stormier parts of the Mediterranean, ends in two scaly and coiling tails. A Maniot grocer told me that the Mavromichalis nereid was possibly a deaf and dumb Venetian princess of the House of Morosini found sitting on a rock by the seashore" (Footnote no. 7, pp. 150–151).

16 Jakub Lipski (ed.), *Travel and Identity: Studies in Literature, Culture and Language*, Cham Switzerland, Springer, 2018, p. 4.

swallowed the peaks of the Taygetus. The valleys rumbled with thunder, and even a few phenomenal drops of rain pattered on the hot planks of the deck." (p. 119). Furthermore, the author observes, "The names over the shops had all changed once more from the *-eas* ending of the Outer Mani to the *-akos* of the Deep: Kostakos, Khamodrakos, Bakakos, Xanthakos." (*M.,* pp. 126/7).

Leigh Fermor does not limit his research and narrative to history, which includes aspects of everyday life, but also explores mythology and popular poetry. In chapter five, "Lamentation", he remarks: "ALL GREECE abounds with popular poetry" (*M.,* p. 152). He describes how it survives in the lives of the Maniots. He thus creates a continuous literary thread between the distant past and the present. It is a "cultivated" poetry, using complex metaphors in popular material and reflecting the speech patterns of the ancient tradition. Most of the texts have never been transcribed, but they are still transmitted orally. Oral culture inscribes itself on the individual soul and shapes it. It is part of the local tradition, part of the ethos of the community. For the transmission of emotions and thoughts in different situations, oral culture remains particularly important:

> It is always sung, and there are different kinds for various occasions – birth, death, marriage, religious feasts, the welcoming of guests, drinking, the pasturing of sheep – and they vary from region to region: the klephtic ballads of Roumeli and the Morea, the oriental *amanés*, the improvised rhyming mantinadas of Crete which the *lyra* accompanies, the romantic Italianate *cantadas* of the Ionian isles, sung to the sound of guitars and mandolins – one could compile a long list. Nearly all of them, however, are written in the decapentesyllabic line, sometimes in rhyming couplets. The metre is slightly monotonous to read – it has something of the jaunty iteration of *Locksley Hall* – but sung, with their peculiar caesurae, repetitions of half lines, long drawn modulations and guttural ejaculations and apostrophes, they are full of life and variety. Many of them accompany Greek country dances (*M.,* pp. 152–153).

The "poet"/"singer" uses metrical cadences and incorporates the oral tradition by narrating or alluding to legends from ancient literature. In other words, the mythical aura of the literary tradition is incorporated into the narration of contemporary events, celebrating what has been gained or lost, as in funeral rites when women perform a dirge, a spoken and recited lament[17]. It seems to be the best tribute that people can pay to

---

17 Gillian Bouras observes "that, in oral Greek culture, it is women who are the keepers of the *logos*, using on every occasion an infinite variety of memorised

the dead. It establishes essential links between ancestral rites and dirges. Fermor notes that "a form of popular poetry does exist in the Mani which has been largely extinct elsewhere since ancient times and this is so singular and remarkable, so representative of the sombre traditions of the peninsula, that it largely compensates for the dearth of all other kinds. The *miroloyia* ('words of destiny'), the metrical dirges of the Mani, are an isolated phenomenon" (*M.,* p. 153). Through the lament, the mourner, who is always a woman[18], traces all the personal qualities, the experiences and the struggles of the deceased; it is a living celebration of the dead person. Thus, dirges appear as short poems or as "long funeral hymns with a strict discipline of the metre. Stranger still, the metre exists nowhere else in Greece. The universal fifteen-syllable line of all popular Greek poetry is replaced here by a line of sixteen syllables, and the extra foot entirely changes the sound and character of the verse" (*M.,* p. 163).

As the author argues, many factors of culture and literature have given shape and form to the dirges of the Mani. Through them the Maniots have created their own identity which is mainly shaped by expressions derived from popular and high culture. Although they cannot be considered canonical literature, Fermor notes that "collections of *miroloyia*, many of them of high poetical value, have been made and new ones are constantly emerging". Moreover, the *dirge singer* shows a remarkable ability to contaminate present language with that of the past. She is able to mix formulaic expressions rooted in the *Odyssey* with rhythm and improvisation.

> The similarity of these *miroloyia* with the themes of ancient Greek literature, most notably with the lament of Andromache over the body of Hector, coupled with the fact that this region remained pagan till six entire centuries after Constantine had made Christianity the official Greek religion, and with the fact that they only exist in the Mani, tempts one to think that here again

---

fragments: myths, legends, customs, traditions, spells, herbal recipes, tales of fairies and ghosts, the swirling mass that is part of religion" in Christina Dokou, "No Place Like Home': Gillian Bouras and the 'Others'" in Vassiliki Kolocotroni and Efterpi Mitsi, *op. cit.,* pp. 199–200.

18 They are sung by women, which is one of the very few occasions in which women have the opportunity to excel, showing their linguistic skills inherent to their role in this specific circumstance. Therefore, Fermor notes: "Only men are mourned at their death, but women wear black for even their remotest male relations" (*M.,* p. 193). This *ritual* – called *klama* – involves the preparation of the body of the deceased for burial.

is a direct descendant of Ancient Greece, a custom stretching back, perhaps, till before the Siege of Troy (*M.,* pp. 164–165).

Thematically and linguistically, the *miroloyia* are an expression of the Maniots' view of the world. The dirge is not simply a way of paying homage to a member of the community. It is also a way to celebrate his life by stressing his importance within the small society that had the opportunity to enjoy his presence. The deep and passionate mourning of the people is expressed in the dirge, in which, as the author points out, "all animate and inanimate, are shedding tears now for their lost master; [...]" (*M.,* p. 167). In the Greek world, words and gestures take on symbolic meanings in the simple form of funeral rites. The ritualised transition is accompanied by symbolic acts intended to protect the deceased and to facilitate his or her safe passage to the underworld. Leigh Fermor draws attention to legends and dreams, ghosts, and witches, and intersperses his account with specific rituals and superstitions. Indeed, he writes that the Maniots believe that "in summer, ghosts are said to roam the Mani in the hottest hour of the day, in winter at the darkest hour of the night. If their mortal predecessors have been killed by an enemy, they wail for revenge. Summer ghosts haunt graveyards, ruined churches and crossroads" (*M.,* p. 188). He also notes that the Maniots believe "in the prophetic importance of dreams, a *pan-Hellenic* superstition" (*M.,* p. 189), and argues that "[it] is even stronger here than in the rest of Greece. In Greece, one 'sees' a dream, but the exegesis of what one sees varies from region to region. In the Mani, in unconscious conformity with many modern theories, it goes by opposites" (*Ibidem*). Dreams, legends, and superstitions strengthen and unite the different parts of the region by presenting the values and dramatising the ideal relationships that animate their culture and society.

The symbols and processes of the rites, in terms of what they meant to the Maniots, were the focus of the author's cultural analysis. His experience reveals a multi-faceted, ever-changing representation of their beliefs. Nevertheless, he observes: "There are some exceptions to this system" (*M.,* p. 190). They have specific cultural meanings. These depend on their association with everyday life. However, the Maniots believe that "life, [...] is wretchedly poor and overcast with sadness" (*M.,* p. 194). Fermor places great emphasis on the essential nature of their pride; indeed, he makes it clear that "in the past, it [life] was entirely shadowed by the blood feud. The thing that kept the Maniots going was their fierce sense of liberty, their pride in living in one of the earliest places in Greece to have cast free of the Turks" (*Ibidem*).

From an anthropological point of view, scholars have tended to emphasise the impact of rites on individuals and the wider community. Similarly, Leigh Fermor's account draws attention to the fact that the rites of affliction demonstrate the Maniot's sense of protection against malevolent forces, thus showing that people can escape from the realm of the evil demon Charon; "one last superstition is very moving" (*M.*, p. 195). He observes, "If a woman has lost a male child (a 'gun'), she carries her next-born son out into the street in her apron shouting, 'A lamb for sale. Who'll buy a lamb?' 'I will,' says the first passer-by. He pays a small sum, stands godfather to him at the font, then hands the lamb back to its mother. It is a ruse to cheat Charon by confusing the familiar track with a false scent" (*Ibidem*). Leigh Fermor notes that while rites, legends and superstitions are particularly effective in preserving the traditional social and cultural order of the community, they also serve to reaffirm the soundness of their cultural motives and the social behaviour of their society. The Maniots seem to make positive ancestral connections in the present in order to (re)construct and narrate their history for both ancestors and contemporary witnesses. Superstition allows the reader to imagine a past world that seems to have disappeared, and to discover instead the meaning of actions, beliefs, and customs. There is no doubt that they are not alien to the modern imagination, nor are they alien to the modern world. Tales of Greek mythology and exemplary documents of an ancient world have always spread throughout Europe. Moreover, as Miguel John Versluys points out, "[...] the ancient world is usually seen as one vast multicultural mosaic with hundreds of equally valuable (local) cultures as constituent tesserae; all interconnected and influencing one another"[19]. Fermor's fascination with a culture that has never been forgotten is evident in the author's collection of a Hellenistic repertoire of images, ideas and stories that are at the heart of this people. His travels take him back to the myths and traditions of antiquity, and his experiences are interwoven with a myriad of scenes that recall the past and reflect the different, modern realities of Greece. In order to share what he has experienced, he prefers to give a detailed account of his journey, focusing on mythological themes and images as constitutive of the Greek context and helping

---

19 Miguel John Versluys, *Visual Style and Constructing Identity in the Hellenistic World*, Cambridge, Cambridge University Press, 2017, p. 25.

the reader to understand their impact on society and history. Fermor's interest in the presence of mythic elements in people's real lives, and his preoccupation with the dead through mourning laments, are evident throughout his observations. Rather than seeing antiquity as mere history, he shows how the past is perceived as a bearer of meaning.

Intersections: Strangers and Hospitality, Superstition, and Religion

Intersections or intergenerational contacts link myths and superstitions to real life. This symbolic linking of time combines memories of the past with experiences of the present. They seem to be circumscribed by visions of a distant time, by icons that keep them alive in the memory and in the culture. The connection between two different worlds is evident in the author's vivid evocations as he brings these images to the reader's mind. In this way, the author pays tribute to the construction of the nation and to the history created thanks to the precious remains of the past, which are returned to modern culture and recalled in chapters such as "The Entrance to Hades", "A Fountain of the Nereids" or "Gorgons and Centaurs", even though, as he remarks, "many things in Greece have remained unchanged since the time of the *Odyssey*" (*M.*, p. 360). *Mani* is Fermor's most explicit exploration of Greek and Mediterranean culture. Nothing is left unmentioned. No omission underlines the distance of time and space from that of the author; and his descriptions and reflections seek to show the historical and cultural evolution of this land. *Mani* is a work in which Fermor never fails to emphasise the habits, the way of life and the way of thinking of the people as a precious legacy of the past since the time of Homer. The hospitality shown to strangers, for example, or the way in which superstition and religion go together are still very much alive in Greek culture. This is why the author stresses that "hospitality to strangers" (cf. ibid.) always represents a sense of belonging that transcends individual boundaries, as he notes,

> [...] the more remote and mountainous the region, the less this [hospitality] has altered. Arrival at a village or farmstead is much the same as that of Telemachus at the palaces of Nestor at Pylos and of Menelaus at Sparta – so near, as the crow flies, to Vatheia – or of Odysseus himself, led by the king's daughter to the hall of Alcinöus. No better description exists of a stranger's sojourn at a Greek herdsman's fold than that of Odysseus when he stepped disguised into the hut of the swineherd Eumaeus in Ithaca. *There is still the*

same unquestioning acceptance, the attention to the stranger's needs before even finding out his name: the daughter of the house pouring water over his hands and offering him a "clean towel, the table laid first and then brought in, the solicitous plying of wine and food, the exchange of identities and autobiographies; the spreading of bed-clothes in the best part of the house – the coolest or warmest according to the season – the entreaties to stay as long as the stranger wishes, and, finally, at his departure, the bestowal of gifts, even if these are only a pocketful of walnuts or apples, a carnation or a bunch of basil; and the care with which he is directed on his way, accompanied some distance, and wished godspeed" (pp. 360–361, my emphasis).

As this passage shows, the Greeks did not change many of their ancestral traditions, strangers could not be ignored, and people were sympathetic to them. Since Homer's time, strangers have been endowed with an enigmatic aura. The author sits and enjoys the offerings of his host, showing his gratitude for the hospitality he has received, in accordance with the ancient tradition. Similarities between past and present are noticed by the author as he observes:

In the *Odyssey*, the newcomer often strikes a banquet in progress, and very often a *stranger* in Greece to-day will find himself led to an honourable place at a long table of villagers celebrating a wedding, a baptism, a betrothal or a name-day and his plate and glass are filled and refilled as though by magic. […] This general hospitality on feast days is less remarkable than the individual care of strangers at all seasons. It is the dislocation of an entire household at a moment's notice that arouses astonishment. All is performed with simplicity and lack of fuss and prompted by a kindness so unfeigned that it invests the most ramshackle hut with magnificence and style (*M.,* pp. 361–363).

In addition, Leigh Fermor stresses the importance of superstition, which is seen as another indication of the Greek/Hellenistic influence on the present. Indeed, he observes: "IN NOTHING is the continuity of Ancient Greece clearer than in the superstitions and pagan religious practices (and many of the 'Christian' ones) that still prevail in the Greek mountains and islands" (*M.,* p. 436). Fermor notes that superstition still echoes from the distant past, despite the differences between the social, economic, and political positions of the Maniots: "I think it is true to say that the educated classes are less and the simple class more superstitious than their English counterparts. The only superstition that really seems to hold its own in the upper reaches of society is the class-defying and pan-Hellenic – indeed, almost world-wide – belief in the Evil Eye. But even in this, the strongest single superstition among the simple, there is a touch of levity (*Ibidem*)". It could be argued that the author has tried to document the whole process from ancestral beliefs to civilisation. He emphasises the presence of ancient superstition even within religion, claiming that superstition and religion were insepara-ble in early civilisations. He does, however, try to give his reconstruc-tion a strict historical and cultural profile. However, he remarks, "It is a wry paradox that the newly urban and semi-educated in Greece, whose knowledge of ancient literature is very limited, [...] are the very people who deplore one's curiosity about such matters and minimize or negate their existence and, in a few cases, try to hinder one's access to them as 'backward,' 'primitive' and above all 'un-European' elements in the modern Greek State (*M.,* pp. 437–438)". Nevertheless, the link between superstition and religion was undeniable, and it continued to exist, almost independently of the civilising process in which Greece was engaged. As the author notes,

> [...] if there is one element in Greek life, after the language and the Greek character itself [...] which points to unbroken continuity, not only from Periclean Greece but from a yet remoter past, indeed, from the very cradle of European culture, *it is the survival of these ancient beliefs* and practices that some seek to patronize out of existence (*M.,* p. 438, my emphasis).

This point, he believes, reflects the ideas of a part of Greek intelli-gentsia that considers traditional and pagan cults a means of exalting Greek culture. Thus, on the one hand, "the aversion of some of the higher clergy – though not of the rustic priests, who see nothing anomalous in Christian and pagan co-existence – is based on much more logical grounds" (*M.,* p. 439). On the other hand, "this side of Greek country life, which evokes the scorn and hatred of some Greeks but few foreign-ers, has attracted, during the last hundred years, the interest and devoted study of a number of Greek and foreign scholars" (*Ibidem*). With more admiration than caution, scholars – such as Alexander Polites and John Cuthbert Lawson, "the Cambridge don" – have studied the works of John Damascene through ancient sources. They have shown that although Damascene condemned pagan practices, they continued to exist. In other words, scholars have raised questions about the relationship between practice and belief, which has been central to the study of religion in Greece. As Leigh Fermor observes after a careful analysis, "it is impossible to wander about in Greece or live for long with peasant families without striking this supernatural background" (*M.,* p. 440).

Apart from this, religion played an important role in determining what was considered superstitious and pagan. After the conversion to Christianity, the older practices associated with beliefs and deities were deemed superstitious. The result was their transformation into something that would have been acceptable to the empire. Through the reinterpretation of their ritual traditions, the polytheistic religion of the Greeks was transformed into a polytheistic religion of the Empire,

> [...] the expulsion of the old gods, after thousands of years of happy tenure and the reduction of the Pantheon to a private cell, was a serious task. There was not much difficulty among the educated: Plato and his successors had prepared the ground; and when Julian the Apostate attempted to re-install the rites of Apollo in the groves outside Antioch, the sophisticated citizens deemed it not only a bad joke, but a rather vulgar one. But what was to be done about the unlettered and conservative masses? How to focus the wide scope of their veneration on a single point? It could not be done, and a compromise was found. Columns and blocks from ancient fanes, hallowed by centuries of worship, were built into new churches and, to ease the change-over, saints were inducted to these old haunts with characteristics or names which corresponded with those of the former incumbents; sometimes both. Dionysus became St. Dionysios and still retains his link with Naxos and his Bacchic patronage of wine. Artemis of the Ephesians became a male St. Artemidos and, like Artemis, his help is sought in the cure of wasting and nymph-struck children, as it was before he changed clothes, when the handmaids of Artemis had wrought mischief among the offspring of mortals (*M.,* pp. 442–444).

The transformation of the pagan world coincided with the conscious growth of social change. The formal religion of the region was circumscribed by new doctrines. Churches and old cults became separate entities, although "the clergy did what they could to reduce the pagan characteristics, but there was more truth in the gods' claims to immortality than is generally thought. The saints satisfied the habit of multiple divinities, and Christianity, although a celestial hierarchy was maintained, became in a sense – in practice if not in theory – polytheistic" (*M.,* p. 446). In other words, "religious organisations" and "ritual traditions" were absorbed into a new religion. There was no outright rejection of the earlier forms of worship, but they were transformed and adapted to a different social order and a different cultural view of the world, which had a different perspective on ritual and its relationship with society. This means that superstition and new religion were never completely separated, but one was contaminated by the other.

In the above context, cultures or cultural phenomena are always related to each other, and consequently the boundaries are porous, open, and fluid. In Fermor's reconstruction, an essential feature emerges that has been focused on and analysed by many scholars: the importance of inclusivism. Inclusivism is a strategy aimed at harmonising cultures or aspects of a particular culture[20]. Greek culture is therefore the result of this fusion. Fermor understands the concept of cultural exchange as a form of interaction. His journey makes him understand that the concept of cultural exchange is a form of interaction. For this reason, his journey seeks above all to see reciprocity, difference, and complementarity, as well as contamination, as unique. No aspect of culture can be relegated to the past, but it coexists with the present, even in its most archaic expressions.

Conclusion

At the end of his long journey, after having described so many landscapes, traditions and customs, Leigh Fermor quickly realised that he had much more in common with the Greeks he had met, in terms of language, history and culture, than he could have imagined. The preservation of a worldview from the ancient past, the fact that it has not disappeared, is emphasised in most of his travel accounts. He points out how the assimilation of past and present is fundamental to the understanding of, for example, ancient Greek religion and Christianity, or the formation of new forms of culture that seek to preserve the identity of peoples, as happens through dirges and other forms of cultural expression, however small but significant.

The author's account shows the complexity of the ancient Greek world in contrast to the more Spartan society of the Mani. Fermor gives a convincing homogeneity to the history of Greece, to its monuments (such as temples and icons) and to its traditions. He attempts to portray the Mani as a natural continuation of the earlier society and culture, representing a community with a shared *ethos*. The author emphasises that modern phenomena do not distort history. Rather, they amplify it and connect it profoundly with modern society and culture. By travelling through Greece and the Peloponnese, Fermor is trying to rediscover and show a country

---

20 On these aspects, see Laila Abu-Er-Rub, Christiane Brosius, Sebastian Meurer, Diamantis Panagiotopoulos and Susan Richter (eds.), *Engaging Transculturality*, New York, Routledge, 2019, p. 9 ff.

whose culture is unlikely to disappear. Moreover, *Mani* seems to express the author's nostalgia for the world of philosophers, literary and mythological figures who have shaped and continue to shape the stories, legends, and traditions of modern Europe. If, as Anthony Kaldellis notes, "[...] the basic cultural parameters of the 'West' are that Byzantium emerges as the quintessential Western civilisation"[21], in the twentieth century, Greek culture demonstrated a clear and unbreakable bond between two distinct perspectives: the ancient and the modern. Scholars have observed numerous instances of this intertwined nature which has led to the evolution of a new concept of Greek tradition and "Grecity"[22] – a concept primarily defined as appropriation and innovation.

---

21 Anthony Kaldellis, *Hellenism in Byzantium: The Transformations of Greek Identity and the Reception of the Classical Tradition*, Cambridge, Cambridge University Press, 2007, p. 2.

22 "Grecity" was a favourite expression by Kierkegaard, and it does mean "the Greek view of life", which in this context appears appropriate to describe the new tendency. Cf. Johannes Sløk, *Kierkegaard's Universe: A Guide to the Genius*, Translated into English by Kenneth Tindall, Copenaghen, Lindhardt og Ringhof, 2013, ch. 10, Kindle.

Neologisms, Wordplays, and *Pastiche* in the Italian Cycle of Tristan Corbière's *Amours jaunes*

Lorella MARTINELLI

Its black drawing on the transparent background of a lampshade had lit his childhood evenings in Brittany at his Aunt Puyo's house. Yet the real Vesuvius did not leave a profound mark on Tristan Corbière's poetry. The Breton poet visited Italy twice[1], following the usual itineraries of the nineteenth century French *intelligentsia*. Between December 1869 and the spring of 1870 the poet stayed for some time in Naples, Castellammare and Sorrento, in the company of the Breton painter Jean-Louis Hamon[2]. With Hamon, an exponent of the neo-Greek or Pompeian school which attracted the attention of Théophile Gautier, Tristan shared an aversion to tearful romanticism, as well as a taste for the *pastiche* and caricatural deformations. We know for certain that the poet also visited Capri in the company of Count de Battine and Herminie, the same Marcelle to whom he dedicated his *Jaundiced Loves* in May 1872[3]. In the poems

---

1   The journeys across Italy by the Breton poet have been widely documented and collected by P. A. Jannini, "Nuovi documenti sul viaggio di Tristan Corbière in Italia", *Sì e No*, 2 luglio 1975, pp. 164–178; by the same author see also *Un altro Corbière*, Roma Bulzoni, 1977, pp. 132–175 and by Lorella Martinelli, *Retorica e argomentazione nelle* Amours jaunes *di Tristan Corbière*, Roma, Carocci, 2017.

2   Afflicted by illness like Tristan, the painter Hamon would sojourn regularly in Rome and Capri starting from 1865. He painted great works such as the *Comédie humaine*, which was exhibited at the Salon in 1852 and draws a clear inspiration from Dante. The Breton poet and the painter had several elements in common: the taste for the *pastiche*, linguistic deformations, and the *calembour*, as well as the dislike for Romanticism.

3   Thanks to Jannini's insightful reading of the testimonies from Capri and Corbière's correspondence, we know for certain that the poet was in Capri again in 1872, this time accompanied by the Count Rodolphe de Battine and the woman who would sign herself in the guestbook of the Hotel Pagano as Herminie de Battine, actress

of the *Amours jaunes*, which preserve traces and memory of them, his journeys across Italy are subject to comic and farcical transfigurations. His lines combine different dialectal registers, melodramatic incursions, and *pratiques pastichantes* that target the Romantic poets Lamartine and Musset, whose works – at once admired and despised – had revived the Mediterranean myth of Italy[4]. The short Italian cycle includes six texts: *Veder Napoli poi mori, Vésuves et Ce, Soneto a Napoli, À l'Etna, Le fils de Lamartine et de Graziella, Libertà*. They all belong to the section *Raccrocs*, and display such similar thematic and stylistic elements that it may be assumed they were composed around the same time.

Corbiére subverts the idea of the Italian tour: Italy no longer stands for a sunny, primitive place, whose sweet, seductive weather and delicate natural and urban landscapes had been written about by so many French authors and intellectuals in their travelogues and memoirs. To the contrary, Tristan conceives of Italy as inherently hostile, in its excesses of colours and confusion: "Ce qui est plus certain c'est que l'Italie lui déplut. […] Il n'y a pas à s'en étonner. Corbière est un chercheur de clair-obscur et il a trop magnifiquement vu le pays d'Armor et chanté les gens de mer pour n'avoir pas dédaigné Naples et ses rives"[5]. To French travellers in the early eighteenth century, Italy was the emblem

---

of Italian descent. Several scholars believe that Corbière was to the woman but an occasional diversion from tiresome days, and that the miserable Tristan, however conscious of his role, could not help but remain close to the two friends.

4 Aside from obvious aesthetic and ideological orientations, Corbière draws part of the linguistic materials and inventions he includes in his collection from a series of texts he would assimilate and turn back to again at different times. The Breton poet's attitude towards the Romantics is akin to his father Édouard Corbière's. Ten or so specific allusions to Musset provide him with the storylines for the section *Sérenade des sérénades*. Nevertheless, Corbière's true view of Musset reveals itself in the seventh of the eight sonnets composing the poem *Paris*, wherein bitterness and sense of helplessness are tinged with angry cynicism, resulting in a sort of handbook for aspiring poets. Furthermore, in the poem *Un Jeune qui s'en va* (included in the section *Les Amours jaunes*), Corbière's ironic solution (the sick young poet who feels close to dying) is a response to Lamartine's tearful *cliché*. Along with the rejection of his aesthetics, Tristan expresses a genuine and visceral antipathy towards the other poet, whose bitter cynicism would take him so far as to speculate on his own daughter's death: ("Lamartine: – en perdant la vie/De sa fille en strophes pas mal", *Un jeune qui s'en va*, in Tristan Corbière, *Œuvres Complétes*, édition établie par Pierre-Olivier Walzer et Francis Burch, Paris, NRF/Gallimard, p. 731).

5 René Martineau, *Tristan Corbière*, avec de nombreaux documents inédits, des portraits, des dessins et un fac-similé d'écriture, Le Divan, Paris, 1925, p. 55.

of charming and picturesque landscapes, precious ancient ruins, the
great masterpieces of figurative arts, and, last but not least, cities such
as Rome, Florence, Venice, Genoa, and Naples, considered to be true
works of art and nature. The educational value of the Italian tour was
indeed found in this ideal representation, as well as in the slow process
of immersing oneself in the Classical tradition[6]. It would have sufficed
him to adhere to his actual experiences, however different these were
from earlier travellers', in terms of how they unfolded, their historical
moment, and his irreverent personality. Instead, far from reinforcing the
Grand Tour iconography, Corbière revels in clichés, as he produces a sort
of comic and spicy Italian rhapsody, a true jumble of commonplaces
more or less linked with the country's geography. The practice of the
quotation, which is of fundamental quantitative and qualitative rele-
vance in the fabric of his *Amours jaunes*, takes on a morbid, disquieting,
and grotesque quality in the Italian cycle. The journey through Genoa,
Naples, and Rome echoes the tones and atmospheres of his crowd
sequences portraying wounded and ulcerated souls, especially in the
Breton poems – *Gens de Mer* and *Armor*. However, the former display, if
possible, less human sympathy and a dimmer hope of redemption. And
yet, "Artiste et poète, il aurait du sympathiser doublement avec l'Italie
sans épithète: il n'en sentit ou n'en voulu sentir, par une infirmité de sa
nature, que les ridicules, la pouillerie et l'emphase, qui lui cachèrent le
visage immortel de la déèsse"[7]. The Italian experience is textualized in an
ironic and desecrating *collage*. This allows him the opportunity to tune
the shrill instrument of poetry, complementing it with the exhilaration
of a Neapolitan *granduignol*: "Masanielli's chorus" – written by Tristan
in the French spelling *Mazanielli* – "torsos of mandolins", "*Signori
Lazzaroni*" e "Pulcinello's prayer cards":

---

6   On the anthropological and heuristic value of the Italian journey, see: Emanuele
     Kanceff, *Alle origini della storia del viaggio in Italia*, in *Mélanges à la mémoire de
     Franco é Simone: France et Italie dans la culture européenne*, vol. III, XIX et XX siècles,
     Genève, Slatkine, 1984; *Le voyage français en Italie*, Actes du Colloque International
     (Capitolo-Monopoli, 11–12 maggio 2007), a cura di Giovanni Dotoli, Fasano,
     Paris-Schena, 2007; Eric J. Leed, *La mente del viaggiatore: Dall'Odissea al turismo
     globale*, a cura di Erica Joy Mannucci, Bologna, Il Mulino, 1992; Marie Madeleine
     Martinet, *Le voyage d'Italie dans les littératures européennes*, Paris, Presses Universitaires
     de France, 1996; Attilio Brilli, *Il viaggiatore immaginario: L'Italia degli itinerari per-
     duti*, Bologna, Il Mulino, 1997.
7   Charles Le Goffic, Preface to *Amours jaunes*, Paris, Messein, 1912, p. XX.

VEDER NAPOLI POI MORI

Voir *Naples et*... – Fort bien, merci, j'en viens.
– Patrie
D'Anglais en vrai, mal peints sur fond bleu-perruquier
Dans l'indigo l'artiste en tous genres oublie
Ce *Ne-m'oubliez-pas* d'outremer: le douanier.

– Ô Corinne!... ils sont là déclamant sur ma malle
Lasciate speranza, mes cigares dedans!
– Ô Mignon... ils ont tout éclos mon linge sale
Pour le passer au bleu de l'éternel printemps!

Ils demandent *la main*... et moi je la leur serre!
Le portrait de ma Belle, avec *morbidezza*
Passe de mains en mains: l'inspecteur sanitaire
L'ausculte, et me sourit... trouvant *que c'est bien ça*!

Je venais pour chanter leur illustre guenille,
Et leur chantage a fait de moi-même un haillon!
Effeuillant mes faux-cols, l'un d'eux m'offre sa fille...
Effeuillant le faux-col de mon illusion!

– Naples! panier percé des Seigneurs *Lazzarones*
        Riches d'un doux ventre au soleil!
Polichinelles-Dieux, Rois pouilleux sur leurs trônes,
Clyso-pompant l'azur qui bâille leur sommeil!...

Ô Grands en rang d'oignons! Plantes de pieds en lignes!
Vous dont la parure est un sac, un aviron!
Fils réchauffés du vieux Phœbus! Et toujours dignes
Des chansons de Musset, du mépris de Byron!

– Chœurs de *Mazanielli*, Torses de mandolines!
Vous dont le métier est d'être toujours dorés
De rayons et d'amour... et d'ouvrir les narines,
Poètes de plein air! Ô frères adorés!

Dolce Farniente!...– Non! c'est mon sac!... il nage
Parmi ces asticots, comme un chien crevé;
Et ma malle est hantée aussi... comme un fromage!
Inerte, ô Galilée! et... *e pur si muove*...

– Ne ruolze plus ça, toi, grand Astre stupide!
Tas de pâles voyous grouillant à se nourrir;

Ce n'est plus le lézard, c'est la sangsue à vide…
– Dernier *lazzarone* à moi la *[sic]* bon Dormir!

Napoli. – Dogana del porto.

The Italian short cycle begins with the poem *Veder Napoli poi mori*, which is marked by a strong, internal dialogism involving several elements of the text. The fragments in macaronic Italian are transcribed according to the traveller's own impression of the sounds he could capture, and they seem to mimic instances of phonetic symbolism: "[…] on peut penser que le soleil, le jeûne, et la liberté chers au *lazzarone* ne sont pas sans rapport avec la rumeur mêlée des rues, ou, ce qui est plus décisif encore, avec les monologues débridés d'une prison (le violon de *Bohème de chic*, la cellule IV bis Prison royale de Gênes de *Libertà*) où il se déclare libre et fier"[8]. The dense, material, bodily soundscape of Naples is often emphasised by means of exclamations: "*Lasciate speranza*, mes cigares dedans!"[9] "*Dolce Farniente!*". The Italian quotations and borrowings within the text are perfectly self-contained. They neither refer to external elements, nor define any kind of denotation or interaction. They are pure indexes to the landscape, and partake in presenting the human environment and the fabric of boisterous voices wherein the speaker is immersed. The *pastiche* indeed unfolds downwards, as the poem collects the vocal magma of a cross-breed language, composed of paraphrases, ironic allusions, calques, and *jeux de mots*. Such linguistic manipulations – translating lyrical matter into the domain of the *Opéra-Comique* – are coupled with a metric-syntactic structure which disrupts rhymes and caesuras, and epitomises the "Poète en dépit de ses vers"[10].

Furthermore, the Italian poems develop a form of painting or visual isotopy that informs several segments of the text. To mention a few: "Patrie/D'Anglais en vrai, mal peints sur fond bleu-perruquier!"; "Dans l'indigo l'artiste en tous genres oublie/Ce *Ne-m'oubliez-pas* d'outremer: le douanier"; "Plus grand, je te revis à l'Opéra-Comique/– Rôle jadis créé par toi: *Le Dernier Jour/De Pompeï* – Ton feu s'en allait en

---

8   Henry Thomas, *Tristan le dépossédé*, Paris, Gallimard, 1972, p. 67.

9   The quotation from Dante – "Lasciate ogni speranza, voi ch'intrate" (*Inf.*, III, ll. 1–9) ("Abandon hope all ye who enter here", trans. by Henry Francis Cary), inscribed on the gate to hell – is a reference to Hamon.

10 *Épitaphe*, l. 19, Tristan Corbière, *op.cit.*, p. 711.

musique,/On te soufflait ton rôle, et… tu ne fis qu'un four"[11]. The latter reference opens up to a reflection on the serial re-production and circulation of images. As such, these end up replacing physical objects, whose factuality is somewhat lessened and challenged (the question in the first line echoes such a weakened sense of reality):

VÉSUVES ET Cie

Pompeïa-Station – Vésuve, est-ce encor toi?
Toi qui fis mon bonheur, tout petit, en Bretagne,
– Du bon temps où la foi transportait la montagne –
Sur un bel abat-jour, chez une tante à moi:
Tu te détachais noir, sur un fond transparent,
Et la lampe grillait les feux de ton cratère.
C'était le confesseur, dit-on, de ma grand'mère
Qui t'avait rapporté de Rome tout flambant…

Plus grand, je te revis à l'Opéra-Comique.
– Rôle jadis créé par toi: Le Dernier Jour
De Pompeï. – Ton feu s'en allait en musique,
On te soufflait ton rôle, et… tu ne fis qu'un four.

Nous nous sommes revus: devant-de-cheminée,
À Marseille, en congé, sans musique, et sans feu;
Bleu sur fond rose, avec ta Méditerranée
Te renvoyant pendu, rose sur un champ bleu.

– Souvent tu vins à moi la première, ô Montagne!
Je te rends ta visite, exprès, à la campagne.
Le Vrai Vésuve est toi, puisqu'on m'a fait cent francs!
……………………………………………………………
Mais les autres petits étaient plus ressemblants.

Pompei, aprile.

The poem *Vésuves et Cie* testifies to Corbière's strong satirical distaste for the cultural trivialities of mass tourism. However, the text particularly highlights Tristan's disenchantment with the adventurous ideals formed during his childhood: "Pompeïa-Station –Vésuve, est-ce encor toi?/Toi qui fis mon bonheur, tout petit, en Bretagne, – Du bon temps où la foi

---

11 On September 21, 1869, the Théâtre Lyrique National in Paris staged *Le dernier jour de Pompeï*, written by Charles Nuittier and Alexandre Baume, with music by Victorin Joncières. Corbière was likely to have attended the performance.

transportait la montagne –/Sur un bel abat-jour, chez une tante à moi". The present does not align with the past, reality proves inferior to fantasy expectations, and truth – the truth of feeling – is but a gracious gift from the past[12]. Accordingly, even in those rare moments of abandonment to the fancy of lost times, Corbière's irony steps in and reminds the reader that nostalgia for one's childhood ultimately holds a kitsch-like quality: "Le Vésuve pérennise la conscience d'un bonheur que l'enfant lui a, dès le départ, associé. Tout le passé s'engloutit alors dans l'évocation d'un moment heureux, donnant la fallacieuse impression que l'existence entière de Tristan a été aussi radieuse que lorsqu'il laissait errer son imagination devant cet abat-jour inaugural"[13].

The poetic project of the Italian cycle has a carnivalesque, satirical, and farcical character. Tristan's collection of caricatures, as well as his delight in combining the contrasting colours of reality, evokes the *arlequin-ragoût*, whose polymorphic face is the very symbol of the poet's *œuvre*, and offers itself as the author's first stylised image.

His painter friends' stories – Hamon's in particular – might have aroused his interest in Italy. The latter relied upon a longstanding tradition: from the Italian-fashion characters featured in the Breton *calvaires*[14] to the *souvenirs* that furnished his family's house and conversations. First and foremost (though not exclusively) was that one lampshade with the image of the Vesuvius which he used to look at as a child and remembers in *Vésuves et Cⁱᵉ* ("Toi qui fis mon bonheur, tout petit, en Bretagne, – Du bon temps où la foi transportait la montagne –").

As noted earlier, the Breton poet sets off for Capri with the painter Hamon in December 1869. Their leisure trip soon turns into a hellish, comic rhapsody. Indeed, while at the customs office in Naples, Corbière is reminded of Dante's words engraved upon the entrance to the Inferno: *Lasciate speranza* ("Abandon hope"), which he later includes in the first poem of the Italian *suite*, *Veder Napoli poi mori*. Thanks to

---

12 Alexandre Arnoux: "Le Vésuve, on le voyait chez la tante Puyo les soirs d'octobre. Sans doute ne mourait-il pas l'été, mais il sommeillait au bout du salon, sans cœur de flamme en veilleuse, la clarté du soleil l'exilant; car il était peint sur l'abat-jour d'une lampe à huile dont le remontoir poussait de doux sanglots". Alexandre Arnoux, *Tristan Corbière*, Paris, Grasset, 1929, p. 45.

13 Pascal Rannou, *De Corbière à Tristan. Les Amours jaunes: une quête de l'identité*, Paris, Champion, 2006, p. 272.

14 See Roger Vercel, *Bretagne aux cent visages*, Paris, Albin Michel, 1959, p. 39.

Pasquale Jannini's careful reading of the evidences from Capri, it is safe to claim that the six Italian poems were all conceived and partly composed during this journey[15].

Out of these, four are devoted to Naples, one to Genoa, and one to Mount Etna, which the poet never visited, however. *À l'Etna*[16]– dated "Palerme. – Aout" – testifies yet again to Corbierè's attempt to distort reality (the connection between Etna and Palermo is definitely imaginary, given the actual distance separating the volcano from the city). The poem, which is built around a farcical comparison between Mount Etna and Mount Vesuvius, contains the revealing phrase "– Tu ris jaune et tousses"[17]. Seen against the theme of sickly love – "Crachant un vieil amour malsain"[18]– this verse points to the title of the collection (*Les Amours jaunes*) and hence clarifies the connotative system of the latter from a semantic perspective.

Therefore, the "Italian" elements sketch extravagant and caustic characters. Neither is Corbière persuaded by the Gulf of Naples and its radiant landscape, nor by the beauty of the city's monuments, buildings, and squares. Rather, he is struck by the dissonance of the language recorded in the field, the irregularities punctuating oral conversation, charged with the discordant expressiveness and unpredictability that characterises instances of *parole*. Nevertheless, as opposed to the Italian borrowings and the Neapolitan eye dialect, his works weave a tangled web of references to traditional literature.

The Italian cycle of the *Amours jaunes* stands as a significant archive of ingenious allusions, twisted quotations, and *pastiche*, targeting the most acclaimed authors from the Romantic and eighteenth century lyrical traditions. Corbière is eager to expose his large and varied set of personal idiosyncrasies, as well as set out his biting satire unequivocally. In *Le fils de Lamartine et de Graziella*, initially set in Capri, Graziella, emblem of Mediterranean beauty and unfortunate protagonist of Lamartine's eponymous 1852 novel, has her story turned into a parody by Tristan. Corbière's *décor* (the touristic one from *Veder Napoli poi mori*) is used as a satirical pretext for Lamartine's tender and delicate sentimentalism,

---

15 See Pasquale Aniel Jannini, 1977, p. 133.
16 Tristan Corbière, *op. cit.*, pp. 784–785.
17 *Ibid.*, p. 785.
18 *Ibid.*

which holds little or no masculinity: "*Le fils de Lamartine!/Si Lamartine eût pu jamais avoir un fils!*".

Direct quotations are used again here, though rid of their original meaning by means of translation into wholly different contexts. Ultimately, they appear as one of the most peculiar traits of Corbière's writing.

LE FILS DE LAMARTINE
ET DE GRAZIELLA

> *C'est ainsi que j'expiai par ces larmes écrites la dureté et l'ingratitude de mon cœur de dix-huit ans. Je ne puis jamais relire ces vers sans adorer cette fraîche image que rouleront éternellement pour moi les vagues transparentes et plaintives du golfe de Naples… et sans me haïr moi-même; mais les âmes pardonnent là-haut. La sienne m'a pardonné. Pardonne-moi aussi, vous!!! J'ai pleuré.*

LAMARTINE, *Graziella*
(I fr. 25 c. le vol.)

À l'île de Procide, où la mer de Sorrente
Scande un flot hexamètre à la fleur d'oranger,
Un Naturel se fait une petite rente
    En *Graziellant* l'Étranger…

L'Étrangère surtout, confite en Lamartine,
Qui paye pour fluer, vers à vers, sur les lieux…
– Du *Cygne-de-Saint*-Point l'Homme a si bien la mine,
Qu'on croirait qu'il va rendre un vers… harmonieux.

C'est un peintre inspiré qui lui trouva sa balle,
Sa balle de profil: – Oh mais! dit-il, voilà!
Je te baptise, au nom de la couleur locale:
    – LE FILS DE LAMARTINE ET DE GRAZIELLA! –

Vrai portrait du portrait du Rafaël fort triste,…
Fort triste, pressentant qu'il serait décollé
De sa toile, pour vivre en la peau du *Harpiste*
Ainsi que de son fils, rafaël raffalé

– *Raphaël-Lamartine et fils* ! – Ô Fornari-
Graziella! Vos noms font de petits profits;

L'écho dit pour deux sous: *Le Fils de Lamartine!*
Si Lamartine eût pu jamais avoir un fils!

– Et toi, Graziella… Toi, Lesbienne Vierge!
Nom d'amour, que, sopran' il a tant déchant!…
Nom de joie !… et qu'il a pleuré – Jaune cierge –
Tu n'étais vierge que de sa virginité!

– Dis: moins éoliens étaient, ô Grazielle,
Tes Mâles d'Ischia?… que ce pieux Jocelyn
Qui tenait, à côté, la lyre et la chandelle!…
Et, de loin, t'enterrait en chants de sacristain…

Ces souvenirs sont loin… – Dors, va! Dors sous les pierres
            Que voit, n'importe où, l'étranger
Où fait paître ton Fils des familles entières
– Citron prématuré de ta Fleur d'Oranger –

Dors – l'Oranger fleurit encor… encor se fane;
Et la rosée et le soleil ont eu ses fleurs…
Le Poète-apothicaire en a fait sa tisane:
            Remède à vers! remède à pleurs!

– Dors –L'Oranger fleurit encor… et la mémoire
Des jeunes d'autrefois dont l'ombre est encor là,
Qui ne t'ont pas pêchée au fond d'une écritoire…
Et n'en pêchaient que mieux! –dis, *ô picciola!*

– Mère de l'Antechrist de Lamartine-Père,
Aurore qui mourus sous un coup d'éteignoir,
Ton Orphelin, posthume et de père et de mère,
Allait – quand tu naquis–déjà comme un vieux Soir.

Graziella! – Conception trois fois immaculée…
D'un platonique amour, Messie et Souvenir,
Ce Fils avait vingt ans quand, Mère inoculée,
Tu mourus à seize ans !… C'est bien tôt pour nourrir!

– Pour toi: c'est ta seule œuvre mâle, ô Lamartine
Saint-Joseph de la Muse avec elle couché
Et l'aidant à vêler… par la grâce divine:
Ton fils avant la lettre est conçu sans péché!…

– LUI se souvient très peu de ces scènes passées…
Mais *il laisse le vent et le flot murmurer,*

Et l'Étranger, plongeant dans ses tristes pensées...
    En tirer un franc – pour pleurer!

Et, tout bas, il vous dit, de murmure en murmures:
Que sa fille ressemble à L'AUTRE... et qu'elle est là,
Qu'on peut pleurer, à l'heure, avec des rimes pures,
Et...– *pour cent sous, Signor* – nommer Graziella !

                                        Isola di Capri. – Gennaio.

As noted earlier, the first stanza both mirrors and subverts the opening of Lamartine's *Le Premier regret*. This poem was deemed so essential to the integrity of the novel and Graziella's incidents that his author included it as a poetic coda to the volume. The original stanza is a lengthy hymn to the beloved woman's purity, and it exploits the great Romantic trope of the unmarked grave where no one ever weeps. It provides Corbière with a set of lexico-phonetic features that he targets for his parody. The following is Lamartine's text:

Sur la plage sonore <u>où la mer de Sorrente</u>
Déroule ses flots bleus aux pieds <u>de l'oranger</u>
Il est, près du sentier, sous la haie odorante,
Une pierre petite, étroite, indifférente
Aux pas distraits de <u>l'étranger</u>!

                A. de Lamartine, *Le Premier regret*, 1830

The underlined words are the ones borrowed by Corbière, who preserved the rhyming pattern, but performed obvious estranging shifts. While the first line's ending of *Le Premier regret* is unaltered – "où la mer de Sorrente" – the rhyme structure (ll. 1–3) is profoundly modified so as to debase its meaning from a lyrical and descriptive context – the tombstone immersed in the heedless beauty of nature: "sous la haie odorante" – to a satirical one. Here, the tourist's foolish credulity is ridiculed – "Un Naturel se fait une petite rente" – also by means of the neologism "En *Graziellant*", which reads as "to beguile". Moreover, Corbière keeps and emphasises the rhyme between "oranger" and "etranger", through which he is able to evoke and recall the former item in different parts of the text: "Dors – l'Oranger fleurit encor... encor se fane" (l. 33); "– Dors –L'Oranger fleurit encor... et la mémoire" (l. 37).

Corbière resorts to the *pastiche* technique, although he becomes increasingly free with the model. The poet makes a polemical or ironically detached summary of the original content, which, as a result, gets trivialised and stripped of its emotional touch. The objective of such a linguistic practice is to expose the poetic sacredness of the landscape. The latter is anthropomorphised in Lamartine's verse, wherein the murmur of the branches and the noise of waves breaking on the sand echo Graziella's tragic fate. Her death is akin to Kore's, the maiden who fell in the prime of her life. Lamartine's bitterness and regret: "Mais pourquoi m'entrainer vers ces scènes passées?/Laissons le vent gémir et le flot murmurer"[19] (which is also part of the refrain of *Le Premier regret* and is repeated in lines 12–13; 44–45; 68–69; 92–93; 124–125; 140–141; 160–161) is turned into "– Lui se souvient très peu de ces scènes passées…/Mais il laisse le vent et le flot murmurer"[20] in Corbière's *pastiche*.

In addition, Corbière's peculiar modes of parody – displayed especially in the opening lines of *Le Fils de Lamartine et de Graziella* – should also be highlighted in order to gain a better sense of their ideological elements. As shown, his imitation preserves Lamartine's structure almost entirely. The line ending is the same – "fleur d'oranger"; so is the geographical context – "la mer de Sorrente". Even the theme of the waves is similar, underlined by a verb of motion at the beginning of the second line – although Corbière's intention of mocking the poet's marked tendency towards sentimentality does not go unnoticed: "[…] un flot hexameter à la fleur d'oranger" clearly suggests a conventional and corny inspiration. Yet, what is less evident in the lexical choices is a further semantic element of Lamartine's text that is the degradation of Graziella's purity, which indeed testifies to her subjection to the rhythms of nature. The metonymic and metaphoric mapping Graziella-Landscape is thus evoked, as well as her kinship to the island's environment – again reinforcing the reference to Classical culture, which pictures Graziella either as a peasant nymph, or, in light of her tragic fate, as Kore (see *Le Premier regret*, ll. 48 onwards):

> Que son oeil était pur, et sa lèvre candide!
> Que son ciel inondait son âme de clarté!
> Le beau lac e Némi qu'aucun souffle ne ride
> A moins de transparence et de limpidité!

This aspect of Graziella's nature is upturned in Corbière's verse. In an iconoclastic manner targeting the dogma of virginity, Lamartine's

---

19 Alphonse De Lamartine, *Graziella*, Paris, Gallimard, 1979, p. 186.
20 Tristan Corbière, *op. cit.*, p. 787.

heroine is transformed into a sort of sacrilegious and unlawful Virgin Mary ("Graziella! – Conception trois fois immaculée...").

The Italian Corbière appears to focus mainly on the pictorial surface of his plays, like a theatre-goer who is grateful enough for the conventionality and *kitsch* anticipated in the well-known script of the performance he/she will attend – a comedy or pantomime: no surprises nor exploration of otherness, but rather a *déjà vu*, as though Italy were an exhausted place, completely colonised by the imagery of the Romantic poets and hence available only as reference or collective memory. In fact, ingenuity and freshness in Corbière's verse stem not from the poet's eyes, but rather from his ears. Hearing, rather than sight, represents the poet's privileged device for recording his impressions of his travels. As opposed to images, his notebook pages are filled with the sounds of language: "Le ton de *Veder Napoli poi mori* est celui de la conversation; ces mots sont ceux que Corbière a entendus ou prononcés, et non de ceux qu'écrit un poète"[21]. Such a propensity indeed inspires one of Corbière's most felicitous verbal creations: the verb *Grazieller*[22] ("En *Graziellant* l'Étranger", quoted previously), whose sarcastic strength places it alongside the rest of the several original denominative forms included in the Italian cycle ("ruolzer, Clyso-pomper, soleiller").

In *Veder Napoli poi mori*, the Breton poet weakens the oleographic image of the Italian blue sky, which gradually turns into a "bleu-perruquier" or an "indigo", up until the final realisation, in the poem *Libertà*, that "le ciel est louche et rose"[23]: it is both shady and pink, an indeterminate hue hinting at the web of subtle games and ultimate deception into which the traveller, charmed by the Italian weather, will fall into. Besides being a caricaturist, Corbière is also a writer equipped with sharp irony, heedless of the realistic, documentary code which should inform travel literature. In his visionariness, and bodily, sullen, and moody attraction for Naples, even the sun – defined alternatively as "vieux Phœbus" or "grand Astre stupide" – sheds a dull and stolid light,

---

21 Albert Sonnenfeld, *L'Œvre poétique de Tristan Corbière*, Paris, Puf, 1960, p. 160.

22 On the semantic value of the verb, see Christian Angelet, who notes: "Tristan Corbière est avant tout un inventeur de mots; le verbe *grazieller* en est un exemple heureux qui désigne par là l'activité d'un *cicerone* qui avait trouvé le moyen de faire débourser les touristes en leur contant les amours de Lamartine et de Graziella. Le trop bienveillant guide allait jusqu'à leur proposer sa propre fille...vénalement!" (Christian Angelet, *La poétique de Tristan Corbière*, Bruxelles, Palais des Académies, 1961, p. 108).

23 *Libertà*, l. 25, Tristan Corbière, *op. cit.*, p. 789.

as if filtered by the disenchantment with the places that were once objects of worship to generations of literati.

While, on the one hand, Tristan ironizes the "touristy" and degraded quality of the Italian landscapes, so dear to the many Mussets and Lamartines, on the other hand, it is indeed in Naples that he meets and singles out the character of the *lazzarone*, whose *laissez-faire* philosophy, as well as free, picaresque, and hectic nature, will give him a central position in *Les Amours jaunes*.

Naples is all of this: a space wherein public scenes are turned into plays, and humanity stands as the background against which, together with its vices and virtues, the grotesque and macabre side of sociality is dramatized. Here, too, does the Neapolitan *lazzarone* seem to recall Brittany. This results from an apparently complex figurative shift, which evokes a parade of Breton cripples and beggars, effectively portrayed by the poet in *Rapsode foraine et le Pardon de Sainte-Anne-de-la-Palud* [...], discussed earlier with reference to its blending of folklore and aesthetic subversion.

The sonnet looks like an unrestrained Italian whim, replete with deliberate grammatical and orthographical deviations, starting with the very title: SONETO A NAPOLI

ALL' SOLE, ALL' LUNA

ALL' SABATO, ALL' CANONICO

E TUTTI QUANTI

– CON PULCINELLA –

Il n'est pas de Samedi
Qui n'ait soleil à midi;
Femme ou fille soleillant,
Qui n'ait midi sans amant!...

Lune, Bouc, Curé cafard
Qui n'ait tricorne cornard!
– Corne au front et corne au seuil
Préserve du mauvais œil. –

... L'*Ombilic du jour* filant
Son macaroni brûlant,
Avec la tarentela:

Lucia, Maz'Aniello,
Santa-Pia, Diavolo,
– CON PULCINELLA. –

Mergelina – Venerdi, aprile 15.

Corbière focusses his attention on the most frequently typified elements – *maccaroni* and *tarantella* – which he provocatively combines in short and rapid lines: "L'Ombelic du jour filant/Son macaroni brulant/Avec la tarentela". The conventional apotropaic gestures, the horn, *Pulcinella*'s (rhyming with *tarantella*) mask – they all provide a support to his caricature, filled with the humours of the Atellan satire: an archive of folklore and stereotypes immersed by the Breton poet in a dazed and sarcastic light, jarringly juxtaposed in unprecedented, intricate, and deformed ways, like in a Breton calvary. Corbière is neither interested in realism nor local colour, but rather in the slanted perspective, in the Dantean distortion of faces, bodies, and landscapes.

Similarly, in Rome he is struck by the place's inexhaustibly festive atmosphere – "Ici c'est fête tous les 5 minutes entre les repas ça arrive comme un nuage et il faut que tout se ferme pour se rouvrir quand la fête est passée"[24] – while he certainly is not by the Eternal City itself. Tristan is little concerned with the Italian political situation. He makes no mention of Rome's transformation and the end of popes' temporal power. Instead, he is satisfied with recording the *Urbe*'s picturesque side, peopled with bishops from all backgrounds, although adding a brief and sarcastic comment on the First Vatican Council. As he tells his aunt about his encounter with Pope Pius IX at the Baths of Diocletian, he notes with his usual sarcasm:

C'est donc là que j'ai vu le Pape, pas dans une vitrine, il marchait tout seul et regardait lui-même à coté de deux cardinaux. Voilà tout [...]. Alors j'ai vu les quelques âmes qui se trouvaient sur son passage piquer des têtes et verser d'abondantes larmes et baiser avec rage tout ce qu'elles pouvaient attraper au vol. Du reste, sa sainteté se laissait faire avec une adorable infaillibilité, et ce sourire de chic que lui ont appris portraits répandus dans le commerce à 7 fr. 50. Enfin le Pape ressemble à tous les papes et un peu à Jeanny Kerbriant.

---

24 The unabridged letter is reproduced in *Hommage à Corbière* (book edited by Alice Le Guéval and André Cariou for the exhibition held in Morlaix from May, 24 to August, 31, 1975, pp. 41–42).

To Corbière, Rome is ultimately a large museum, lacking any appeal
to the emotions: "Je ne regrette pas d'avoir vu Rome, parce que j'aurais
toujours regretté de ne l'avoir pas vue. Mais je n'ai senti rien là"[25].

As the curtain falls on his Neapolitan and Roman experiences,
Corbière closes the Italian cycle with the poem *Libertà*, which bears at the
bottom the dedication "À la Cellule IV Prison royale de Gênes"[26], paradoxical tribute to the royal prison of Genoa. From his ship anchored in
the roadstead and which he cannot leave, he writes to his parents: "Mon
cher papa et, de plus, ma chère maman, je ne dois pas vous dissimuler
l'État de Gênes où je me trouve depuis deux jours en relache avec le
paquebot qui porte César et sa fortune"[27]. The *gêne*, i.e., the constraint
of feeling uncomfortable in one's own skin, is familiar to the poet. The
irritating conjuncture must have given him the opportunity for a *calembour* in his manner ("état de gêne/État de Gênes"), hinting at the
prison of inner exile. Associations do not stop there: prisoner of both
his *gêne* and the *État de Gênes*, Corbière must have remembered he had
heard or read somewhere about the habit in Genoese prisons of writing
the motto "Libertà. Ce mot se lit au fronton de la prison de Gênes"[28].
First and foremost, his literary memories are inhabited by Dante, whom
he uses as a stylistic reagent to colour comic and telluric atmospheres.
Furthermore, echoes of de Musset are found in *Vers inscrits dans la cellule
n. 14* (the parallel with Corbière's "la cellule" is evident, as well as the
numerical reference in "À la cellule IV bis"). Still, as he takes pride in
his own uncomfortableness, "at last, is not pretending to be at ease in
his constraint also the entire substance, the entire freedom of his inner
prison?"[29]. There appear reunited, in light of these circumstances, all the
elements of a paradox: the bitter pleasure of privation, as acknowledged
by the poem's ending: " – Va: reprends, froide et dure,/Pour le captif
oison,/Ton masque, ta figure/De porte de prison.../Que d'autres, basse

25 *Ibid.*

26 Tristan Corbière, *op. cit.*, p. 788.

27 The letter is not part of the *Correspondance* edited by Pierre-Olivier Walzer and
   Francis Burch included in the *ŒC.*, but a transcription can be found in Jannini,
   1980, p. 192.

28 For further information see the note documented by Pierre-Olivier Walzer in Tristan
   Corbière, *op. cit.*, pp. 1321–1322.

29 Giuseppe Bernardelli, *La poesia a rovescio: Saggio su Tristan Corbière*, Milano, Vita e
   Pensiero, 1981 p. 100, my translation.

race/Dont le dos est voûté,/Pour eux te trouvent basse,/Altière déité!"
(*Libertà*, ll. 89–96)[30].

Therefore, while Corbière's *Grand Tour* has its educational value and
its function of refining one's culture and taste ultimately marred, as a
result of his rejection of the canon historically established in the Romantic
Age, that is not the case with its language. In fact, the latter interests him
and gets stuck in his memory, almost to the point of obsession. Italian,
with all the poet's grammatical and orthographical deviations, consistently informs *Soneto a Napoli*, whose subtitle also reads: "ALL'SOLE,
ALL'LUNA/ALL'SABATO, ALL'CANONICO/E TUTTI QUANTI/
CON PULCINELLA"[31]. Giovanni Bogliolo[32] recorded 86 loanwords or
foreignisms, most of them Italian, or approximately so. However, fac-
toring in titles, indications at the foot of poems, and variations (especially the ones noted down by Corbière in the specimen of the *Amours
jaunes* studied by Yves-Gérard Le Dantec and registered by Pierre-Olivier
Walzer[33]), the final number rises considerably. Thus, it must be observed
that a certain lexical musicality, although pictorially charged, is peculiar
to the *Amours jaunes*. Corbière develops such a linguistic repertoire, of
which only a few samples have been explored here, during his travels
across Italy. Whereas this experience leaves no memorable impressions
in terms of pictorial suggestions or literary influences, it does result in a
strong and clear imprint of the Italian (and Neapolitan) language and its
sonority on Corbière's works.

---

30 Tristan Corbière, *op. cit.*, p. 790.
31 *Ibid.* p. 784.
32 Cf. Giovanni Bogliolo, *Lessico corbieriano: Indice analitico del vocabolario delle Amours
     jaunes*, Urbino, Argalìa, 1975.
33 Tristan Corbière, *op. cit.*, pp. 1308–1322.

Metaphors of Ecotourism: The Use of Figurative Language in the Promotion of Ecotourism Activities in the Mediterranean

Lorenzo BUONVIVERE

Introduction

Among ever-increasing concerns for the state of the environment in the modern world, ecotourism has been developing as an opportunity to address conscious travel and support sustainable mobility. Although the International Ecotourism Society (TIES) provided its first definition as early as 1990, its actual meaning – and benefit – is still somewhat disputed[1]. It is sometimes interpreted as a synonym for nature-based tourism, and thus regarded only as a set of traditional leisure activities to be carried out in natural contexts. For this reason, the labels of "sustainable" or "responsible" tourism are alternatively preferred, since they are seen to emphasise its conservational aspect. Nonetheless, TIES's most up-to-date framing of ecotourism does include references to environmental protection, as well as actions aimed at foregrounding the active role of people in the host country. Hence, ecotourism can be understood as "responsible travel to natural areas that conserves the environment, sustains the well-being of the local people, and involves interpretation and education"[2].

The Mediterranean epitomises the lure of summer holidays and coastal mass tourism is indeed the most prominent in the area. However, its geographical and ecological diversity make it a privileged destination for ecotourism. The European Union is particularly engaged in this

---

1   Cf. *The Routledge Handbook of Ecotourism*, edited by David A. Fennell, London and New York, Routledge, 2021.

2   The International Ecotourism Society, "What Is Ecotourism", https://ecotourism. org/what-is-ecotourism/, 2019. Accessed July 23, 2022.

respect, and it has been funding projects to promote sustainable touristic enterprises in the region[3]. As with all forms of touristic activity, these also result in the publishing of promotional material which offers an interesting opportunity to investigate ecotourism discourse.

From the perspective of linguistic analysis, ecotourism has received marginal attention, and research has often pointed to the inconsistencies of its discursive practices. In his seminal work on the language of tourism, Dann includes ecotourism texts as an instance of what he calls "Greenspeak", or one of the registers of tourism language. He refers to the "three Ns of ecotourism", namely "nature, nostalgia, and nirvana"[4]. Accordingly, linguistic strategies of ecotourism texts strive to present natural destinations as uncontaminated, romantically set in pre-modern times, and equated with an earthly paradise. In Stamou and Paraskevopoulus, ecotourism discourse is understood as a "third space" placed along a continuum that has environmental and tourism discourses at its poles[5]. Thus, its lexis and pragmatic strategies are alternatively aimed at construing a need for conservation and leisure. Ruffolo's investigation supports these results, as she shows that in travel promotion texts concerned with nature, the latter is mainly described as an unspoilt space, and the recreational function is prominent with respect to linguistic items aimed at stressing preservation[6]. Malavasi observes that in texts promoting sustainable tourism on the web, values generally associated with tourism such as novelty, attractiveness, and exclusiveness are complemented by reference to sustainability through the use of highly evaluative language[7].

---

3   A list of projects currently receiving funding from the EU is available at https://ec.europa.eu/growth/sectors/tourism/offer/sustainable/transnational-products_en, Accessed July 23, 2022.

4   Graham Dann, *The Language of Tourism: A Sociolinguistic Perspective*, Oxon (UK), CAB International, 1996, p. 247.

5   Anastasia G. Stamou and Stephanos Paraskevopoulos, "Images of Nature by Tourism and Environmentalist Discourses in Visitors Books: A Critical Discourse Analysis of Ecotourism", *Discourse & Society*, 15, no. 1, 2004, pp. 105–129.

6   Ida Ruffolo, *The Perception of Nature in Travel Promotion Texts: A Corpus-Based Discourse Analysis*, Bern and New York, Peter Lang, 2015.

7   Donatella Malavasi, "'No One Can Be the Invisible Tourist – But We Like That You're Trying': An Analysis of the Language of Sustainable Tourism", in *Ways of Seeing, Ways of Being: Representing the Voices of Tourism*, edited by Maurizio Gotti, Stefania Maci and Michele Sala, Bern, Peter Lang, 2017, pp. 363–377.

Furthermore, some studies have tackled the issue of metaphorical language within ecotourism discourse. Analyses have been carried out across different genres, including oral communication by both guides and tourists during "ecowalks" or whale watching expeditions, as well as written examples from online promotional articles. Mühlhäusler and Peace find three main types of metaphors in ecotourism activities, representing nature as "a war zone", as anthropomorphic, and as a circus[8]. Milstein focusses further on this latter type of conceptualisation, whereby ecotourism is shaped around a "performer metaphor" that builds on tourists' expectations of being entertained by nature[9]. Spinzi analyses recurrent metaphorical framings on websites advertising ecotourism, reporting on the figurative use of the word "travel" to be intended as "conduit", "discovery", and "immersion" in abstract and sensory experiences, particularly through the act of walking[10]. Lazzeretti's contrastive analysis of English and Italian web texts highlights the recourse to metaphorical language in the latter to offer a negative evaluation of mass tourism, whose practitioners are addressed as "invaders" or "criminals"[11].

Traditionally, metaphors have been understood as a powerful tool in supporting the suasive objective of tourism texts. Although a comprehensive picture is still lacking, some authors have addressed the promotional purpose of metaphorical language. Mattiello suggests that in tourism discourse metaphors may have a "metarepresentational" function and thus be interpreted literally, so as to "activate a mental image that evokes a mental world"[12]. Dann's claim that metaphors are especially relevant in minimising the distance between tourist and destination by "reducing the unfamiliarity"[13] of the latter is confirmed by Jaworska. Through

---

8   Peter Mühlhäusler and Adrian Peace, "Discourses of Ecotourism: The Case of Fraser Island, Queensland", *Language & Communication*, 21, 2001, pp. 359–380, 365.

9   Tema Milstein, "The Performer Metaphor: 'Mother Nature Never Gives Us the Same Show Twice'", *Environmental Communication*, 10, no. 2, 2016, pp. 227–248.

10   Cinzia Spinzi, "Treading Lightly on the Earth: Metaphorical Frames in the Discourse of Ecotourism", in *Tourism and Tourist Promotion around the World: A Linguistic and Socio-Cultural Perspective*, edited by Elena Manca and Francesca Bianchi, Lecce, Salento University Publishing, 2013, pp. 81–94.

11   Cecilia Lazzeretti, "Communicating Sustainable Tourism in English and Italian: A Contrastive Analysis", *Lingue & – Rivista Di Lingue e Culture Moderne*, 19, no. 2, 2021, pp. 133–154.

12   Elisa Mattiello, "Metaphor in Tourism Discourse: Imagined Worlds in English Tourist Texts on the Web", *Textus*, 25, no. 1, 2012, pp. 69–84, 81.

13   Graham Dann, *op. cit.*, p. 171.

corpus-assisted analysis, she observes that texts advertising "faraway" places show an increase in metaphorical items if compared to domestic travel[14].

In my study, I propose to investigate metaphorical expressions in a corpus of nine ecotourist guides promoting travel in the mountainous regions of the Mediterranean. My first aim is to assess whether metaphors occurring in the texts have nature as their main target domain. Second, I seek to identify the most productive source domains with the purpose of understanding if and how ecotourism discourse differentiates itself from the language of traditional tourism texts in its figurative representation of destinations. Furthermore, taking into account the principles inspiring ecotourism, I wish to find out if metaphors can partake in an ecologically-conscious representation of natural destinations, or whether they only act as promotional devices to attract customers. Results confirm expectations concerning the relevant frequency of figurative devices describing nature in the texts analysed. In terms of function, however, these metaphors are aimed mainly at advertising the natural space as recreational. Some considerable exceptions point out to an interpretative function peculiar of ecotourism that targets, for example, local inhabitants as well as the tourists themselves. Still, their role in increasing ecological awareness is hardly noticed, since linguistic metaphors framing nature in ecotourism texts mainly uphold traditional conceptualisations that generally disregard nature's ecological complexity.

Data and Methodology

The corpus of the analysis consists of the nine ecotourist guides produced within the EMbleMatiC Project. This was a programme co-financed by the European Union Regional Development Fund originated in 2013 with the creation of EMM, the network of Emblematic Mediterranean Mountains. Aiming to offer an alternative to sea holidays in the Mediterranean, the EMbleMatiC project (which lasted from 2015

---

14 Sylvia Jaworska, "Metaphors We Travel by: A Corpus-Assisted Study of Metaphors in Promotional Tourism Discourse", *Metaphor and Symbol*, 32, no. 3, 2017, pp. 161–177. Jaworska uses the UK as her point of reference. On the matter see also: Yaniv Belhassen, "Metaphors and Tourism Paradoxes", *Tourism Management*, 79, 2020. Belhassen understands metaphors as enacting the "familiarity paradox" of tourism, by which tourists wish to experience familiar feelings in unfamiliar contexts.

to 2019) brought together different regions from the Mediterranean hinterland for the purpose of designing "eco-itineraries" that could allow tourists to experience the natural features of their territories while preserving their ecology. It involved nine mountains located across five countries: Canigó and Sainte-Victoire in France; Olympus and Psiloritis (Crete) in Greece; Etna and Gran Sasso in Italy; Pedraforca and Serra de Tramuntana in Spain; and finally Çika in Albania. Each produced a guide in which the suggested eco-itinerary is described, together constituting the material outcome of the project[15].

My analysis falls within the theoretical framework of Conceptual Metaphor Theory (CMT), addressing metaphors as a broad cognitive phenomenon through which we make sense of reality[16]. Simply put, conceptual metaphors consist of structuring and understanding one concept in terms of another. For example, saying "I don't know *where I'm headed* with my life" equals to describing the concept of life by comparing it to a journey. In CMT, this mapping between concepts or "conceptual domains" would be schematised as LIFE IS A JOURNEY, and labelled as a conceptual metaphor[17]. More precisely, the concept of journey is called "source domain", and it represents the set of knowledge from which we draw expressions to talk about life, which in turn makes up the "target domain", the one we aim to represent and understand through the metaphor. Therefore, the expression "I don't know where I'm headed with my life" is a "metaphorical linguistic expression"[18], one of the possible

---

15 All the guides are available online and can be downloaded from the "Deliverable Library" section of the EMbleMatiC website: https://emblematic.interreg-med.eu/what-we-achieve/deliverable-library/, Accessed July 8, 2022. Except for Çika, guides in English are provided along with versions in the language of the area promoted. Therefore, it is assumed that the texts composing the corpus are actually translations, although the name of the translator is either omitted or reference is made to a translation agency, so that it is actually unclear whether these were performed by native speakers of English.

16 Cf. George Lakoff and Mark Johnson, *Metaphors We Live By*, Chicago, University of Chicago Press, 1980; Raymond W. Gibbs Jr., *The Poetics of Mind: Figurative Thought, Language, and Understanding*, Cambridge, Cambridge University Press, 1994; Zoltán Kövecses, *Metaphor: A Practical Introduction*, 2nd ed., Oxford, Oxford University Press, 2010; Zoltán Kövecses, *Extended Conceptual Metaphor Theory*, Cambridge, Cambridge University Press, 2020.

17 It is an established convention of CMT to indicate conceptual metaphors by using small capital letters.

18 Zoltán Kövecses, *Metaphor: A Practical Introduction*, cit., p. 4.

realisations or wordings in language that the conceptual metaphor LIFE IS A JOURNEY can have.

Once regarded as merely stylistic and hence decorative devices circumscribed to literature, CMT contributed to assess the ubiquity of metaphors in every type of discourse. Not only do they allow us to reason concretely about abstract or complex areas of life, but they also fulfil discursive functions. It follows that the study of linguistic metaphors, i.e., of authentic metaphorical realisations in discourse, can address questions concerning the role they perform when associated with particular media, registers or texts[19]. For instance, metaphors are often exploited as persuasive devices in political discourse, wherein they partake in the definition of "scenarios" that justify political actions as either good or inevitable[20]. With reference to environmental communication, Proctor and Larson argue that linguistic metaphors act as "nomadic terms" that link scientific and public discourse[21], although some of the conceptualisations they afford, particularly in news discourse, may distort the correct understanding of issues such as climate breakdown[22].

What is more, implications of the pervasiveness of metaphorical reasoning in all domains of experience have led to account for realisations of metaphors beyond language, as well. These include, for example, visual metaphors[23], and Jensen and Greve's "ecologically informed approaches to metaphors", that see the latter as a "figure of action" involving simultaneously thought, body, and environment (in its spatial sense)[24].

In my study, I seek to single out linguistic metaphors from the corpus of ecotourist guides and group them according to the different source domains to which they belong. Because I am particularly interested in

19 Cf. *The Routledge Handbook of Metaphor and Language*, edited by Elena Semino and Zsófia Demjén, London and New York, Routledge, 2017.

20 Cf. Andreas Musolff, "Metaphor and Persuasion in Politics", in *The Routledge Handbook of Metaphor and Language*, cit., pp. 309–322.

21 James D. Proctor and Brendon M. H. Larson, "Ecology, Complexity, and Metaphor", *Special Thinking of Biology*, 55, no. 12, 2005, pp. 1065–1068, 1066.

22 Cf. Nelya Koteyko and Dimitrinka Atanasova, "Metaphor and the Representation of Scientific Issues: Climate Change in Print and Online Media", in *The Routledge Handbook of Metaphor and Language*, cit., pp. 296–308.

23 *Visual Metaphor: Structure and Process*, edited by Gerard Steen, Amsterdam-Philadelphia, John Benjamins, 2018.

24 Thomas Weben Jensen and Linda Greve, "Ecological Cognition and Metaphor", *Metaphor and Symbol*, 34, no. 1, 2019, pp. 1–16, 2.

assessing how these texts use metaphors to describe the natural features of the destinations they advertise, I focus on expressions having nature as their target domain. I am providing an example to clarify this. Since I interpret the metaphorical wording "The landscapes around Montalba *are carved out* of the granite" (from the Canigó guide) as describing the shape of the mountain by comparing it to a sculpture that has been carved out of the rock, I deem it as an instantiation of the conceptual metaphor NATURE IS ART.

However, the identification of metaphors is not always straightforward, and is indeed faced with some methodological challenges. These include concerns of metaphoricity and conventionality. Firstly, there is the problem of how to establish whether a word or set of words has a metaphorical meaning. In order to provide a systematic method to do this, the Pragglejaz Group has devised a Metaphor Identification Procedure (MIP), which is the one I adopt in my study[25]. It consists of a four-step approach that may be summarised as follows: (1) read the entire text; (2) determine its lexical units; (3) establish the contextual and basic meanings of the lexical unit; (4) mark the item as metaphorical if its basic meaning contrasts with its contextual meaning. The definition of the contextual and basic meanings of the lexical units represents the core of the MIP. Their recognition will also depend on the resources used, i.e., the dictionaries and/or electronic corpora that have been searched for definitions and examples of usage. In my case, I employ the online edition of the Collins English Dictionary[26]. Occasionally, I resort to the British National Corpus (BNC) and the Corpus of Contemporary American English (COCA)[27].

Secondly, once assessed the metaphoricity of an expression, claims can be made regarding its degree of conventionality, that is to say, how actually widespread (and predictable) the metaphorical meaning of a unit is. For instance, Steen's study of metaphors contrasts grammar, which "contains form-meaning pairings that are relatively fixed" and therefore conventional, with usage, which is in turn "more situated and specific" and displays a certain "uniqueness"[28]. However, he admits that conventional

---

25 Pragglejaz Group, "MIP: A Method for Identifying Metaphorically Used Words in Discourse", *Metaphor and Symbol*, 22, no. 1, 2007, pp. 1–39.

26 https://www.collinsdictionary.com/dictionary/english.

27 Both available at https://www.english-corpora.org/corpora.asp.

28 Gerard Steen, *Finding Metaphor in Grammar and Usage: A Methodological Analysis of Theory and Research*, Amsterdam and Philadelphia, John Benjamins, 2007, p. 5.

expressions may be found both in grammar and usage, and that it will depend on the particular "level of uniqueness" defined by the analyst[29]. Willing to focus on metaphorical language peculiar to the genre under examination, for the purpose of my study I consider only novel metaphorical expressions. I discriminate between conventional and novel metaphors following Semino's classification[30]. Accordingly, conventional metaphorical expressions are those whose "relevant metaphorical meaning has become lexicalized, so that it is normally included in the dictionaries alongside nonmetaphorical (basic) meanings"[31]. On the contrary, novel metaphorical expressions are those "whose relevant metaphorical meaning has not become lexicalized, and is therefore not included in dictionaries"[32]. For example, I do not include in my results conventional metaphors from the corpus like "The peaks of Galatzo, Teix, Ofre, Puig Tomir, which dominate the valleys of Puigpunyent, Valldemossa, Soller and Pollenca" (Tramuntana). This is because the meaning of "dominate" with reference to "a building, mountain, or other object" as to be "so large or impressive that you cannot avoid seeing it", while metaphorically derived from the basic meaning of "to have power over", is indeed listed in the dictionary and therefore conventional.

Electronic corpora are useful in determining some metaphorical uses, as well[33]. For instance, the adjective "photogenic" in "the church of Sant Miquel and the Ensija mountain range like a backcloth, altogether comprising a *photogenic* location" might have been identified as metaphorical, since, according to definition and examples found in the dictionary, in its basic meaning it refers almost exclusively to a human subject. A quick search on both the BNC and the COCA, however, shows a relevant number of occurrences of "photogenic" modifying also geographical places. For this reason, the item is left out of the analysis.

Consideration of the context in which the metaphorical unit appears, as prescribed by the MIP, is also especially relevant in determining the novelty of some expressions. This is the case with the noun "face" used with reference to the mountain. The face of a mountain is its "vertical

---

29 *Ibid.*, p. 6.
30 Elena Semino, *Metaphor in Discourse*, Cambridge, Cambridge University Press, 2008.
31 *Ibid.*, p. 19.
32 *Ibid.*
33 Cf. Alice Deignan, *Metaphor and Corpus Linguistics*, Amsterdam and Philadelphia, John Benjamins, 2005.

surface or side", according to the dictionary. Consistently, instances like "The escarpments of the north *face* of the Cadí mountain range are one of the most significant elements" (Pedraforca) are not taken into account. On the contrary, "mount Olympus shows its beautiful *face* of its northern side" is marked as a metaphorical expression. The adjective "beautiful" and the verb "show" depict mount Olympus as actively displaying its "facial features" to the tourist, hence construing an instance of personification.

Finally, in my identification of metaphorical expressions, I decide to include other linguistic phenomena which, although not strictly recognisable as metaphors, still involve a mapping between different conceptual domains. These are simile and metonymy. Similes are often contrasted with metaphors in terms of their explicitness, but can in fact be seen as equally producing a connective leap between different domains[34]. Metonymies, on the other hand, have been included in CMT since Lakoff and Johnson, who claimed that "metonymic concepts allow us to conceptualize one thing by means of its relation to something else"[35]. While cognitive linguistics may now treat them separately[36], with regard to my study, the inclusion of similes and metonymies makes it possible to consider occurrences that draw from the same source domains as the metaphorical expressions found in the corpus, so that a better understanding of the productivity of each domain – and accordingly mapping – can be hopefully gained.

Having made the necessary methodological clarifications, I now move on to present the findings of my study.

Results

Results confirm the considerable presence of metaphors in tourism discourse. As expected of ecotourism, metaphorical expressions targeting natural elements of the destination outnumber the others (Table 1)[37]. As much as 16 relevant source domains have been identified in the corpus[38].

---

34 Cf. Elena Semino, *Metaphor in Discourse*, cit.

35 George Lakoff and Mark Johnson, *op. cit.*, p. 39.

36 Cf. Francisco José Ruiz de Mendoza Ibáñez, "Conceptual Metonymy Theory Revisited: Some Definitional and Taxonomic Issues", in *The Routledge Handbook of Cognitive Linguistics*, edited by Xu Wen and John R. Taylor, London and New York, Routledge, 2021, pp. 204–227.

37 Target domains not related to nature include, for instance, TOWN, FOOD, and TOURIST.

38 By "relevant" I refer to those source domains which count at least two occurrences.

Of these, five are found to be particularly productive, namely the source domains of WAR, ART, GUARDIANSHIP, COMPETITION, and HUMAN BODY (Table 2). Whereas some of them have been already observed to feature in traditional tourism texts (ART and HUMAN BODY), others may be seen as peculiar to ecotourism. In fact, expressions from the source domains of GUARDIANSHIP and COMPETITION may especially appeal to potential eco-tourists seeking adventure rather than relaxation, and instances from the source domain of WAR seem to shift the perspective from the guests to the local community, as in the case of the Etna guide. In order to present my findings as systematically as possible, I will follow Jaworska's example and discuss results by examining each of the most prominent source domains on its own[39]. Where relevant, reference to minor source domains will be made, as well.

Table 1. Number of metaphorical expressions found in the corpus.

Metaphors	C1	C2	P1	GS	O	E	T	P2	SV	Total
All	24	16	31	34	15	47	42	7	39	255
Targeting nature	19	9	23	15	13	33	35	3	33	183
Proportion (%)	79 %	56 %	74 %	44 %	87 %	70 %	83 %	43 %	85 %	72 %

C1=Canigó; C2=Çika; P1=Pedraforca; GS=Gran Sasso; O=Olympus; E=Etna; T=Tramuntana; P2=Psiloritis; SV=Sainte-Victoire.

The Source Domain of WAR

Surprisingly, the source domain of WAR proves to be the most productive in the corpus, as shown in Table 2. Identified as early as Lakoff and Johnson's initiation of CMT as mapping one of the most basic conceptual metaphors, ARGUMENT IS WAR, research has testified to the impressive pervasiveness of the concept of war in structuring representations of the world in a great variety of discourses[40]. In Kövecses's terms, the source

---

39 Sylvia Jaworska, *op. cit.*

40 These include advertising (cf. Laura Hidalgo-Downing, Blanca Kraljevic Mujic and Begoña Nuñez-Perucha, "Metaphorical Creativity and Recontextualization in Multimodal Advertisements on E-Business across Time", *Metaphor and the Social World*, 3, no. 2, 2007, pp. 199–219), politics (cf. Nicholas Howe, "Metaphor in Contemporary American Political Discourse", *Metaphor and Symbolic Activity*, 3, no. 2, 1988, pp. 87–104), the news (cf. Nelya Koteyko, Brian Brown and Paul Crawford, "The Dead Parrot and the Dying Swan: The Role of Metaphor Scenarios in UK Press Coverage of Avian Flu in the UK in 2005–2006", *Metaphor and Symbol*,

domain of WAR has a wide metaphorical "scope"[41], i.e., it shows to apply to a great variety of target concepts.

Nonetheless, the generally negative connotations of war in touristic texts seem to clash with the aim of tourism language to construe destinations as appealing to potential travellers. In fact, the use of the source domain of WAR appears to be culture specific, or at least strongly dependent on the geographical area being targeted. In the corpus, the great majority of metaphorical expressions concerned with war (60 %) occur in the Etna guide. Given the volcanic nature of the mountain, the text resorts to the metaphor of war to characterise the complicated relationship between local inhabitants and Etna's frequent explosions: "Walking through the middle lands of Etna means crossing *the disputed territory* between man and nature". While describing the different stages of the ecojourney, the guide refers to past eruptions which survived in the collective memory of the local community and shaped features of the landscape. The latter is presented as bearing the traces of ancient battlefields: "go along for a hundred meters [...] and enter the *lava field* of 1923, the eruption that covered a large cultivated area". Dwellers are praised for their endurance and pictured as survivors: "[...] those who saw their lands *spared* by the *fury* of the volcano".

The clustering of these expressions in the Etna guide builds up an instance of "extension", which Semino understands as one of the textual patterns that metaphors can construe in discourses[42]. Extension involves the clustering of different metaphorical expressions in a text which evoke the same broad source domain and relate to the same target domain. In this case, not only does extension contribute to the consistency of the metaphor within the guide, but it also provides criteria for interpreting ambiguous instances. For example, although the adjective "tenacious" in "The vegetation of this zone consists essentially of *tenacious* evergreen trees" could have been assigned to the source domain of HUMAN EMOTION (see below), its closeness to other expressions of the kind highlights it as belonging to the "extended" war metaphor. This is in line with Cameron and Low's idea of "attraction" among clusters of metaphorical

---

23, no. 4, 2008, pp. 242–261), and healthcare (cf. Elena Semino, " 'Not Soldiers but Fire-Fighters': Metaphors and Covid-19", *Health Communication*, 36, no. 1, 2021, pp. 50–58).

41 Zoltán Kövecses, *Metaphor: A Practical Introduction*, cit., p. 136.

42 Cf. Elena Semino, *Metaphor in Discourse*, cit.

expressions[43]. Therefore, abundance of peculiar vegetation in the area is described as the result of the ability of nature to win over the human enemy and resist their attempts at taming through agriculture: "a large area once cultivated with vineyards and now fully *re-conquered* by natural vegetation"; "environmental conditions were *hostile* for the farmers of the nineteenth century and [...] today the forest *dominates unchallenged*".

The geo-cultural specificity of war metaphors with reference to Etna may be confirmed by occurrences found in the other guides of the corpus, where the use of the source domain of WAR has a more positive connotation and indeed aligns with the promotional aim of tourism texts. In the case of Sainte-Victoire, for example, it presents nature as an intelligent strategist: "clever nature *deploys* gems of ingenuity to implement one of the fundamental law of living things: to protect oneself and one's species"; "nature comes to *develop* amazing *strategies* to attract pollinators". In the Canigó guide it frames an alliance between dwellers and landscape: "The hillside inhabitants know this and *have allied* with the land to make it a nurturing home".

Table 2. Number of occurrences and distribution.

Source domain	C1	C2	P1	GS	O	E	T	P2	SV	Total
WAR	2	0	0	1	0	12	2	0	3	20
ART	4	0	7	0	1	2	2	0	3	19
GUARDIANSHIP	0	0	2	3	0	3	5	0	2	15
COMPETITION	2	0	1	1	1	0	2	0	6	13
HUMAN BODY	1	3	2	0	1	1	1	0	3	12
HUMAN CHARACTER	0	0	0	1	0	0	5	0	3	9
LOVE	0	0	2	1	1	2	1	0	1	8
BUILDING	3	1	1	1	1	0	0	0	1	8
PERFORMANCE	0	1	3	2	1	1	0	0	0	8
RESOURCE	0	0	0	0	2	2	3	1	0	8
RELIGION	0	1	1	3	0	0	1	1	0	7
LANGUAGE	2	0	0	0	0	0	1	0	3	6
CONCEALMENT	0	0	1	0	3	0	0	1	1	6
MAGIC	1	0	1	0	1	0	0	0	0	3
FOOD	0	1	1	0	0	0	0	0	1	3
HUMAN EMOTION	1	0	0	0	1	0	0	0	0	2

43 Cf. Lynn Cameron and Graham Low, "Figurative Variation in Episodes of Educational Talk and Text", *European Journal of English Studies*, 8, no. 3, 2004, pp. 355–373.

The Source Domain of ART

Whereas almost equivalent with the previous one in terms of productivity, the source domain of ART is actually found to be the most pervasive, since metaphorical expressions belonging to this domain figure in six out of the nine guides which make up the corpus (Table 2). Indeed, the total number of occurrences would further increase if not only unique types were included in the count. The noun "monument", for example, is used metaphorically six times across different texts to describe either peculiar features of the natural landscape, such as Gjipe Canyon in the Çika guide, or the mountain itself, as in the case of Sainte-Victoire. All these instances contain a form of hedging: "natural *monument*" (3), "geo-*monument*" (2), "rocky *monument*" (1). Hedges are actually perceived to weaken the metaphoricity of the expression by making the underlying comparison between source and target more explicit[44].

Within the source domain of ART, the latter is interpreted alternatively both as process and product. In the former case, metaphors are mainly realised by means of verbs which describe the act of modelling the landscape. The actor, or "artist", performing the effort is either the concealed agent of passive structures: "The landscapes around Montalba *are carved out* of the granite" (Canigó); "It is a landscape *designed* for walking" (Tramuntana); or it is identified with the wildlife and other natural elements of the place: "goats *have sculpted* the Provençal landscape" (Sainte-Victoire); "The erosive action of mountain streams and glaciers [...] *redraws* the valley landscape" (Canigó).

Most of the occurrences in the source domain, however, portray the mountainous destination as the outcome of artistic processes, in particular sculpture, photography, and literature. The reference to sculpture, already evident in the examples provided above, is especially salient (and perhaps inspired by the solid character of the massifs). Adding to the metaphorical "monument" discussed earlier, a pair of other examples is found: "There is no lack of *castings* of [Etna's] activities"; "always overlooked by the solitary *figurehead* of St. Victoire". The comparison with works of art has the effect of presenting the scenery as if carefully assembled to please the

---

44 Cf. Sam Glucksberg, *Understanding Figurative Language: From Metaphor to Idioms*, Oxford, Oxford University Press, 2001; Jeroen Vandaele, "Cognitive Poetics and the Problem of Metaphor", in *The Routledge Handbook of Cognitive Linguistics*, edited by Xu Wen and John R. Taylor, London and New York, Routledge, 2021, pp. 450–483.

tourist's eye. Indeed, the beauty of the landscape is often addressed by attributing to it the quality of a photograph: "the church of Sant Miquel and the Ensija mountain range *like a backcloth*, altogether comprising an extraordinarily photogenic location" (Pedraforca); "It is a lovely water-fall, a magnificent *background* for a photograph you may want to take at this point" (Pedraforca); "trees, boxwood and moss, forming a *picture-postcard image*" (Pedraforca); "a succession of fantastic *frames*" (Etna). In other occurrences, visual arts are replaced by literature. In one example, this is an attempt at picturing the tourist's journey as an experience which will prove worth narrating: "the rivers Llobregat and Bastareny, and the countless corners with pools and places to bath, are the *protagonists* of family stories" (Pedraforca). Elsewhere, it is the mountain itself to be rec-ognised a narrative power through the comparison with a hand-written book: "Every corner of the mountain harbours a place name and a story. The ridges are *calligraphy*, the geological folds are *pages* from *an ancient book*" (Tramuntana).

What is more, two sub-domains can be associated with the pres-ent one: the source domains of PERFORMANCE and LANGUAGE. While it contains a relatively small number of instances (8), the presence of the PERFORMANCE domain within the corpus confirms Milstein's findings. These identify the performer metaphor as widespread in Western nature tourism contexts, with the effect of framing tourists as the audience to a spectacular nature. In line with this, examples from the present cor-pus show nature as "intentionally exhibiting"[45] for tourists: "As much as it may seem an unvisited destination certain parts of its territory *are performing a One-Place show* in the regional and international arena of tourism" (Çika); "The river which *takes centre stage* in Berguedà is the Llobregat" (Pedraforca); "Mount Olympus *shows* the beautiful face". In the case of the Gran Sasso guide, popular culture is exploited to advertise mountain places like Campo Imperatore and Rocca Calascio, which were used as shooting locations for several film productions. Hence, the land-scape becomes "an *open-air set*" or "a natural *cinematographic set*" and is given the fame of a celebrity: "mountain passes that *have* already *starred* in important professional events". According to Milstein, "popculture" is useful in ecotouristic promotion because it can offer context to tourists who miss "bioregional reference points"[46].

45 Tema Milstein, *op. cit.*, p. 233.
46 *Ibid.*, p. 235.

The source domain of LANGUAGE develops figurative expressions that contribute to the metaphorization of nature as a book. This is due to the fact that these charge nature destinations with a communicative ability, as in the case of Galatzó, whose peak is "the first *word* of an endless *narrative*" (Tramuntana). Sometimes, features of the landscape inform tourists of what they are going to see along their ecojourney: "The foothills of the Canigó, the *promise* of a slow and curious walk full of natural scents"; "Today 'Elikonas-Vafryas' is called Orlias or Ourlias and its bed, near Dion, remains dry, and nothing *announces* the water's beauty higher" (Olympus). More often, metaphors are used to describe the land as being rich in cultural past: "the trail *recounts* the stories of this inhabited region" (Canigó). In turn, tourists are invited to decipher the language of the places they visit: "this country, which has not yet found an *interpreter*"; "Wherever you are in the Pays d'Aix area, there is some point where the mountain is visible, and everyone *reads* it in their own language" (Sainte-Victoire).

The Source Domain of GUARDIANSHIP

Although not as prominent as those of the source domain of WAR, metaphorical expressions belonging to the source domain of GUARDIANSHIP are more homogeneously distributed across the corpus. Moreover, their mappings align with the expectation of the positive value associated with promotional tourism discourse. Two different sets of metaphorical expressions are identifiable. First, metaphors that represent natural elements as a source of protection. These mostly consist in the mountain being described as a benevolent entity watching over its human inhabitants and travellers: "All under the *attentive watch* of the Pedraforca"; "The Gran Sasso *has always protected* its people"; "[Valle del Bove is] an imposing presence from the landscape point of view (even more than a thousand metres high), but able to *offer comfort* to the inhabitants of the volcano" (Etna). In particular, this is evident in the presentation of Galatzó, the highest mountain of the range of Serra de Tramuntana: "Under the *shelter* of the majestic Mount Galatzó, which rises above the sea, you will wander on a land of legends"; "The route goes through the skirt of Galatzó. Its peak will always *be nearby*. It will *walk with you, next to you*. Galatzó will be [...] your *watch*" (Tramuntana). It is interesting to note here how metaphors are not employed to build up the value of the place only insofar as it constitutes a touristic destination, but are equally aimed at characterising it with respect to the local communities who already inhabit it.

The second type of metaphors portray the mountains as offering a point of reference along the tourist's hike, and accordingly assign to them the role of a guide: "a summit emerging *like a focal point*, a *lighthouse*" (Canigó); "It is not possible to get lost. The Pedraforca always *shows* you *the way*"; "Galatzó will be your *guide*"; "Sainte-Victoire is a kind of *signal*, visible from far and wide in fine weather".

The Source Domain of Competition

A considerable number of metaphorical expressions (13) fall within the source domain of COMPETITION. First, this is intended in the sense of a game between tourist and destination, with natural scenery presented as a recompense. Because the destination advertised is a mountain, all the eco-itineraries proposed by the guides involve hiking across steep routes and therefore require some physical effort. In order to make this appealing to potential travellers, figurative language is often resorted to: "You then go up quite a steep passage heading south for 630 metres. Your *reward* will be a panorama over Força Real, with the Roussillon plain bordered by the Mediterranean at its foot" (Canigó); "the effort to ascend the Apennines peaks *is repaid* when, in front of the plateau, unlimited landscapes open" (Gran Sasso). Making it to the end of the route is equalled with achieving the first prize: "Once the *trophy* has been won, these are the places from which the most enamoured ramblers will get the best view of the beautiful Sainte-Victoire". Conversely, failing to see some of the natural views along the journey is conceptualised as a defeat: "Through the road we can enter higher paths, reducing thus the distance to the peaks, but *losing* some of the mountain's beautiful ecojourneys lower" (Olympus).

By the same token, further occurrences describe nature as a challenge against which tourists can test out their strength. Most of these metaphorical expressions cluster in the Sainte-Victoire guide: "Sainte-Victoire – everyone has their own feelings about this mountain. For some, it's [...] a *challenge*, [...] a *playground*"; "its [Saint-Victoire's] *game of hide-and-seek*"; "Walkers, climbers, and runners *measure themselves against it*". I suggest that the use of metaphors here may reflect the cultural character of ecotourism itself, which is often found to overlap with adventure tourism[47]. Fletcher refers to the experience of ecotourists as a "paradox", since practitioners "elect to spend their free time engaging in activities that often require more exertion, more hardship, more stress, and, at times, even more suffering than they encounter in their regular activities"[48].

In addition, one interesting example drawing from the present source domain metaphorises the increase in popularity of areas of the Pedraforca region as a competition among natural landmarks: "Thus, places such as the springs of the Llobregat, Dou del Bastareny, Els Empedrats, La Gallina Pelada or the Pedraforca itself, all *compete* for the maximum number of visitors". This may be understood as a metonym, with the destination used as a substitute for the tourist businesses operating there. Contrary to the ends of ecotourism, it has the effect of depicting the natural space as if willingly offering itself to mass of tourists.

The Source Domains of HUMAN BODY, HUMAN CHARACTER, and HUMAN EMOTION

The fifth and most productive domain is that of HUMAN BODY, which will be discussed alongside instances belonging to the domains of HUMAN CHARACTER and HUMAN EMOTIONS to examine the use of personifications within ecotourist guides.

Metaphorical references to body parts are highly conventionalised in tourism discourse[49], as in the equation "heart"/"centre" in expressions like "In the *heart* of the Alcantara valley" (Etna). Except for one occurrence referring generally to the landscape in Canigó, all instances of anatomical metaphors in the corpus have the mountain as direct target. For example, in the Çika guide, the Ceranian Mountains are said to stretch "as a *natural spine*", whereas Çika itself, which is actually the highest peak of the Cike-Lungare range, is located "in the *arms* of the mountain".

47 Robert Fletcher, "Ecotourism", in *Companion to Environmental Studies*, edited by Noel Castree, Mike Hulme and James D. Proctor, London and New York, Routledge, 2018, pp. 591–594.

48 Robert Fletcher, *Romancing the Wild: Cultural Dimensions of Ecotourism*, Durham, Duke University Press, 2014.

49 Cf. Sylvia Jaworska, *op. cit.*

In some instances, metaphorical references to the "bodily" appearance of the massifs result in their sexualisation. Consider this excerpt from the Sainte-Victoire guide:

> Its south face unfurls in waves the intense green of its *curves*. [...] In the north valley, whatever the season, the light can be **honey-coloured**, or the sky tinted in **dragee shades**. Girl or boy, it never decides, blue <u>flirting with</u> pink. Forever. [...] It is from the surrounding heights – the mountains of Concors, Etoile or Régagnas – that it offers up its *silhouette*, its *profile*, from start to finish of the trail. Once the trophy has been won, these are the places from which the most enamoured ramblers will get the best view of the beautiful Sainte-Victoire. (my emphasis)

This stretch of text contains three metaphorical expressions from the BODY domain (in italics) that present Sainte-Victoire as having – and indeed "offering" – a luscious figure. Moreover, these combine with one (underlined) metaphor belonging to the source domain of LOVE and two expressions (in bold) from the source domain of FOOD (note how the adjective "luscious" applies also to food with a rich and sweet taste)[50]. The combination of metaphorical items drawing from different source domains and which are "compatible" can produce "a single more complex metaphorical scenario"[51]. The effect is that the mountain of Sainte-Victoire can "seduce" tourists into visiting and ascending it. Similarly, the Tramuntana guide includes a metaphor which describes mount Galatzó as "raising his *head*" – its peak – to receive "the golden *kiss* of the sun"; this is however a quotation from Salvador Galmés's short story "Between Two Worlds", and hence it belongs to literature, although it offers an interesting example of intertextuality.

Metaphorical expressions drawing from the source domain of HUMAN CHARACTER are all realised by adjectives that describe characteristics typical of human behaviour. These are mostly positive traits, with only a few exceptions: "the sun is *lavish*" (Gran Sasso); "Galatzó is *human, vigilant, benign, indifferent*" (Tramuntana); "Its north face is mineral and *merciless*"; "Other plants, such as wild orchis, are more *discreet*" (Sainte-Victoire).

---

50 The adjective "enamoured" describing the ramblers' admiration for mountaineering also has a metaphorical origin, although since its meaning is lexicalised I deem it as conventional and therefore do not count it as a metaphor. However, I believe that it contributes to the sexual representation of the mountain in the text.

51 Elena Semino, *Metaphor in Discourse*, cit., p. 26.

Instead, only two metaphors derive from the source domain of HUMAN EMOTION: "The erosive action of streams and glaciers *tears up* and carries away the elements" (Canigó); "The river, Elikonas, was *ashame*" (Olympus). Nevertheless, it is worth singling them out because, together with the two other source domains using human qualities to conceptualise nature, they make personifications the most productive type of metaphor within the corpus, totalling 23 occurrences.

Conclusions

Overall, findings confirm that metaphors are mainly aimed at adding perceived value to the destination advertised, therefore fulfilling a persuasive function. If the purpose of tourism discourse is to present a reality that has to be judged by potential tourists "as authentic and which can give them the illusion of really living an 'off-the-beaten track' holiday experience"[52], this is especially true of ecotourism's claim for adventure. This is shown by the considerable presence of metaphors from the source domain of COMPETITION, which describe the Mediterranean mountains as playgrounds for tourists willing to test out their physical endurance. Furthermore, the productivity of the source domain of ART also reaffirms the tendency to sell out nature for its aesthetic qualities, which are described as pleasing both the eye and soul of the observer. The source domain of LANGUAGE may present nature as a book to be read from, although contrary to Mühlhäusler and Peace[53], interpretation is not left to experienced guides, rather to tourists themselves. Minor domains such as that of RELIGION align with Jaworska's previous findings[54].

However, the source domain of WAR may reveal peculiar discursive strategies. While Mühlhäusler and Peace describe it as reinforcing the idea of nature as a struggle for existence[55], with reference to the Etna guide it can be seen as characterising the relationship between the volcano and the local communities, with the effect of praising both the strength of nature and the endurance of the inhabitants, who are grateful to the land where they reside despite Etna being a constant threat to

52 Elena Manca, *op. cit.*, p. 2.
53 Cf. Mühlhäusler and Peace, *op. cit.*
54 Cf. Sylvia Jaworska, *op. cit.*
55 Cf. Mühlhäusler and Peace, *op. cit.*

their lives. The source domain of GUARDIANSHIP partly contributes to this, as well. Nature is presented as a source of protection for its dwellers, who are dependent on it. Therefore, I suggest that metaphorical items in ecotourism discourse may have an interpretative function. I refer to ecotourism's emphasis on "interpretation", or the promotion of "greater understanding and appreciation for [...] local society and culture"[56]. This means that these expressions are used to characterise the land with respect to the people inhabiting it, so that the destination does not lose its worth after it is "consumed" by the tourist, but is presented as a place of continued value, as testified to by its ties with the local people. Contrary to the general "ego-targeting" aim of tourism language which stresses the individuality of the tourist[57], they reveal a tendency to focus on a third subject, local communities.

Ultimately, the role of figurative language in answering the efforts of ecotourism towards ecological education remains to be assessed. On the one hand, source domains such as those of GUARDIANSHIP and HUMAN BODY, CHARACTER and EMOTION activate natural elements and describe them as vivid subjects of the landscape, worthy of attention and respect. The source domain of WAR also participates in problematising the relationship between human subjects and nature by stressing the dwellers' dependence on the latter. On the other hand, culturally established "unecological" metaphorizations of nature tend to surface. For instance, the presence of the source domain of RESOURCE signals that nature is sometimes addressed merely as a "supplier" for local businesses, especially within the food sector – e.g. "The lands that [...] were the large *supply area* for the Riposto wine industry" (Etna). Moreover, only one occurrence in the Tramuntana guide is used to condemn mass tourism practices, by means of comparing nature to an industry: "The island, at times, *looks like* a liveable land rather than *some unbridled industry* [...] *stuffing* tourists into *concrete casings*". While metaphors in ecotourism discourse do show some differences with traditional tourism discourse, as they are not limited to performing a persuasive function, further research is needed to evaluate the actual implications in terms of ecological awareness of figurative devices in ecotourism texts. Furthermore, tourism as a specialised discourse is comprised of a variety of text-types, whereas the corpus under consideration accounts only for tourist guides. Given the

---

56 The International Ecotourism Society, *op. cit.*
57 Cf. Graham Dann, *op. cit.*

central role played by language in shaping our experience of reality, it is hoped that figurative representations of the natural world in all manifestations of discourses will receive increasing attention[58]. This is somewhat urgent in ecotourism, wherein the promotional factor meets – or rather clashes – with the ethical aims of the activity itself. Provided that the persuasive aim can never be entirely suppressed, linguistic metaphors, having the ability to explain, theorise and provide alternative conceptualisations of environmental matters, may be exploited as a valuable educational device within ecotourism discourse.

---

58 Cf. George Lakoff, "Why It Matters How We Frame the Environment", *Environmental Communication*, 4, no. 1, 2010, pp. 70–81.

The Representation of Sicily in Tourism Discourse

Antonio GURRIERI

Introduction

Sicily and tourism represent an inescapable binomial in today's collective imagination and beyond. This great island has been at the centre of complicated socio-historical dynamics, and as the historian Giuseppe Barone recounts in his "world history" of Sicily, the island has also been one of the objectives of the European Grand Tour vogue since the eighteenth century[1]. Visiting Germans, Englishmen, and Frenchmen, created a wide-ranging travel literature made up of diaries, correspondence and depictions, consolidating a collective imagination, which in turn "transfused and multiplied itself into the first tourist guides for travellers and fixed certain international stereotypes"[2].

Travel guides legitimate stereotypes and impose their own world view. They also feed, however, on what is around them and the intertextuality that characterises them. Laurent Jenny defined intertextuality as: "le travail de transformation et d'assimilation de plusieurs textes opéré par un

---

1   Cf. Hélène Tuzet, *Voyageurs français en Sicile au temps du romantisme (1802–1848)*, Boivin, Paris 1945; Id., *La Sicile au XVIIIᵉ siècle vue par les voyageurs étrangers*, Heitz, Strasbourg, 1955.

   The nineteenth century saw the development of the "Voyage en Orient", and Sicily was one of the stops on this new itinerary. Cf. Brigitte Urbani, "Auberges siciliennes au XIXᵉ siècle dans quelques récits de voyageurs français", *Revue du CAER* , 17, 2007, pp. 415–442. http://journals.openedition.org/etudesroma nes/932.

2   Cf. Giuseppe Barone (ed.), *Storia mondiale della Sicilia*, Bari-Roma, Laterza, 2018, pp. 11–12: "si trasfonde e moltiplica nelle prime guide turistiche per i viaggiatori e fissa alcuni stereotipi internazionali". Here and elsewhere, all translations from Italian in the chapter are my own.

texte centreur qui garde le leadership du sens"[3]. The tourist guide is a text that makes use of numerous intertextual references, especially literary ones, to tell the story of a people and their culture, inevitably exploiting the reader's preconceived notions. Cicero himself already made extensive use of them, as in the well-known orations against Verres, where he defined the character of the Sicilians as "genus nimis acutum et suspiciosum"[4]. But we may also take a leap forward in time and think of the three great Sicilian writers, namely, Verga, Pirandello and Quasimodo. Each, in their own way, conveyed an aspect of Sicilian reality: the virile and lucid resignation of Padron 'Ntoni in the *Malavoglia,* for instance; the particular spirituality of Pirandello; or even the island as inspiration for Quasimodo's poetry.

To begin, our research intends to investigate these aspects of the Sicilian reality. Particularly, it will focus on a touristic imaginary, understood as "imaginaire de lieux géographiques dans lesquels se déroule l'activité touristique"[5], which construes Sicily as the centre of the world, a place of exchange and passage, and as a mythical and magical place that attracts visitors enraptured by its thousand-year history. As another important historian, Santi Correnti, wrote, it is not easy to write the history of Sicily without turning "all of Sicilian history into a projection of the Mafia"[6], so we will avoid going into this aspect in depth; it has, moreover, been extensively dealt with in a previous study[7]. The second part of our analysis will focus on Sicily as a Mediterranean island, taking into account its landscape and climate, that is, a Sicily with a temperate Mediterranean climate that is so attractive to French-speaking tourists.

---

3   Jenny Laurent, *La stratégie de la forme,* in "Poétique", 27, p. 262. For more on intertextuality, see the following works: Julia Kristeva, *Semeiotikè. Recherches pour une sémanalyse,* Paris, Éditions du Seuil, 1969; Roland Barthes, *Théorie du texte,* in "Encyclopaedia Universalis", XV, Paris, 1973; Michaël Riffaterre, "La trace de l'intertexte", in *La Pensée,* 215, pp. 4–18; Gérard Genette, *Palimpsestes,* Paris, Éditions du Seuil, 1982.

4   Cf. Marcus Tullius Cicero, *In Quintum Caecilium divinatio,* IX. "Certainly those, people beyond sharp and suspicious". Here and elsewhere, all translations from Latin are my own.

5   Maria Gravari-Barbas and Nelson Graburn, "Imaginaires touristiques", *Via* I, 2012.

6   Santi Correnti, *Storia di Sicilia,* S.G. La Punta, CE.DI.L., 1995, p. 9.

7   Antonio Gurrieri, "Le discours touristique en Sicile", *Le Forme e la Storia,* XIII, 1, 2020, pp. 221–236.

Our corpus is based on a limited selection of those well-known and reputable paper guides that are readily available on the French-speaking publishing market: *Géoguide Sicile*[8], *Guide Le Routard: Sicile*[9] and *Guide Vert Michelin*[10]. The structure of these guides is rather similar in content and approach to the description of tourist attractions, with rich historical and cultural introductions. These guides still find ample space both in physical bookshops and in electronic versions on digital platforms, despite the numerous websites or digital content that make the need to buy a printed guide less and less necessary. Today, they also contain numerous hypertext references to related sites, in which there are forums for exchanging travel experiences or in-depth articles or videos. These elements make these publications more competitive. Finally, they are well indexed and thus immediately available for users to search.

Sicily as a Cultural Crossroads or Mythical Place

Sicily, the Greco-Roman *mare nostrum*, has been the focus of many travel narratives, and even today the fascinating nature of its history and culture seduces the modern traveller. The tourist guides in our corpus build on these historical and cultural aspects in order to frame their own tourism discourse. *Géoguide*, for example, includes the following description in its section on Sicilian geography:

> Non, la Sicile n'est pas qu'une succession de plages de sable fin. Vous découvrirez avec surprise – au même titre que tous ses visiteurs, à commencer par les premiers colonisateurs, jusqu'aux voyageurs du Grand Tour – qu'elle est constituée à 85 % de montagnes et de collines et à 14 % de plaines. Alors, terre bénie des dieux ? Il est difficile de répondre, mais, en tout cas, elle n'a cessé d'alimenter ce mythe et d'accueillir toutes les civilisations depuis que les divinités y ont élu domicile en raison de la fertilité de ses vastes plaines à blé (la Sicile était considérée dans l'Antiquité comme le grenier de la péninsule)[11].

---

8   Aurélia Bollé, Gilles Guérand and Raphaëlle Vinon (eds.), *Sicile: Géoguide*, Paris, Gallimard Loisirs, 2017.

9   Philippe Gloaguen and Michel Duval (eds.), *Sicile: Le Routard*, Vanves, Hachette, 2019.

10 Maura Marca and Sophie Lhéraud (eds.), *Sicile: Guide Vert*, Boulogne-Billancourt, Michelin Travel Partner, 2017.

11 Aurélia Bollé, Gilles Guérand and Raphaëlle Vinon, *op cit.*, p. 10.

As we can see, within a purely descriptive discourse on the characteristics of the natural environment, the *topos* of Sicily as a mythical land, the object of admiration on the part of Grand Tour travellers, is evoked. This discursive mode is typical of tourism guides. Indeed, "finalement, le discours des guides s'apparente aux discours *promotionnels* [...] Le touriste voyage *pour son plaisir*, seuls les lieux "plaisants" méritent donc de lui être indiqués et décrits; le tourisme est aujourd'hui une *industrie*, et les guides sont un des rouages de ce réseau complexe d'institutions et d'organismes ayant pour but de promouvoir l'activité touristique" [12].

Critical analysis of tourism discourse shows us how that persuasive component of language seduces the tourist-reader through an appeal to the emotions. It must be said, however, that, as extensively studied by Mariagrazia Margarito, Sicily is often described by resorting to the *topos*[13] of the land of contrasts[14]. The very rhetorical question in *Géoguide*'s quotation – "Alors, terre bénie des dieux?" – paves the discursive way towards the introduction of the typical dysphorias linked to the land. These dysphorias have the function of making tourism discourse more credible, and not simply a panoply of valorising adjectives[15] that may represent the place described as unreal. However, our intention in this work, as already mentioned, is to analyse the euphoric elements of these texts that enhance certain historical and cultural aspects of Sicily. It is precisely this that the *Guide Vert* Michelin through its use of landscape contrasts presented in a seductive manner: "Si le vert des alpages finit par se mêler au bleu enivrant de la mer, si les figuiers de Barbarie poussent sur les pistes de ski chauffés par le volcan ou si, en plein hiver, la blancheur des amandiers en fleur vous éblouit, pas de doute à avoir : vous êtes en Sicile!"[16].

12 Catherine Kerbrat-Orecchioni, "Suivez le guide! Les modalités de l'invitation au voyage dans les guides touristiques: l'exemple de l'île d'Aphrodite'", in *La communication touristique: Approches discursives de l'identité et de l'altérité*, Paris, L'Harmattan, 2004, p. 135.

13 Cf. Ruth Amossy and Anne Herschberg Pierrot, *Stéréotypes et clichés*, Paris, Nathan, 1997; Paris, Armand Colin, 2014, pp. 96–99.

14 Mariagrazia Margarito, "Éléments dysphoriques dans les guides touristiques: La Sicile des guides français", *Synergies Italie*, I, 2003, pp. 102–114.

15 Cf. Catherine Kerbrat-Orecchioni, *L'énonciation*, Paris, Armand Colin, 1999.

16 Maura Marca and Sophie Lhéraud (eds.), *op. cit.*, p. 445.

Nevertheless, even in this guide, there are occasions when Sicily is presented as a mythical place by means of an intertextual reference to Ovid's *Metamorphoses*:

> Durant son combat contre le géant Typhée, Zeus lui lança la Sicile dessus et l'orgueilleux Typhée, qui dans son audace osa lui disputer l'Olympe, gémit et souvent s'agite en vain sous cette énorme masse. Sur sa main droite est le cap de Péloros; sur sa gauche, le promontoire de Pachynos; sur ses pieds, l'immense Lilybée. L'Etna charge sa tête. C'est par le sommet de ce mont que sa bouche ardente lance vers les cieux des flammes et des sables hurlants. Il lutte pour briser ses fiers[17].

The simple description of the natural landscape is enriched with mythical references that activate in the reader an evocative, almost magical filter, through which tourists perceive the destination advertised. Texts of this type have a descriptive and at the same time introductory function, and activate a form of what Annabelle Seoane defines as "validating dialogism", which uses literary quotations to "place d'emblée le lecteur dans une situation plutôt valorisante"[18]. As a result, the reader becomes enthusiastically and positively involved in their reading experience.

A similar way of mythologising the landscape is found in *Le Routard* guidebook, which refers to the story of the giant Typhoeus:

> Les Grecs la nommaient *Trinakria* ("Trois Pointes"), symbolisée par son emblème : une tête de Méduse sur trois jambes repliées. Ce signe de la Trinakria est présent sur le drapeau de la Sicile depuis la fin du XIIIᵉ s. Carrefour des civilisations, la plus grande île de la Méditerranée s'est forgé un cadre bien à elle où, sous un même soleil, se retrouvent de fabuleux temples grecs, des châteaux et des cathédrales érigés par les Normands dans un style empruntant à la fois au roman, aux Byzantins et aux Arabes, des jardins orientaux semblant tout droit sortis de la lampe d'Aladin, des palais et des églises au baroque tardif hispanisant[19].

Through this, we are invited to see Sicily as the cradle of ancient civilisations and a land of passage in the centre of the Mediterranean.

These three examples show us how tourism discourse succeeds in effectively appropriating natural elements, as well as, and especially in

---

17 *Ibid.*, p. 447.

18 Annabelle Seoane, *Les mécanismes énonciatifs dans les guides touristiques: entre genre et positionnements discursifs*, Paris, L'Harmattan, 2013, p. 143.

19 Philippe Gloaguen and Michel Duval (eds.), *op. cit.*, p. 11.

this case, the historical-cultural ones, in order to construct a narrative that captivates the traveller. In so doing, it arouses a feeling of discovery and fuels a well-defined touristic imaginary that will act as an emotional thermometer every time tourists find themselves admiring the natural landscape or gazing at a Greek temple or an Arabesque-style church. Moreover, the *topos* of the island as a cultural crossroads can be seen not only in the historical-geographical aspects taken as an example, but also in other cultural elements such as gastronomy: "le métissage des cultures a aussi enrichi la gastronomie de l'île"[20] and even: "la découverte de ses recettes, issues d'une longue tradition et du mélange de multiples influences, est un véritable voyage dans le voyage"[21]. Finally, "la cuisine sicilienne est métissée et a subtilement intégré les apports de toutes les civilisations qu'elle a vues se succéder"[22].

The island as crossroads is an isotopy that recurs throughout the text, haunting the reader. We also find it in descriptions about the population: "tant de fois envahis et s'étant fait imposer tant de choses, les Siciliens se sont forgé un caractère indépendant et malicieux"[23]. Or even: "les Siciliens sont, à l'image de l'île, riches de culture croisées, d'histoires juxtaposées"[24].

Thus, tourism discourse represents Sicily as a place that is culturally stimulating and interesting in the eyes of the tourist-reader, who, persuaded by so much richness, seeks to immerse themselves in the cultural crossroads herein so lavishly extolled.

Mediterranean Culture between Climate and Landscape

The Mediterranean Sea is an immense expanse of water overlooked by a myriad of peoples whose trade and cultural exchanges have made this part of the earth the centre of the world for many centuries. Fernand Braudel asked the question of what the Mediterranean is, and the answer is certainly a complex one:

20 *Ibid.*
21 Maura Marca and Sophie Lhéraud (eds.), *op. cit.*, p. 516.
22 Aurélia Bollé Gilles Guérand and Raphaëlle Vinon, *op. cit.*, p. 32.
23 Philippe Gloaguen and Michel Duval (eds.), *op. cit.*, p. 502.
24 Maura Marca and Sophie Lhéraud (eds.), *op. cit.*, p. 444.

Mille choses à la fois. Non pas un paysage, mais d'innombrables paysages. Non pas une mer, mais une succession de mers. Non pas une civilisation, mais des civilisations entassées les unes sur les autres. Voyager en Méditerranée, c'est trouver le monde romain au Liban, la préhistoire en Sardaigne, les villes grecques en Sicile, la présence arabe en Espagne, l'islam turc en Yougoslavie. C'est plonger au plus profond des siècles, jusqu'aux constructions méga-lithiques de Malte ou jusqu'aux pyramides d'Égypte. [...] Tout cela parce que la Méditerranée est un très vieux carrefour. Depuis des millénaires tout a conflué vers elle, brouillant, enrichissant son histoire: hommes, bêtes de charge, voitures, marchandises, navires, idées, religions, arts de vivre[25].

There is, consequently, a Mediterranean culture that manifests itself in our corpus through very specific linguistic references. Genuine linguistic clichés are noted: "climat méditerranéen, cuisine méditerranéenne; maquis méditerranéen". These are all words that call to the tourist's mind landscapes, flavours and colours of the Sicilian land. Such linguistic clichés have not always existed. As the geographer Martine Tabeaud observes: "la création du climat méditerranéen va de pair avec l'invention du beau temps dans les années 1920, et les bienfaits corporels supposés de la chaleur. Aujourd'hui encore, vacanciers et retraités d'Europe plébiscitent la Méditerranée pour ses étés, malgré un arrière-plan de réchauffement climatique qui devrait les porter peut-être à privilégier plus de fraîcheur"[26].

Furthermore, the myth of the Mediterranean climate is certainly present in the corpus in question. Indeed, it makes French-speaking tourists, especially those accustomed to more continental and harsh climates, dream of the Sicilian land:

Le climat en Sicile, typiquement méditerranéen, a fortement contribué à la naissance du mythe sicilien. Ses hivers sont doux et ses étés sont longs et chauds. Cependant, à l'image de l'île, les températures sont riches en contrastes et se laissent aller à de fréquentes sautes d'humeur[27].

Méditerranéen par excellence, le climat est (un peu) tempéré par l'influence marine. Au printemps, la Sicile est toute verte et pleine de fleurs. Celles des orangers embaument alors sublimement l'air. En été, c'est le climat africain : pelé, végétation rase et desséchée. Il fait alors chaud, très chaud (40°C

25 Fernand Braudel, *La Méditerranée: L'Espace et l'Histoire*, Paris, Champs Flammarion, 2017, pp. 8–9.

26 Martine Tabeaud, "Voyage sous des cieux pas tous bleus", in *Le Monde*, *L'Histoire de la Méditerranée*, Hors-série, 2019, p. 16.

27 Aurélia Bollé, Gilles Guérand and Raphaëlle Vinon (eds.), *op. cit.*, p. 14.

ou plus), luminosité est aveuglante, l'air brûlant. Comme l'écrit Lampedusa dans *Le Guépard*, "il neige du feu"[28].

Pensez surtout à emporter l'attirail complet de protection contre le soleil car, même en hiver, il peut être traître: lunettes de soleil, chapeau, vêtements clairs, éventail à glisser dans le sac et crème solaire. Les soirées sont assez fraîches et un gilet ou une étole peuvent être utiles. Si vous voyagez à la fin de l'automne et en hiver, un coupe-vent est indispensable[29].

As we can easily understand, the three guides cannot fail to mention the Mediterranean climate, but each of them enacts a slightly different discursive procedure. In the first example, we note how reference to myth is immediately taken up, precisely to make the climatic narrative much more realistic. In addition, a personification linked to mood swings is used, with clear reference to the aforementioned *topos* of the land of contrasts, characteristic when describing Sicily[30]. The second excerpt, instead, presents the reader with the actual climatic reality of the island but, in order not to upset the reader too much, adds a literary reference at the end of the description that distracts attention and makes the whole thing more poetic and in fact almost alluring. Lastly, the third guide chooses not to devote a specific paragraph to the Mediterranean climate, but includes a paragraph in the section on things to do before setting off, dedicated to useful objects that make it possible to cope with the particular Sicilian climate.

However, the image of Sicily as an emblem of a Mediterranean rich in native plants is widely exploited in the various guidebooks. In this regard, we present further specific examples relating to the natural environment, each with different nuances:

La Sicile renferme une variété extraordinaire de plantes, propres à la fois aux climats méditerranéen et subtropical. Le long des côtes, vous serez subjugué par la palette des citronniers, des orangers, des champs de vignes et d'oliviers [...] la tomate, qui est devenue l'élément indispensable de la cuisine méditerranéenne [...] règne le maquis méditerranéen qui vous émerveillera par ses genêts, sa lavande, son romarin, ses palmiers nains, ses lentisques, ses caroubiers[31].

---

28 Philippe Gloaguen and Michel Duval (eds.), *op. cit.*, pp. 51–52.

29 Maura Marca and Sophie Lhéraud (eds.), *op. cit.*, p. 526.

30 Cf. Mariagrazia Margarito, "Éléments dysphoriques dans les guides touristiques: La Sicile des guides français", cit., pp. 102–114.

31 Aurélia Bollé, Gilles Guérand and Raphaëlle Vinon, *op cit.*, pp. 12–13.

> Puis ce fut au tour des Arabes […] qui ont apporté nombre d'arbres et d'ar-
> bustes comme ils l'ont fait dans tout le Bassin méditerranéen. Ils introduisi-
> rent de meilleures techniques d'irrigation et un grand nombre de nouvelles
> cultures : le bigaradier (orange amère), le caroubier, la canne à sucre, le coton,
> le dattier, le citronnier et le sumac, producteur de tanins et de laques[32].

> […] son climat très doux, la Sicile a une végétation typiquement méditer-
> ranéenne, du moins près des côtes et dans la plaine. D'une saison à l'autre,
> c'est une véritable symphonie de couleurs et de parfums qui se joue. […]
> On y trouve en abondance buissons de myrte, arbousiers, lentisques et l'eu-
> phorbe de Bivona […] les caroubiers (surtout dans la région de Raguse),
> caractérisés par leurs baies brunâtres ; les eucalyptus […] les oliviers sau-
> vages […] les pins maritimes[33].

The description of the Mediterranean landscape seems to be fundamental to tourism discourse, in that it lays the foundation for the reader's
Mediterranean imagination, or rather reinforces it by enriching it with
new and vivid elements. The enumeration of plants and trees that adorn
the Sicilian landscape, often with precise indications of the areas where
they are found, is useful for presenting, above all, the typical products
associated with the local flora. The olive tree, for example, recalls the
production of oil, which has remote historical roots: "Columelle, célèbre
agronome latin du Ier siècle, considérait l'olivier comme le premier des
arbres. Cette place éminente montre bien tout l'intérêt que portaient les
sociétés méditerranéennes à cet arbre, et ce depuis des millénaires"[34].

This tree is part of the cultural heritage of Mediterranean societies,
and a strong spiritual symbolism, especially in the religious sphere. As for
Mediterranean fauna such as wild boars, porcupines, badgers, foxes, deer
and numerous bird and insect species, it is noteworthy that the guides in
our corpus devote little space to it:

> Si les richesses naturelles sont menacées par l'homme, les animaux, en par-
> ticulier les plus sauvages, ont déjà déserté l'île. D'autres ont choisi de résister
> en "prenant le maquis", comme le chat sauvage, la marmotte, la belette, le
> porc-épic. Quant aux oiseaux, tels le faucon, le milan, l'aigle, le corbeau
> royal, ils observent ce spectacle d'en haut, ou se limitent à des étapes, s'ils
> sont voyageurs, comme la mouette rosées, l'hirondelle de mer ou la spatule[35].

---

32 Philippe Gloaguen and Michel Duval (eds.), *op. cit.*, p. 480.

33 Maura Marca and Sophie Lhéraud (eds.), *op. cit.*, p. 450.

34 Stéphane Anglès, "Sur la branche de l'olivier se niche l'identité", in *Le Monde,
    L'Histoire de la Méditerranée,* Hors-série, 2019, p. 18.

35 Aurélia Bollé, Gilles Guérand and Raphaëlle Vinon, *op cit.*, p. 13.

Pour contenir la dégradation des territoires et leur usage irrationnel, plusieurs zones protégées ont été instituées. On dénombre aujourd'hui 5 parc naturels régionaux et 72 réserves régionales, représentant environ 10,5 % du territoire sicilien. Parmi ceux-ci, le parc de l'Etna […] Celui des Madonie, lui regroupe la moitié des espèces végétales et animales […] Quant à la réseve du Zingaro […] elle abrite une partie de la flore sicilienne endémique, beaucoup d'oiseaux et une vaste faune marine côtière[36].

The first example is perhaps the only one that contains a long enumeration of animal species typical of the Mediterranean maquis, while in the second, reference is rather made to local fauna without going into detail. The focus is rather on the preservation of the natural environment. Tourism discourse, in this case, points to one of the Sicilian dysphorias linked to the lack of respect for the natural environment, mitigated by a change in the trend observed among the population: "L'écologie est devenue un sujet sensible, car la Sicile, dotée d'un patrimoine naturel, végétal et historique extraordinaire, a dû s'armer pour lutter contre la destruction de son environnement"[37].

Le Guide Vert, on the other hand, makes almost no reference to local fauna, except when describing traditional dishes linked to the area described: "du côté des Madonie et des Nebrodi, les élevages de cochons et de chevaux à demi sauvages sont à la base de la fabrication d'une excellente viande"[38]. The Mediterranean in terms of touristic imagery is therefore evoked almost exclusively through the natural landscape, with its many species of natural trees and plants.

Therefore, in the investigation of our corpus, we found that *Géoguide* and *GuideVert* make more use of the Mediterranean discourse. On the contrary, we observed some difficulty in finding extensive references to the former in *Le Routard*, which focuses more on landscape dysphoria with an extremely critical slant, which, although realistic, fails to evoke the magic of the Mediterranean landscape, a landscape which is in fact idealised in the other guides:

Agriculture, industrie, urbanisation, intensification du réseau routier […] les paysages siciliens ont, comme tant d'autres, été fortement modifiés par l'homme, entraînant une fragilisation des sols et des versants. On a même

36 Philippe Gloaguen and Michel Duval (eds.), *op. cit.*, p. 482.
37 Aurélia Bollé, Gilles Guérand and Raphaëlle Vinon, *op. cit.*, p. 13.
38 Maura Marca and Sophie Lhéraud (eds.), *op. cit.*, p. 518.

inventé dans les années 1980 le concept de «construction illégale par néces-
sité» [...] Néanmoins, la sensibilité des citoyens face aux problèmes d'environnement grandit au fil des années[39].

Le Routard's approach to tourism discourse is certainly different from
the other two. In highlighting the critical aspects of the destination, it
leaves room for an authenticity that might win the most demanding
reader over, but nevertheless gives a tentative hint of hope, mitigating the
negative aspects by shifting the reader's attention to the growing sensi-
tivity of the local population. The approach is certainly ethnocentric and
the guide's editor acts as an impartial critic revealing a lack of environmental culture.

Instead, the other guides recreate the *topos* of Mediterranean culture
and climate. Some descriptions allude to the ideal Sicilian climate, in the
ancient Greek's sense of the word: "*Klima* ne signifie rien d'autre qu'une
bande de latitude recevant la même quantité d'énergie solaire. Au nord,
il fait trop froid et au sud, trop chaud, si bien que les Hellènes habitent
l'espace au climat idéal. Le propos est clairement méditerranéocentré"[40].

Therefore, objectivity is not always maintained, and sometimes deviations from reality are detectable.

Conclusion

Our analysis highlights how one of the significant elements of tourism discourse is its euphoric function, which is clearly observable in
the extracts investigated. Their method is certainly persuasive, and the
tourist-reader falls in love with the tourist destination. Lorenzo Devilla
speaks in this regard of a "loi de positivité" that makes everything pleasant and bearable, as illustrated in particular by the examples referring
to the climate, despite the fact that in summertime temperatures reach
unbearable levels. The fascination of discovering this land as a crossroads
of different cultures is undeniable.

We are in the presence of an epideictic discourse that aims to "accroître
l'intensité de l'adhésion à certaines valeurs [...] L'orateur cherche à créer
une communion autour de certaines valeurs reconnues par l'auditoire,

---

39 Philippe Gloaguen and Michel Duval (eds.), *op. cit.*, pp. 481–482.
40 Martine Tabeaud, *op. cit.*, p. 16.

en se servant de l'ensemble des moyens dont dispose la rhétorique pour amplifier et valoriser"[41].

The positive values found in the texts are precisely linked to the *topos* of Sicily as a mythical land, a crossroads of language and culture, and a land symbolising the Mediterranean with its physical and climatic characteristics. Tourist guides are texts that have a "haute densité stéréotypique (autrement dit, et en souriant, à haut risque de stéréotypes)"[42]. However, as repeatedly pointed out, especially with regard to the *Le Routard* guide, the guides' descriptions try to overcome the stereotype of Sicily as a happy island where the climate is pleasant all year round, even though the positive aspects of the Mediterranean climate continue to be emphasised and valorised. Bessière ultimately reminds us how "l'imaginaire touristique traduit également la recherche d'un cadre rassurant, sécurisant, compréhensif, 'maternant', d'un univers de protection et de sensations oubliées"[43].

In conclusion, the ultimate goal of tourism discourse is the promotion of the tourist destination and the satisfaction of the desires of the future tourist who needs to latch on to a pre-established imagery that succeeds both in reassuring them and arousing their curiosity about new aspects and unique experiences.

---

41 Chaïm Perelman and Lucie Olbrechts-Tyteca, *Traité de l'argumentation*, Bruxelles, Éditions de l'Université de Bruxelles, 2008, p. 67.

42 Mariagrazia Margarito, *La bella Italia des guides touristiques: quelques formes de* stéréotypes, in Bova, Sergio, Margarito, Mariagrazia (eds.), *L'Italie en stéréotype*, Paris, L'Harmattan, 2000, p. 35.

43 Jacinthe Bessière, *Valeurs morales et imaginaires touristiques*, Rachid Amirou and Philippe Bachimon (dir.), *Le Tourisme local, une culture de l'exotisme*, Paris, L'Harmattan, 2000, p. 77.

Western Travellers of the 19th and the 20th Centuries Encounter the Bedouins: A General Overview

Miriam Al Tawil

> "The Orient and the Orientals [are considered by Orientalism] as an object of study, stamped with a constitutive otherness of essentialist character".
> Anouar Abdel-Malek, "L'Orientalisme en Crise", 1963.

Introduction

Travel literature (or hodoeporics, from the ancient Greek adjective *hodoiporikós*, der. from *hodoiporía* 'travel') is a historically ancient genre in which, on a literary level, a personal, peculiar experience of observation of the world is realised. This observation is certainly never neutral nor objective, on the contrary, it seeks for a confirmation of what the authors expect according to their previous notions or models of references and pre-set schemes. This is particularly true if we consider a specific category inside the hodoeporics, which is travel reports (or travel memoirs), written by travellers or explorers who were interested in experiencing new regions of the world.

Travels reports exist since men started to travel and explore areas which were new to them and then felt the need to write about what they had experienced. Travelling as a pedagogical and educational experience started during the Renaissance (with the famous *voyage d'Italie*)[1]. Examples of this kind of work are those of Rifāʿa al-Ṭahṭāwi (1801–1873),

---

1   Luigi Monga, "Travel and travel Writing: An Historical Overview of Hodoeporics", in Luigi Monga (ed.), *Annali d'Italianistica*, vol. 14, *L'Odeporica/Hodoeporics: on Travel Literature*, Chapel Hill, NC, *Annali d'Italianistica*, 1996, pp. 6–54.

about whom we will discuss later, who travelled to acquire knowledge to use in his homeland to make his country progress. Travelling as discovery and cross-cultural contacts is what interests us the most in regard to the vision western travellers had about the Bedouins they met during their travels in the Near East regions.

The present chapter, after a preliminary excursus about the history of the hodoeporics genre and some information about the very first sources that give us some notions about the Bedouins and their society, aims to analyse the fascinating reports of European travellers who visited the Near East region during the nineteenth and twentieth centuries. In particular, the focus of the article will be the encounter between the western explorers and the nomad tribes in present Syria, Iraq, Palestine and Egypt, whose descriptions are accompanied by personal comments of the authors.

These authors were mostly explorers and travellers and have been selected among others because of their different ways of approaching the themes, the different time periods and their diverse backgrounds. John Lewis Burckhardt and Gertrude Bell had prior knowledge of the topic they wrote about, and spent a long time in those regions before writing their reports. Robert Montagne gave us a stimulating insight of oral literature and cultural customs. They were able to keep the right distance to write virtually objective descriptions, even when reporting personal experiences, without avoiding sensitive comments.

F. J. Mayeux was the editor of the notes of Don Raphael, who was an Egyptian that travelled and made researches, while Charles Texier, being an archaeologist, was not specialists of the customs of the area.

Historical Context

Historically, the second half of the nineteenth century represents the moment when European forms of society have been systematically taken into consideration and borrowed in the Ottoman empire. In this period the "western" influence was more or less direct in Egypt, Tunisia, Syria, and Lebanon, slowly acquiring more and more power, and spreading the reform ideals. The process was not easy and smooth, since the young intellectual of the 1860's were aware of the contradictions they had to deal with. As a matter of fact, the modern world they wanted the Ottoman Empire to enter had to face the reality of the Islamic roots of their homeland[2]. Combining the Islamic and western ideologies, trying to justify the latter was the aim of the movement of the Young Ottomans.

The Encounter with the Bedouins

The very first works that document the encounters with the ancient Bedouin society are the Egyptian hieroglyphic sources. These are, nonetheless, too much unprecise to be considered as reliable. Assyrian and Babylonian cuneiform texts mention for the first time the term *aribi* referring to nomad populations in the Syrian desert and in the Arabian Peninsula, even though differentiating between Arab and Aramaic ethnic populations is not an easy task. Of the same period are the first mentions of Bedouin in the Ancient and New Testament even if, in this case also, it is not clear if they refer to ethnically Arab populations. Greek and Latin sources rarely mention the populations of inner Arabia, if it is not for Herodotus, Strabo, Ptolemy, and Diodorus of Sicily, who mentioned the nomad populations of Central Arabia and for the first time with them the term Arab started to be used as an ethnic name and not as an epithet. Epigraphic and literary Arabic sources in proto-Arabic are the first reliable sources on the pre-Islamic Bedouin life[3].

An important and influential reference of the Middle Ages, at the time of the early Abbasid regime, is for sure the epistle of al-Ğāḥiz (m. 869) *Risāla fī radd al-naṣāra* which reflects the anti-Christian polemic of the time. This literary piece has been considered a referential model of ethnographic works for travellers, geographers and literature intellectuals when describing human ethnic groups -in terms of language, religion, territory. The medieval scholar al-Ğāḥiz was able to elaborate objective and accurate descriptions that are added to the already known *topoi* of that period and these are made reliable. In the epistle written against the non-Muslims, he gives account of the other ethnic groups, such as Turks, Chinese, Jews, Christians, Greeks and the Arabs, listing their main features. The characteristics he mentioned about these ethnic groups may have had an impact on the vision of the categories through which Arabs

---

2   Cf. Albert Hourani, *Arabic Thought in the Liberal Age 1798–1939*, Cambridge, Cambridge University Press, 1983.

3   Cf. Joseph Henninger, *La société bedouine ancienne*, in Francesco Gabrieli (ed.), *L'Antica società beduina*, Roma, Centro di Studi Semitici – Istituto di Studi Orientali, 1959.

have classified ethnicities and communities in the next centuries. The Arabs he describes may be identified with the Bedouin tribes, since they are depicted as proud people dwelling in the desert, acquainted with astronomy, war and horses. Moreover, according to the Medieval tradition, they are also custodians of the pure Arabic language, which they master and use in the art of panegyrics and insults[4]. Medieval scholars have long thought that (only) Bedouin dialects were the archetype of Classical Arabic:

> In the early centuries of the Islamic empire the Bedouin dialects were regarded as the only true representatives of the Classical language. The Bedouin were supposed to speak pure Arabic – that is, with the declensional endings, ʾiʿrāb, literally 'making it sound like true Bedouin Arabic' – but in the course of time the Arabic grammarians conceded that not even the Bedouin could escape the effects of sedentary civilisation[5].

These commonplaces could possibly have a role in accepting some ethnologic prejudices of the colonial period acquired by some intellectuals that also influenced the Arabic Renaissance of the nineteenth century, such as al-Ṭahṭāwi[6].

Another well-known phenomenon (which started in the sixteenth century, with the establishment of the Maronite seminary in Rome) is the presence of many figures of eastern intercultural intermediaries between the Near East and France and Italy. They were mostly Syrian Christians and Copts, who were often sent to Europe, especially to Rome, to be trained as missionaries or priests. Since the end of the sixteenth century, scholars were trained at the Maronite seminary. Not only did this institution boost oriental studies in Europe, but also made the European culture be known in the East. When the scholars would return home, they would spread the culture they had acquired and be reliable intermediaries thanks to their deep knowledge of the language and the culture. Moreover, in the eighteenth century, many missionary schools were funded in Syria, Egypt, and Lebanon.

---

4   Cf. Biancamaria Scarcia Amoretti, "Modelli autorevoli: L'epistola di al-Jāḥiẓ (m. 869) contro i cristiani. Qualche osservazione", *Rivista degli Studi Orientali*, 78, 2005, pp. 63–75.

5   Kees Versteegh, *The Arabic Language*, Edinburgh, Edinburgh University Press, 1997.

6   Biancamaria Scarcia Amoretti, *op. cit.*, p. 75.

On the other hand, there were Egyptian students who would go to France to study modern sciences. Among them, it is impossible not to mention Rifā'a al-Ṭahṭāwi, who was part of the group of students sent to France by Muhammad Ali in 1826. When back in Egypt, he spread French Enlightenment ideals to his Egyptian audience. What interests us most in this context, it is however his humoristic and vivid description of the French customs and manners in his "*Taḫlīṣ al-ibrīz fī talḫīṣ Bārīz*" (The Extraction of Gold or an Overview of Paris), which is to be considered as one of the first modern accounts about the French customs by a Muslim scholar who lived five years among them. In his work he praised their intellectual curiosity and critical thinking.

Numerous scholars have written their travel memoirs about their encounters with the Bedouin in the Arabian Peninsula[7]; nevertheless, here we will limit to recall reports about travellers, explorers, geographers, diplomats, archaeologists, and academics who visited the Near East. In terms of linguistic remarks, the most interesting comments are to be found in the works of those travellers (e.g. William Gifford Palgrave, Georg August Wallin, Richard Francis Burton, Charles Montagu Doughty) that visited the inner regions of present Saudi Arabia, describing the spoken language they happened to hear as "almost the pure language of the Coran" or at least "purer than that the language the citizens", "more correct than the low language of the Syrian and Egyptian mob"[8]. Almost all these writers comment upon the differences between the Bedouin and sedentary dialects and the mutual unintelligibility.

One of the finest travellers that analysed the Arabic language is without any doubt Charles M. Doughty, who, in *Arabia Deserta*[9], defined

---

7   John Lewis Burckhard, *Travels in Arabia: Comprehending an Account of Those Territories in Hadjaz which the Mohammedans Regard as Sacred*, London, Henry Colburn, 1829; Alois MUSIL, *Arabia Petraea, 1,2,3*, Vienna, Alfred Hölder, 1907–1908; Max von Oppenheim, *Die Beduinen*, Leipzig, Harrassowitz, 1968; William Gifford Palgrave, *Narrative of a Year's Journey Through Central and Eastern Arabia (1862–1863)*, London and Cambridge, Macmillan, 1865.

8   Heikki Palva, *Linguistic Observations of the Explorers of Arabia in the 19th Century*, in Elie Wardini (eds.), *Built on Solid Rocks, Studies in Honour of Professor Ebbe Egede Knudsen on the Occasion of his 65th Birthday April 11th 1997*, Oslo, Novus Forlag, 1997, pp. 226–239.

9   Charles Montagu Doughty, *Travels in Arabia Deserta* (new and definitive edition), with an Introduction by Th. E. Lawrence, I-II, London, J. Cape, 1936 (New York, Dover, 1979).

the Arabic variety spoken there as "archaic" and rather close to Classical Arabic, especially because of the *tanwīn* that gave the language a special, pleasant taste[10]. This idiosyncratic feature of the *naġdi* variety has been confirmed and examined in depth in recent studies by scholars such as Palva and Ingham[11], as well as the affrication of *kāf* and *qāf* and an accuracy of 70 % for the lexicon data also confirmed by recent studies[12]. A part of this lexicon has been reported and described by Contini in his study[13], in which he mentions the *hapax legomena* (both lexical and semantic) individuated by Doughty, together with words already known that Doughty, as an European scholar, reported for the first time in the speech of Northern Arabia.

Some of this lexicon is relevant not only for Arabic linguistics, but also for ethnolinguistic, historical linguistics, and dialectology, thanks to the accuracy and awareness of Doughty, who refers to the Bedouin dialect as "nomad ears". Some of his remarks also allow us to obtain ethnographic data. We know for example that Bedouins were not practicing Muslims, and knew little about the religion practised in the sedentary areas. This is, at least, what we can still hear in some comments about Bedouin society in the recent past nowadays and it is confirmed by Doughty in the chapter of *Arabia Deserta* dedicated to the nomad life in the desert: "These sometime emigrated Beduins, have no suspicion of Nasrânies, whom they have seen in the north, and heard them reputed honest folk, more than the Moslemîn"[14].

---

10 Riccardo Contini, "... like an Attic sweetness in the Arabian tongue": Charles M. Doughty e l'arabo naġdi, in F. Mazzei – P. Carioti (a c.), *Oriente, Occidente e dintorni ... Scritti in onore di Adolfo Tamburello*, Napoli, Università di Napoli "L'Orientale", Dipartimento di Studi Asiatici/Istituto Italiano per l'Africa e l'Oriente, 2010, pp. 641–662.

11 Cf. Bruce Ingham, *Najdi Arabic. Central Arabian* (London Oriental and African Language Library, 1), Amsterdam – Philadelphia, J. Benjamins 1994 (= I); Heikki Palva, "Linguistic Observations on the Explorers of Arabia in the 19th Century", in E. Wardini (a cura di), *Built on Solid Rock. Studies in Honour of Professor Ebbe Egede Knudsen on the Occasion of his 65th Birthday*, April 15, 1997, Oslo, 1997, pp. 226–239

12 Cf. Saad Abdullah Sowayan, "The Arabian Oral Historical Narrative. An Ethnographic and Linguistic Analysis", *Semitica Viva*, 6, Wiesbaden, Harrassowitz, 1992; Marcel Kurpershoek, "Oral Poetry and Narratives from Central Arabia, vol. V, Voices from the Desert: Glossary, Indices, & List of Recordings", *Studies in Arabic Literature*, XVII/v, Leiden, Brill, 2005.

13 Cf., Riccardo Contini, *op. cit.*

14 Charles Montagu Doughty, *op. cit.* p. 216.

The use of the term Muslims does not only indicate that the speaker does not recognise himself in that social group but also, he considers the Christians more honest than the Muslims.

Contini also dedicated an article to another traveller, probably one of the most famous British travellers of the Victorian period, Richard Francis Burton, also known for his imperialistic views. Burton was also known for being an excellent polyglot and, according to some of his friends, an excellent linguist (even though his abilities have been recently questioned)[15].

Apart from describing the Harari language, and the neo-Aramaic spoken in Maʿlūla, he wrote a careful and accurate description of the linguistic situation in central and northern Arabia. His works contain many lexical data, place names, and etymologies referring to Arabic dialects[16]. His data also mention names of animals and plants, clothes and food, as well as the Midianite linguistic variety, and the Omani dialect spoken in Zanzibar by merchants and settlers, even if it is still not clear to what extent his knowledge in different scientific fields was solid and accurate. What is sure, it is his vivid interest for the spoken Semitic languages, a certain knowledge for the methodology of language sciences and its technical literature[17].

As for the Near East, one of the works we chose are the tomes based on the unpublished notes of Rufāʾil Anṭūn Zaḫūr, also known in Europe as Dom Raphael de Monachis (1759–1831). Born in Cairo to a Syrian Melkite family, he attended the Greek seminary in Rome, and was also a poet and translator. Later he entered the Monastery of the Saviour in Sidon and came back to Egypt in 1794. He taught Arabic at the École de Langues Orientales in Paris. His unreleased notes were then reworked and published in 1816 by F. J. Mayeux in three tomes with the title "Les Bédouins, ou Arabes du désert"[18]. According to the author, being Bedouin means belonging to a caste. The author divides the work into two books. In the first one he describes and comments upon all the

---

15 Riccardo Contini, "Richard Francis Burton esploratore delle lingue neosemitiche", in A. Bausi et al. (a c.), *Aethiopica et Orientalia. Studi in onore di Yaqob Beyene* (*Studi Africanistici – Serie Etiopica*, 9), Napoli, UNIOR, DAAM, Napoli, I, 2014, pp. 223–249.

16 *Ibid.*

17 *Ibid.*, p. 244.

18 F. J. Mayeux, *Les Bédouins, ou Arabes du désert*, Paris, Ferra Jeune Libraire, 1816.

tribesmen met in Egypt and in Syria (and present Palestine, and Jordan). One of the first comments is that these nomad populations do not have a history, they have just been present in some ancient and modern works that describe some events of that area. Nevertheless, these events cannot constitute a real historical recount since there is no cohesion. For this reason, the author explains that he will primarily focus on what he is certain about, that is their qualities and their daily occupations. Describing the tribes for example, he portrays their settlement and the reasons they are famous for (e.g. selling dairy products in Alexandria).

Interestingly, according to the author, this people is very similar to the Tunisians in the spoken language (which is a corrupted one), in the accent and even in the costumes. Another tribe is known for the language they speak that the author defines as "barbaresque". The author usually starts with moral comments about the tribes, then usually compares them with similar or neighbour tribes. Afterwards he specifies the place where they encamp, the cattle they possess, what are their occupations (agriculture, breeding) and if they pay a tribute (and to whom they pay it).

When recounting the Mawāli tribe he depicts them as cleaner than the other tribes of the desert and having taste for jewellery and the appearance because nature has been kinder to them. They are also famous for their eloquence and they are good at poetry despite their illiteracy: they cannot write nor read. The editor adds there a note explaining how difficult it is to write Arabic poems, since Arabic is a language that has many dialects and needs long studies; moreover, poems must contain unknown expressions, subtle puns, unnatural metaphors and inexistent associations.

The work of Mayeux seems to be a sort of list of tribes with the features they are characterised by, but apart from that it seems like the author does not have a deep knowledge of the people he describes, their culture, and their language. He is an external, detached spectator.

This kind of work says more about the author's view than about the subject of his account. In this case, the comments of Mayeux contain prejudice and racism ("Ces gens ne sont pas civilisés" when referring to the Berbers; "Célèbres pour les courses sur les terres voisines, paresseux, et grands voleurs [...]") (p. 61) when describing the Arab of the West; "Les Arabes de Thour ne sont point [...] les pires que l'on connaisse; Les Arabes Haoaitate (Ḥuwayṭāt) [...] ils sont plus belliqueux que malfaisants et, les temps de guerre exceptés, leur rencontre passe pour assez peu dangereuse" (p. 72).

This text is, among the others, the less scholarly accurate and the richest in personal comments, feelings, and judgements, as well as stereotypes and discriminations. It is the least scientific because the terms regarding the names of the places or the names of the tribes are often transcribed improperly. The laryngeal consonants are never transcribed; the uvular stop *q* is transcribed as *c*, interdentals are often transcribed as dentals and long vowels as short vowels, so that it is often quite difficult to recognise which tribes he is writing of.

Despite the intellectual position of the author, the account he gives seems to be written by someone who did not have a vast experience on this area of the world. Compared to the other authors, Mayeux uses instead a lively and strong style describing the Bedouins as robbers, perverse tribes, or uses verbs like "wander" that has a negative implication or "infest" which is usually employed for weed or insects. Audacious and intrepid are also positive terms that are used to describe the members of the tribe, but, despite the positive value of the terms, they have nonetheless a wild connotation.

The Bedouins of Karak are described just in terms of number of the members, the big quantity of camels they possess and their beauty which is said to be hereditary. The author explains that the difference between the tribes depends on the nature of the soil where they live and not just education and traditions. Thus, the tribes living in the desert are defined as cruel, dangerous and grasping (again, as if he was describing animals) and concludes writing that they just can be defined as "more Arab" than those living on fertile soils such as the tribes living on the present Israeli-Jordanian border. Neighbour tribes are described as having many horses and cattle and as being good horsemen. Concerning the Christian tribes converted to Islam, he describes them as half-Arabs because the Bedouin perversity and fanatism seized them.

He denies the previous accounts depicting the Bedouin as heroic: they are very brave, audacious but they are also brigands, so that it is difficult to the author to define them as heroic. This *topos* reminds also the narrative about the ṣaʕālīk, poor, brave and enduring brigand-poets[19].

The language of the Bedouin is described by the author as "more or less pure" depending on the area they lived in, their isolation and how much time they spent with neighbour people, who are said to distort

---

19 Albert Arazi, *Suʿluk*. "Encyclopaedia of Islam", vol. 9, 2nd ed., 1997, pp. 863–868.

the *š* to *s*. Finally, the author goes into a detailed description about other peoples of that region, such as the Yazidis.

Burckhardt John Lewis (1784–1817) is a famous Swiss-born explorer. In 1830 he published *Notes on the Bedouins and Wahhabis* collected during his travels in the East, where he spent seven years. According to the author, Bedouins are one of the noblest nations he ever became acquainted with. After all that time, it made more sense to him not to compare them with Europeans but with the neighbour Turks. The Bedouins despite their avarice possess many virtues that Turks do not possess. If the former are characterised by freedom, the latter are characterised by despotism. After enumerating all the tribes of Greater Syria, their alliances, and their places of encampment, he also expresses some comments about the dialect of the Bani Saḥar tribe, saying that it has "still more of a chanting expression than that of the ʿAnaze". After that, he starts describing their way of encamping and the way they build the tents. Also, some expressions used by the Bedouins referring to the raids are said to be unknown by the sedentary Syrians, thus alluding to the lack of connections between the two groups. Then, the author starts with the detailed description of the parts of the tent, moving then to the detailed description of clothes and weapons. In describing the Bedouin diet, he mentions dishes that are not common anymore, based on camel's milk. Moreover, even goat-skin names have changed. What is surprising is the description of the stage when Bedouin in Najd just ate dates and milk, before producing other dairy products, such as butter, cheese and yogurt, as in the early twentieth century. Others used even to eat rats and gazelles. Comments upon their manners are not frequent, but for example, their way of eating is defined as slovenly, since they rarely wash their hands after the meal and prefer licking their fingers or cleaning them with the tent. He recounts that at the beginning he was seldom satisfied and disgusted by the custom of eructation. Women used to eat the rests of men's dishes.

What makes the recounts of Burckhardt original is that he has a vast knowledge about different tribes of Syria, Iraq and present Jordan, so that he is able to make comparisons and name the different terms through which objects are known according to the tribes or the nations. Moreover, he has a deep knowledge of the customs of the different tribes and he is able to describe the tradition, for example, of the tattoo according to the tribe. Hospitality and generosity are the most valuable virtues among the Bedouin, despite their wealthy. As for education, most of them are illiterate and have no books, even the author admits to know more about Arabic reading and poetry. Bedouins are famous for their musical and poetical talents. Differently from Europeans, the author says that the love of the Bedouin is known to everyone, and it is not a mystery. The melody was so different from the European or Turkish music that the author was not able to note it down. At a certain point, speaking of ophthalmic diseases, he mentions that Bedouin have less ophthalmia than people in Damascus or Aleppo because they sleep covered in wraps, while people in the cities sleep outside on high terraces uncovered. One way of curing diseases is the cauterization and inoculation. Leprosy is also diffused. Parents do not teach civil manners but they are taught how to steal and beat strangers who come to the tent and the more they are troublesome, the more they are praised. Divorce is common and even if polygamy is a Bedouin privilege according to the Turkish law, but they rarely have more than one wife. They easily separate from their spouses even during their pregnancy. Then, the author continues with the description of the Bedouin laws and the warfare between tribes, saying that they are constantly in war against each other. The most interesting part of the travel report is that in which he describes the moral character of the Bedouins, since here we can understand more of his personal view and get some comments about the people. First of all, he writes that there are many contradictions when describing Bedouin manners: throughout the book they are described as generous but also robbers, not practicing polygamy nor betraying but easily divorcing their wives, and in the description of their moral character these contradictions continue: they live free and independent (even from material life) but they would do anything (including lying and cheating) to acquire wealth and this is considered as a common trait of Levantine people. Then a series of comparison with the Turks gives us more details about the Bedouin who are of kind temper, merry, helpful, used to abstinence and sufferance, jocose and decent in familiar conversations, while Turks are depicted as the opposite: cruel, sanguinary, insinuating, making obscene allusions. Burckhardt denies the representations built by other travellers who depict the Bedouin as silent person: he is, instead, a joyful companion, who may be silent during the travels only not to get thirsty, and is usually talkative during evenings spent in the tent. What is also very interesting is that the Bedouin changes his way of speaking (employing expressions that he never uses in the Desert) and acting when he goes to the town. Nevertheless, according to the author, the Bedouin speech is more original and concise compared to that of the city-dwellers. Bedouin are wittier more moderate and easily pleased in terms of food and sensual enjoyments. They are more abstemious, knowing neither infidelity nor prostitution nor any kind of luxury. Men are depicted as lazy, just taking care of guests, while women are tireless in taking care of all domestic matters. What differentiates Burckhardt's report from the others, is that he has a deep knowledge, and he is able to prove other travellers (as Laurent D'Arvieux, 1635–1702)[20] wrong and explains why they misunderstood their behaviours. He enumerates all the diseases of the cattle in Arabic and all the names of the horses, the herbs, and the winds. He compares them with those of Yemen, Nubia, Sinai, Najd, Iraq and Syria Bedouins. He even gives advice regarding how to behave in their respect: travellers should imitate their hospitality but without being exaggerate in kindness, treat them as equal and be friendly. Travellers are attracted by the frankness and uncorrupted manners of the Bedouin, despite their laziness in the tents, when they just smoke and play games. After a while, their passivity and idleness become unbearable to western people. That is why, that experience has been to the author the happiest and the most irksome at the same time, spending entire days doing nothing. Finally, the language of the Bedouin is described as purer and more correct than that of the sedentary Arabs. Among the Bedouins themselves there is a great variety of dialects and he remarks the Bedouin pronunciation of the interdentals. Differently from the Egyptians and the Syrians they do not use any slang terms. He concludes that Bedouin Arabic, as well as Bedouin manners are purer, despite their illiteracy, thanks to their love for poetry that they have preserved and transmitted orally.

Charles Félix Marie Texier (1802–1871), who was a French historian and a brilliant archaeologist, conducted an expedition to Persia, Armenia, and Mesopotamia. In 1860 he published *Les tribus arabes de l'Irac-Arabi*[21], in which he accurately describes the people he met in present Iraq, during his visit to Baghdad and Basra. He initially admits a certain generalisation shared by western scholars for whom all tribes are "Arabs", although, as soon as they encounter them, the differences are remarkable, in terms of both culture and physiognomy. He was as a matter of fact able to distinguish between what he calls "races": Chaldeans, Assyrians (sedentary and Christians) and the Arabs (defined as nomads).

---

20 A French traveller and diplomat, who is famous for his travels in the Middle East.
21 Charles Félix Marie Texier, *Les tribus arabes de l'Irac-Arabi*, Lyon, Soye et Bouchet, 1859.

He stated that at the beginning they all looked the same, but then the variety was easily visible, especially in terms of facial traits. They also differed in terms of food habits. Sometimes, the author is tactless in his descriptions since, for example, women are described as Gorgons, and human as animals ("les turcs pur sang").

The aim of Gertrude Bell (1868–1926) was not just to write a travel report of what she saw, but she aimed at writing about the people she met, to describe the reality in which they live and how they perceive it. This declaration of intent at the beginning of her work, makes her a pioneer ethnographer, whose intent is not to write just about the people but also to investigate their emic perspective, their opinions about the world surrounding them. What makes G. Bell modern is her relativist judgement of these people that she does not label as undeveloped or barbaric as the other authors did in the previous centuries, but just as different from the European. Her relativism makes her work more objective, she says that these people have different understandings of practicality and utility and are more inspired in their behaviours by traditions and morality. She then concludes that, apart from these differences, they are like the Europeans and human nature does not change and it is rather easy to be friends with them. She also goes against the western stereotypes of that period, clarifying the distinction between the Turks and the Arabs that tend to be regarded as a unique entity or a homogenous empire, making comparisons with England and its colonies, which contain different peoples, speaking different languages and having different nationalities. She even makes a good portrait of the Turks, describing them as virtuous and hospitable, contrary to the severe critic expressed by Burckhardt, who has a totally different opinion about them. Despite her modern and sharp analysis of these people, she expressed some colonialist remarks when she argued that if Syria were governed by the British instead of the Turks, they could have made it more successful.

What distinguishes the travel report of Gertrude Bell are her meticulous and thorough descriptions of archaeological ruins, fortresses, castles, forts, ruined sites, that are due to the interest and the professional tendency of the author who was also an archaeologist. These descriptions are mixed with her personal comments, the anecdotes she tells about the hosts or people she met or historic anecdotes told by her guides. All the scenes she describes are rich in visual details and the feelings she experienced, to the point that sometimes the travel report looks like a mix between a daily report and a diary where she transcribes all her thoughts and perceptions. She even relates the dialogues and the stories she heard. She does not express comments about them in terms of ignorant people, if it is not for "unlettered" referring to their lack of knowledge of the poets, knowing but Antara. On the other hand, they have a deep knowledge of the desert and all its features, and they are then distinguished from the European mentality, for which it is just wildness and an empty desolated land. In some parts of her descriptions she employs a sensitive and imaginative style that differentiates her from the other authors, who are more objective and concise. She also tends to describe the Bedouins as warmongers but also free and strongly independent as it had been previously stated by Burckhardt whose opinions she corroborates. What is compelling are her minute descriptions of the encounters she made during her travels from one city to another and the descriptions of the cities as she expected them to be (from her previous readings on the architecture of those regions), giving much information about who were the inhabitants of those villages (e.g. Druzes, Christians, Muslims, etc). These recounts also show the ease through which they used to move in areas that today are separated by borders (like the Syrian-Jordanian border). If Burckhardt limited himself to objective descriptions of the diseases and the cures Bedouins had, Bell describes episodes that happened to her, like ill or injured people asking for her help or her medicines, leaving her with a sense of helplessness. She does not avoid irony and sarcasm in her descriptions of the people she met, who tried to impress her speaking a few words in French and wearing European accessories.

The last author who wrote a report of what he had collected is Robert Montagne (1893–1954). As the title of his work "Contes poétiques bédouins (Recueillis chez les Šammar de Ǧezīré)"[22] suggests, published by the Institut Français du Proche-Orient in *Bulletin d'études orientales*. He focused not only on the ethnographic descriptions of the tribes he encountered, but also on their oral literature, in particular, Bedouin poetic tales that he collected on both sides of the Syro-Iraqi border. What makes Montagne's work, original and different from the others, is first of all the specificity of the geographic area which is well defined, as well as the tribes, two camel-breeder tribes originally from northern Najd. Another peculiarity of the work of Montagne is the analysis of the society

---

22 Robert Montagne, "Contes poétiques bédouins (Recueillis chez les Šammar de Ǧezīré)", *Bulletin d'études orientales*, t. 5, 1935, pp. 33, 119.

starting from the language and the content of the tales. He somehow anticipates sociolinguistic descriptions (a science that will be officially developed in the forties), explaining that some tribes are more isolated and thus their oral literature is not influenced by contacts with settled Bedouins. He is interestingly able to detect if the tales contain sedentary influences or not. Nevertheless, before explaining the meaning of the poetic tales, he wants to retrace the history of the tribes basing himself on travellers' suggestions, direct investigations, and the tradition. He then focuses on the general conditions of life of these tribes and their occupation (i.e. the pillage). From a linguistic point of view, the author describes the slow and little noticeable changes in lexicon, loan words from sedentary varieties and phonetic changes that show the influence of the *Šāwi* tribes. According to Montagne, all these changes (which he considers almost invisible) reveal the evolution that will bring the Bedouin to the decadence in less than a century. In that historical period, when pillage was prohibited, the most urgent need was to find other new economic resources, for which they had to found villages to cultivate the soil and little by little they started to have a semi-sedentary way of life, by virtue of the influences of settled neighbours (i.e. *šawāya*, Kurds, and Christians). These first decades of the twentieth century mark an important socioeconomic transition toward sedentarization that the author analyses and describes examining all factors.

The poems[23] denounce the influences of the sedentary civilisation – described as lacking any virtue – on the pure Bedouin and the consequent abandonment of the noble nomad traditions. All poems' situations take place in the desert and have real and known persons as characters; main themes are love stories, wars and pillages. From a linguistic perspective, the author underlines the difference between sheep-breeders and camel-breeders, saying that the variety spoken by the Shammar tended to be altered and levelled in terms of phonetics and semantics toward the so-perceived "low-variety" of *šāwi* Arabic.

According to what he observed both in the history of the tribes and in their poems, the conclusion is the same: there is a sort of intellectual or moral boundary between the sheep-breeder tribes and the camel-breeders. The formers have more contacts with the rural populations, and their poems are more focused on love, coffee and tobacco. The latter

---

23 *Ibid.*

instead, who consider themselves the real and pure Bedouins, make the effort to maintain their language, their traditions, and their poems reflect this mentality with which they are obstinate to make their tribes survive. As for the linguistic remarks, he writes that the poems are too scarce to make a proper analysis of the linguistic evolution. The aim of the poems' collection was actually to just gather and not to analyse them. Nevertheless, he comments the evolution saying that it is due to the external influences on the variety (Kurdish, Turkish and Armenian influences) that are observable through some phonological phenomena like, for example, the *ġalġala* (q > ġ), *kaškaša* (k > č), as well as the passage from *ʕa* > *ha*. These are the sole linguistic comments he made, beside the mention of the semi-sedentary lexicon employed.

Conclusions

Despite the fact that the authors in question were not anthropologists, their works constitute nowadays an interesting, useful source for researchers since they provide notions about the customs of the past, as well as the names of the tribes that lived in the area, so that it is possible to reconstruct their recent history and movements. Nevertheless, these texts are doubly compelling since they do not just offer an overview about what the authors depicted, but also display the approach they adopted to compose their travel reports and their manner of dealing with different cultures. What we see in these accounts are descriptions that are influenced by the social constructions and the historical period in which they were written.

Social constructivism has led most intellectuals of the last centuries to consider the believes and lifestyles as odd or primitive, neglecting the focus on the object of study itself, employing internal categories. Indeed, nowadays ethnography (after decades of post-modernist theories) poses epistemological questions about the different representations of the world. In the present day, most anthropologists believe that a correct and unambiguous representation of the world does not exist and that every perspective is valid and true. Although today it is still challenging to utterly ignore old classifications when dealing with the object of study, contemporary reflections on sociology and anthropology have improved researchers' understanding of how they should investigate. Moreover, post-modern speculations provided with the intellectual tools to interpret sources and categories with major critical consciousness, often in a multi-disciplinary perspective.

In this sense, today ethnographers display more accurate information, not only because they conduct long fieldwork campaigns, but also because they consider the emic point of view and do not neglect perspectivism. Albeit they do not (necessarily) omit personal impressions, feelings and assume a subjective, biased narrative, they possess the instruments to develop a qualitative research, which usually focuses on one subject (rather than commenting upon different areas and tribes). Today most Bedouins, in the SWANA region, are settled and generally live the same life as other sedentary communities. Due to their definitive settlement and the social mobility introduced also by education, social differences have been levelled and what makes them still different from the others are their culture, their diet, and their proud sense of belonging to the tribes, which is what anthropologists seek to investigate the most nowadays.

TounsiaDigordia by Hiba Boujnah: Digital Travelogue of a Mediterranean Journey

Elisa GUGLIOTTA

Introduction

Thanks to its position in the Mediterranean Basin, the Tunisian territory has historically been regarded as a strategic place of political and economic value. Tunisia has always been a land of passage, of historical encounters, human and linguistic contacts and a basin of ancient civilizations, such as Carthage[1]. All these factors, over the centuries have enriched its culture, giving it a varied and nuanced character, which has always attracted many tourists from all over the world. Tourism has early become an essential sector of the Tunisian economy. Mainly concentrated on the coast, it has experienced a coherent development plan since the 1960s, resulting into the construction of large hotel complexes to facilitate the development of mass and low-cost tourism[2]. However, the political instability that followed the 2011 revolutions and the terroristic attacks that hit Tunisia (especially in 2013 and 2015), have caused tourism in Tunisia to fall dramatically. In fact, the tourism sector, which absorbed 15% of the workforce, was already losing ground in the aftermath of the 2011 uprisings, but following the 2015 Bardo attack, it suffered a considerable loss (–25,7 %)[3].

---

1 William D. Marçais, "Le parlers Arabes et Berbères, I. Les parles arabes", in A. Basset (ed.), *Initiation à la Tunisie*, Paris, Adrien-Maisonneuve, 1950, pp. 195–219.

2 Robert A. Poirier, "Tourism and Development in Tunisia", *Annals of Tourism Research*, 22, no. 1, 1995, pp. 157–171; Dribek, Abderraouf, *Vers un tourisme durable en Tunisie: le cas de l'île de Djerba*, Doctoral dissertation, Brest, 2012.

3 "Il modello Tunisia", *Il Libro dell'anno 2015 – Treccani*. https://www.treccani.it/encic lopedia/il-modello-tunisia_%28Il-Libro-dell%27Anno%29/. Consulted the 7/12/ 2022.

The focus of this article is a travel blog, published by a young Tunisian girl, Hiba Boujnah, in 2014[4]. As just mentioned, Tunisian tourism in 2014 was in the midst of a severe crisis. Hiba's blog is named "TounsiaDigordia", which can be translated literally as "a Tunisian girl in the know"[5]; however, by reading it, what emerges as the subject of the narrative is Tunisia; or rather, Tunisia as seen through the eyes of a Tunisian young girl. The girl is defined as "in the know" since she has the courage to embark on this journey, which is presented, from the outset, as a journey with the aim of discovering the southern Tunisia. Contextualizing this literary-digital product in a moment of geopolitical crisis related to the Tunisian post-revolution context, it can be defined as an act of rehabilitation of Tunisia itself, rediscovered bit by bit along the stages of the journey, and finally as an act of Tunisian identity affirmation. The topic of the journey is indeed the thread that connects the narrated steps, but the modality of broadcasting the "message" is also a constituent element of this product. It is in fact a digital narrative. One issue addressed by transmedial narratology is the question of how narrative practices are shaped by the possibilities of the medium in which the story is presented. In attempting to determine the different dimensions of narrative, proponents of this narratology look to plays, films, narrative poems, fiction, cartoons, ballets, video clips, paintings, statues, *et cetera*[6].

In order to delve deeper into the discourse on narrative, and digital communication in general, realised in Tunisian Arabic, one must first of all consider the implications behind the use of this Neo-Arabic variety and the issues related to Arabic diglossia[7]. Tunisian Arabic is generally described as mainly employed for oral conversations; in fact, it is only

---

4   Available at: https://tounseyyadigordeya.wordpress.com/.
5   The adjective "digordia" can be traced back to the French *dégourdi*, which has the meaning of "smart".
6   Cf. Jan Alber and Monika Fludernik, *Postclassical Narratology: Approaches and Analyses*, Columbus (Ohio), The Ohio State University Press, 2010, pp. 8–9.
7   Given the vastness of the topic and number of studies on this subject, for a general overview on diglossia, we invite the reader to refer to Charles A. Ferguson, "Diglossia", *Word*, 15, no. 2, 1959, pp. 325–340; and to Kees Versteegh, *The Arabic Language*, Edinburgh, Edinburgh University Press, 2014, pp. 189–208. While, for the Tunisian specific case, see Daoud, Mohamed, "The Sociolinguistic Situation in Tunisia: Language Rivalry or Accommodation?" *International Journal of the Sociology of Language*, no. 211, 2011, pp. 9–33; and Lotfi Sayahi, *Diglossia and Language Contact: Language Variation and Change in North Africa*, Cambridge, Cambridge University Press, 2014.

recently that it has begun to be used for literary production, which, however, remains limited to a few examples, such as *Le Petit Prince*, which was translated in Tunisian Arabic by Hédi Balegh[8]. This new employ of Tunisian Arabic is motivated by the needs of Tunisian identity affirmation. Concerning the modality selected by Hiba to share her experience with the digital community, namely the blogosphere, we must also consider it as a diastratically influenced writing choice. Indeed, digital writing is a widespread practice among the younger generation of users of digital spaces such as forums and social networks; where the latter are most favored by the Generation Z, i.e. the digital natives. Regarding the Generation Z and their digital channels, an interesting case in point is the Tunisian Youtube channel "Boubli"[9], which offers several formats focusing on current youth and social issues in Tunisia, one of which is called indeed "Generation Z***", where topical political issues are addressed. Another format is instead dedicated to taxi stories, this is called "Fi Thnity", literally "On my road". The latter, together with others, are provided with subtitles, which are actually a central part of the graphics and animation of the video, in Arabizi. Words are in fact the real subjects of these videos. Concerning the writing system defined as Arabizi[10], this uses the Roman alphabet and numerals, and it is another element that can be traced back to the theme of identity assertion by writing in Tunisian Arabic. In fact, mass written communication in Tunisian Arabic began with the spread of social networks, and Facebook in particular, and it is strongly associated with themes of freedom of expression, given the role these media played during the Arab revolutions[11]. Eid claims that the media "creates in between spaces that serve as excellent sites for the negotiation of identities"[12]. Moreover, social media has given the new

---

8 Cf. Giuliano Mion, "La versione del piccolo principe in arabo tunisino", *Ricerca e didattica tra due sponde, atti della Convenzione Internazionale tra l'Università "G. d'Annunzio di Chieti-Pescara" e l'Université '7 Novembre à Carthage' di Tunisi*, Lanciano, Carabba, 2007.

9 Available at the following link: "https://www.youtube.com/@BOUBLI". Consulted the 7/12/2022.

10 Yaghan, Mohammad A. "Arabizi": "A Contemporary Style of Arabic Slang", *Design Issues*, 24, no. 2, 2008, pp. 39–52.

11 Cf. Heather Brown, Emily Guskin and Amy Mitchell, "The Role of Social Media in the Arab Uprisings", *Pew Research Center*, 28, 2012.

12 Mushira Eid, "Arabic on the Media: Hybridity and Styles", in *Approaches to Arabic Linguistics*, Brill, 2007, p. 405.

Tunisian generations the opportunity to create spaces for expression and identity affirmation in their mother tongue[13]. Indeed, for digital and informal contexts of communication, writing in Tunisian Arabic is not experienced as inadequate, even more so when it is encoded in Arabizi, since it is a non-standardised orthographic system, created specifically for digital and informal communication[14]. This thematic is also strongly related to the concept of youth speech, or with the words of Léglise _et al._ _parlers jeunes_, which, according to the scholars, reflects the idea of resistance to the dominant adult or political order[15]. Young people may not be the only ones who are young at birth, but they are meant as the driving force behind rebelling against the order of a society within which they cannot see themselves reflected, or in which they cannot find a _space_ where they feel to belong[16].

The Blogosphere as a "third space"

It has been observed by Burnett _et al._ that the practice of writing and sharing intimate life stories, such as a collection of memories, travel stories or lived experiences, can be assimilated to taking spiritual journeys, keeping a traditional diary, as well as to psychotherapeutic practices, where people in therapy are invited to explore their experiences through writing[17]. People have an innate ability to represent their experiences in the form of stories, being storytelling like conversing or communicating with other people in a way that everyone knows and perceives as natural[18]; it requires less effort than other types of sharing, especially when

13 Cf. Teresa Pepe, _Blogging from Egypt: Digital Literature, 2005–2016_, Edinburgh, Edinburgh University Press, 2019.

14 Cf. Reem Bassiouney, _Arabic and the Media: Linguistic Analyses and Applications_, Brill, 2010.

15 Cf. Isabelle Léglise, Caubet, Dominique, Bulot, Thierry, Billiez, Jacqueline and Miller, Catherine. _Parlers jeunes ici et là-bas_, Paris, L'Harmattan, 2004, p. 15.

16 Cf. Elisa Gugliotta, _Realization of a Tunisian Arabish Corpus with Use Within the Scope of NLP-Natural Language Processing_ (PhD dissertation, Università Sapienza di Roma and Université Grenoble Alpes), 2022.

17 Cf. Simon Burnett, Sarah Pedersen and Robert Smith, "Storytelling through blogging: a knowledge management and therapeutic tool in policing", SIPR Research Summary, Dundee, Scottish Institute for Policing Research, School of Social Sciences, University of Dundee [online], 2011.

18 Cf. Walter J. Ong, _Orality and Literacy_, London, Routledge, 2013.

complex content is to be shared. Indeed, the practice of sharing written stories implies readers, and sharing experiences provides a positive connection between them and the writer, allowing readers to feel part of the writer's life. The readers, on the one hand, can experience new things thanks to the fictitious freedom to slip into the writer's shoes, and the writer, on the other hand, gains the empathy of his readers, who share the emotions of his stories with him[19].

Stories nowadays can be stored and shared digitally, and some platforms such as blogs and forums fit the prototypical storytelling model, while more synchronous modes, such as social media and in particular chat rooms, represent more of a textual micro-genre, which challenges the traditional view of storytelling. Blogs, in comparison with other digital tools, show particular potentials, allowing not only the identity expression, but also experiment new identities[20]. The relation between blog and identity has been analysed by various studies and much information exists about how identity develops on blogging websites[21]. For instance, the role played by blog in identity building process has been studied by observing the dialogical choices of participants. Indeed, as Delahunty observes, they project an impression of themselves, negotiate their positioning within the group and set the rules of the context[22]. She states that the discourse analysis of the forums reveals how identity is simultaneously constructed through interpersonal handling. Researchers agree with the concept that narrating meaningful experiences on blogs enables the realisation of shared identity-building processes. This takes place through narrative strategies, giving voice to the human need to narrate mentioned above. In fact, it has been observed by Di Fraia, that the link between narration and blogs is so close that different types of narration can be used to classify blogs[23]. We can assume that self-image

---

19 Cf. Radzuwan Ab Rashid and Azweed Mohamad, *New Media Narratives and Cultural Influence in Malaysia: The Strategic Construction of Blog Rhetoric by an Apostate*, New York, Springer, 2019.

20 Cf. Cristina Solimando, "E-Writers and Arabic: New Genres and Linguistic Renewal", *La Rivista Arablit*, VII, no. 13, 2017, pp. 35–50.

21 Cf. Reem Bassiouney, *Arabic Sociolinguistics*, Edinburgh, Edinburgh University Press, 2020; Albirini, Abdulkafi. *Modern Arabic Sociolinguistics: Diglossia, Variation, Codeswitching, Attitudes and Identity*, London, Routledge, 2016.

22 Cf. Janine Delahunty, "'Who am I?': Exploring Identity in Online Discussion Forums", *International Journal of Educational Research,* 53, 2012, pp. 407–420.

23 Cf. Guido Di Fraia, *Blog-grafie. Identità narrative in rete*, Milano, Guerini, 2007.

construction is an important part of social media, and language also plays a key role in it. Users have the ability of multilingual speakers to switch from one language to another, treating the different languages that form their repertoire as an integrated system. On the other hand, the dynamics of digital language practices and identity constructions of multilingual users in social networking communities should be further studied. Biró observes that social media users creatively adopt the multimodal resources offered by social media and use their linguistic repertoires to construct their online linguistic identity, which do not necessarily coincide with their real offline identities. This mainly concerns people belonging to an ethnic minority. Biró thus describes the linguistic identities of users as fluid and dynamic, considering that multilingual users switch from one language to another to communicate with different audiences or to share aspects of their identity[24].

The digital context, much more accessible for the new generations, also provides a space for expression that protects bloggers from completely exposing themselves[25]. This element eases addressing issues of a complex and sensitive nature, more or less across the narrated history. What is evident, is that digital spaces constitute a situation in which conventional social structures and relationships are suspended, while others take over, allowing new identities and meanings to emerge and contributing to the creation of a "third space".

> When we talk about this we will go back to the source of the term (Bhabha 1994) and we […] want to suggest that this third space has a literal and metaphorical meaning. We understand it as a space which is a negotiated and contested area in which meanings are made and shared, some of which may relate to encountering new knowledge, learning or developing new skills and dispositions. Its literal, physical location could also be an after-school club, a museum, a lunchtime activity[26].

---

24 Cf. Enikő Biró, "Linguistic Identities in the Digital Space", *Acta Universitatis Sapientiae, Philologica,* 11, no. 2, 2019, 37–53.

25 Tan, Wee-Kee and Teo, Hock-Hai, "Blogging to Express Self and Social Identities, Any One?", *ECIS,* 2009, pp. 267–278.

26 John Potter, and Julian McDougall, *Digital Media, Culture and Education: Theorising Third Space Literacies,* London, Palgrave Macmillan, 2017, p. 7. Concerning the reference included in the citation, this is the following: Horni K. Bhabha, *The Location of Culture,* London, Routledge, 1994.

One of the "third space" meaning is a place for "learning or developing new skills"[27], which is the result of being first of all a space "in which meanings are made and shared". Our hypothesis is that the blog analysed in this study wants to convey new meanings, deconstruct stereotypes and reconstruct a vision of Tunisia together with its readers. The blogger does that in an indirect manner, by narrating the experience of a girl, who undertakes a journey, organised in several stages. It is a journey, not only in the physical sense, but also in the metaphorical sense, a journey of rediscovery of Tunisia, that could not have been realised in a better place than in a digital-third space.

The Blog "TounsiaDigordia", a First Glance

Before addressing a preliminary linguistic analysis of the blog, we would like to describe some of its characteristics. The blog narrates a journey undertaken by Hiba in 2014, exactly from the 10th to the 31st of May. Hiba did not travel alone, but with a friend of hers. The trip consisted of several stages, starting from Tunis, with Kerkennah as the first destination, then going down to Djerba, Tataouine, Chenini and up again to Aïn Draham, passing through Tozeur and El Kef. As mentioned earlier, one of the elements that raises curiosity about this blog is the fact that the stages of the journey are addressed in several languages, Tunisian Arabic, encoded in both Arabizi and Arabic characters, English and French. In fact, the first thing that may come to mind as the motivation behind this choice is that Hiba may have had at least a dual target readership in mind when creating the blog, an "internal" reader and a reader "external" to the Tunisian context.

The first page of the blog is the presentation in Arabizi of the young Tunisian girl who is the protagonist of the trip. The same introduction to the blogger is reported in English, on the second blog's page. There are some meaningful differences in these two autobiographic pages; we will first introduce them, and then we will discuss them, in the second part of this paragraph. In the English version of her presentation, Hiba calls herself *Tounseyya Digordeya*, describing herself as a girl who "simply loves

---

27 In fact, Gutiérrez *et al.* used this expression to describe a particular type of zone of proximal development. For details, see: Kris D. Gutiérrez, P. Baquedano-López and C. Tejeda, "Rethinking Diversity: Hybridity and Hybrid Language Practices in the Third Space", *Mind, Culture, and Activity*, 6, no. 4, 1999, pp. 286–303.

life, travelling the world and leaving a personal touch wherever she goes".
The last concept in Arabizi appears as reported in Example 1.

1)   *ykhaali fi kol blassa l marque mte3ou*

/yxalli   fi   kull   blāṣa əl-*marque*   mtāʕ-u/

He:leaves   in   all   place DET-mark   of-him

In Arabizi the subject of the verb *to leave* is male, because the structure
of the sentence is not exactly the same as in English, and we could trans-
late it as: "TounsiaDigordia is you, is me, is any young Tunisian or non-
Tunisian who loves the travels and the adventure. Any young who wants
conquer the world, visit all its corners *and leaves everywhere his mark*".

Returning to the English version, already in the third line, the blogger
makes a pact with the reader, who, in order to make this journey with
her and to walk in her shoes must recognise himself as *young*, where for
young she means "youth of spirit [...], age is nothing but a number", *wild*
and *free*. This pact with the reader does not exist in the Arabizi version.

Afterwards, the blogger explains the reasons that led her to write this
blog. She explains that following a period of dissatisfaction in her studies, somewhat by chance she discovered her passion for travelling. So,
when she had some free time to travel again, she decided to do it in
Tunisia: "But why does it have to be abroad? Why not travel *closer* and
enjoy *a very beautiful country*? Why not his *own country*, Tunisia?" (My
emphasis). The same concept is also expressed in the Arabizi version, as
shown in Example 2.

2)   *5ammet chwayya w kalet alech « lbaarraa »? yekhi sfar meyetsama sfar ken
« lbarra »? aleh mouch Tounes?*

/xammət   šwayya w   qālət   ʕlāš "əl-barra"? yāxi sfar   ma-yətsamma

She:thought   a bit   and   she:said   why "abroad"? Thus travel   not-it:is called

sfar   kān   "əl-barra"? ʕlāš   muš   tūnis/

travel   only   "abroad"? why   not   Tunis

Already from the first example, i.e. the first sentence of both versions,
the theme of identity affirmation, through the concept of leaving a *personal touch* (*marque* in the Arabizi text), i.e. a trace of one's identity, appears
central. The first personal goal that Hiba intends to realise through the
journey, and which she expresses through this concept, is therefore to

offer something of herself. Moreover, the concept of *young* (and *jeune* in the Tunisian version) is mentioned, specifying that it is not a question of age but of spirit. The fact that this clarification is only made in English seems to indicate that the theme of youth, in Tunisia, automatically refers to very specific concepts. Without forgetting the digital context and the orthographic system in which these words are shared, and thus the potential youth target of Tunisian readers, we should remind the concept of *youth speech* and its opposition to the established order, mentioned earlier. Hiba thus seems to fit into this social discourse and appeal to these kinds of "youthful" claims, apparently largely shared with her culture (so much so that it does not require specifics in the Arabizi version). This hypothesis seems to be confirmed by the two further concepts, related to the sense of freedom, expressed through the words *wild* and *free*, present, again, only in the English version. This seems to be a further explanation of what was previously expressed through the concept of *youth*. We are here within what we have defined as the pact with the foreign reader. That reader, who, if he comes across her travel blog in Tunisia, is probably a potential tourist of Tunisia, and probably attracted precisely by the wild character of that Mediterranean country. The way in which, in the Arabizi text, Hiba identifies TounsiaDigordia as "[…] you, […] me, […] any young […]" and the fact that she speaks about TounsiaDigordia in the third person, as something that does not belong to her, but to the community, makes this text appearing much more empathetic towards the Tunisian reader, whereas she feels the need to make a pact with the reader of the English text. However, at this point, this appears a little less like a pact, but rather like a guide to empathise with her, her community, her country and her narrative. She is suggesting him to bring with him the tools he will need for the journey. For the reader of the English text, more effort is required in order to understand her story, as he does not share the same cultural background with the blogger.

Also, in the third remark, about why to travel in Tunisia, the difference in approach between English and Tunisian is evident. In English, Hiba guides the reader step by step to let him understand the concept. Starting with more "emotionally distant" topics, she first introduces the concept of proximity (*closer*), then describes a generic *very beautiful country*, which is later defined as her *own country*, and finally named (*Tunisia*). She does not need this step-by-step approach when expressing herself in Tunisian. Moreover, in the Tunisian version, the word for "abroad" (*lbarra*) is emphasised both by vocalic repetition (*lbaaraa*) to reproduce the prosodic features typical of an exclamation, namely a suprasegmental information such as the intonation contour, and by the repetition of the word itself twice, as well as by the angle brackets that highlight both words. This is a further element of otherness, or rather of identity opposition. What is more, this concept of otherness is expressed by the phrase itself, that could be translated as: "She thought a bit and said why 'abrooaad'? Thus, a travel is not considered as a travel if it is not 'abroad'? Why not Tunis?". On the one hand, it is possible that the issue of tourism plays a role in this choice to travel in Tunisia rather than abroad. In fact, it is possible that the economic difficulties due to the drop in tourism may have been perceived as a foreign "condemnation" of Tunisia, due to its situation, seen as unstable.

What is evident is that there is much more empathy and emotional sharing with the reader in the Tunisian text even in this final part of the text in Arabizi. Sentence 3 and 4 both present a number of positive concepts related to Tunisia as seen through Hiba's eyes, and these positive emotions are only shared with the Tunisian readers.

3) *Tounes bled mezyena w men Sud le Nord aandek bech tamla 3inek!*[28]
4) *Tounseyya Digordeya bch ta3tii toute son energie et bonne humeur à une Tunisie qui saura certainement la charmer!*[29]

Could it be that the aim of Hiba's blog is to encourage other Tunisians to travel more in Tunisia to compensate for the gap left by foreign tourism? We will try to answer this question, through an early linguistic and discourse analysis of the Hiba's travel blog, putting on her shoes and following her suggestions.

Hiba's Journey and Signs of Identity Construction, a General Overview

The biography does not leave much doubt about what Hiba perceives as being part of or not, or where she stands in the process of constructing her own identity. But it is also true that she starts out as a traveller discovering Tunisia, thus almost as an "external" participant, or at least external

---

28 Translation: Tunis is a wonderful country and from the South to the North you have a lot to see!

29 Translation: TounsiaDigordia will give all her energy and positivity to a Tunisia that will surely enchant her!

to the characteristics of southern Tunisia, coming from the north of the country. A tourist of the more traditional part of the country[30]. Reading Hiba's blog, we seem to detect a path of evolution that the traveller/narrator makes, along the stages of her journey, which perhaps can also be understood as stages of formation. For example, all along the hitchhiking route, Hiba and her travelling partner meet many drivers who help them get to their destinations. Hiba reports their names, ages and stories. These always appear as examples of life for her. Several social issues are tackled in Hiba's thoughts, such as unemployment among young Tunisians, or the difficult living conditions due to poverty. Furthermore, it is possible to place this blog within the narrative of the female journey, as a metaphor for change, rupture and transformation. The narrator explicitly expresses solidarity with women's issues several times, mainly in English, as we can see in the following example, 5A, from the Kerkennah stage, and 5B, from the El Kef one. Both of these insights of the narrator are absent in the Tunisian narration of the respective stage of the journey.

5) A. [...] *She even got an award from Women's minister some years ago for her creativity. I'm teling you about this lady because she is an example of women keeping hope on life, not giving up.*

   B. [...] *showing mainly how much women were clever in daily life making everything possible out of nothing* [...]

Therefore, in this section, we have tried to highlight the traces of this process, observing Hiba's journey and trying to reveal her positioning, as a narrator addressing different topics and target readers, in relation to her own journey. We mainly considered the languages and spelling systems used in the course of the narration; the personal or impersonal style of the narration (empathy and participation); the connotative/explicative connotations and/or insights developed in the narration, the textual structure and finally the plot, i.e. TounsiaDigordia's journey as a whole. For reasons of space, we report below only a few excerpts from the blog, those we consider most significant in leading the reader along the path of analysis we have undertaken.

---

30 The north-south (and east-west) dichotomy of the country, where the north is the progressive part of the country both economically and socio-politically, and the south is the conservative part of the country from a socio-political and religious point of view, is a dichotomy that has been very much stressed during the Tunisian political processes of the last two centuries. For more details on the Tunisian geographical dichotomy see: Belhedi, Amor. The spatial influence of Tunisian cities via the diffusion of innovative multi-site companies. *Cybergeo: European Journal of Geography*, 2011.

If we wanted to look for a common thread throughout the blog, we could say that it is Hiba's positive attitude, which runs through the whole trip. The narrator does not hesitate to show Hiba's enthusiasm for this journey, right from the first stage, in both languages, as can be seen in the next example, from the Djerba stage.

6) A. *mates2louch kifeh, emchiw plutôt et découvrez ça sur place ! sad9ouni, ça en vaut la peine ?*[31]

B. *It's really a place worth to visit, a must seen in Djerba, a place which can tell you more about Tunisian culture and arts.*

As can be seen from Example 6, empathy towards the Tunisian target is greater than towards the English one. Empathy in Tunisian is evident from the warmer and more informal tones used, highlighted for example by the use of exclamation punctuation, the frequent French insertions, the imperative verbal mode and the use of the semantic sphere of trust. Hiba seems to have a message to spread, particularly to her peers and compatriots from the capital, namely to do the same as she did: leave and go to rediscover her own culture and origins, as is evident from Example 7, where she gives information about the youth hostel she found in Tozeur.

7) A. *3tawna bit mta3 3 menness w fiha douche et wc mte77a w 7atta l wifi zeda w hetha lkol b 4 alef ellila ki tebda étudiant. ETheka aleh ena nchajja3 ay étudiant tounsi bech yestghal les avantages mta3 statut mte3ou fi bledou w y7awwes w yetfarhed w yen3em belli 3andou 7a9 fih.*[32]

B. *Everything was perfect with the room; was clean, comfortable, with its own shower and wc for only 4dt per person for tunisian students, 7dt for non students and 15dt for foreigners. So, yeah tunisian students, go for it!*

The first stages of Hiba in fact have a very "touristic" character: tours of the touristic market in Medenine (Djerba), days spent at the hotel, *perfect sea food, wonderful view, jet sking and sunbathing*, visit to the Ghriba synagogue, city tours or typical tourist attractions, such as the ride on the pirate boat to Ras Rmal, a visit to Chebika, the *Lézard Rouge* train trip to the canyons and finally the desert.

---

31 Translation: Don't ask how, go instead and find out on the spot! Trust me, it's worth it!

32 Translation: They gave us a room for three people, in which there is a shower and a toilet and also the wifi connection and all this for only 4 dinars per night for students. This is why I encourage every Tunisian student to take advantage of the benefits of his status, in his own country, and to travel and enjoy what he is entitled to.

Instead, the last two stages are much more connected to the core of Tunisia ancestral beauty: its history and nature. Towards the end, we find a narrator much more intent on describing Hiba's inner feelings of peace and tranquillity that this journey, globally, has given her. The last two stages are centred on these two elements, and perhaps it is no coincidence that the author of the blog chooses to narrate these two stages not only in English, and the last one also in French, but also in Tunisian encoded in Arabic characters. It is as if, in a way, the target of the Tunisian public with whom she empathises has changed, and thus the mode of communication, at first much more playful and focused on youthful and amusing themes, then much more introspective, reflective, calm and traditional. We report brief excerpts from the El Kef stop, the first one in Arabic characters, from which this change in attitude and the topic of identity discovering are evident.

8) وتزيد أدور في الآثار و تزور متحف، من أزين و أثرى المتاحف التونسية، وين ترا
عادات و تقاليد جدودك يا تونسي أصيل.
و كيف تتعب قد قد، تعطيها حمام، في حمام ملاق، حمام روماني أصل، آثار، مازال
إكيما هو ، الماء جاي مل العين بالكبريت، والراس على 500 فرنك!

/w tzīd tdūr fi-l-āθār w tzūr matḥaf, mən āzyen w āθra l-matāḥif ət-tūnsəyya, wīn tra ʕādāt w taqālīd ždūd-ek ya tūnsi āṣīl. w kīf tətʕab qad qad, taʕṭī-ha ḥammām, fi ḥammām Mallāq, ḥammām rūmāni āṣl, āθār, mā-zāl kīma huwa, l-mā žāy mə-ll-ʕayn bə-l-kibrīt, wə-r-rās ʕala 500 frank!/

"And keep walking around the ruins and visit a museum, among the most beautiful and richest Tunisian museums, where you see the customs and traditions of your ancestors, authentic Tunisians. And as soon as you get tired, take a bath, in the Turkish bath of Malleg, of Roman origin, a ruin, which has remained intact, the water flows from the sulphurous spring, and costs only half dinar per person."

Conclusions

In this study, we have laid the groundwork for analysing a blog that presents interesting characteristics in several respects. First of all, it is a travel blog, the central pivot of which is Tunisia. Around this pivot, various social issues are addressed. Based on our preliminary analysis, we can say that this is in fact a journey of identity formation, of a young Tunisian girl who sets out to discover her origins. This work of digital literature

shares common traits with masterpieces of Mediterranean travel literature, where the journey as an experience of personal growth is a central
theme; among the many examples, there is As-Sindibād, the sailor of the
One Thousand and One Nights, or Odysseus, as well as the protagonists
of Boccaccio's *Decameron*. All these travelers sought in their journeys a
meaning for their existence. In particular, the voyage is the instrument
of knowledge and inner formation, which frees man from his fears; the
means of realising man's constant need to go further, to go elsewhere
out of a desire for knowledge of the unknown, but above all of himself.
On the other hand, the word Mediterranean nowadays is frightening,
divisive, but every journey is worth it for the experience it brings and the
questions it forces us to ask. A little courage is always needed in facing a
journey and a little desire for transformation is always needed to bring a
personal experience to the public plane.

Notes on Contributors

Miriam Al Tawil is an Italian researcher at the University of Vienna, where she also teaches Arabic Language at the Institute of Oriental Studies. She obtained a PhD from "Sapienza" University of Rome and the University of Vienna in October 2023, with a thesis on *Bedouin Arabic Varieties in North-Eastern Jordan*. At present she is employed in a project investigating the Bedouin Arabic dialects in south-eastern Anatolia and in the Middle-Euphrates region.

Silvia Antosa is Associate Professor of English and Director of the Centre for Foreign Languages at the University for Foreigners of Siena. She has published on Victorian fiction, nineteenth-century travel accounts and translations, and contemporary British novels. She is the author of *Frances Elliot and Italy: Writing Travel, Writing the Self* (Mimesis 2018); *Richard Francis Burton: Victorian Explorer and Translator* (Peter Lang, 2012) and *Crossing Boundaries: Bodily Paradigms in Jeanette Winterson's Fiction 1985–2000* (Aracne 2008). She has edited several inter- and transdisciplinary volumes on queer theories and practices, which include: *Queer Crossings: Theories, Bodies, Texts* (Mimesis 2012); *Gender and Sexuality: Rights, Language and Performativity* (Aracne 2012) and *Omosapiens II: Spazi e identità queer* (Carocci 2007). She is the co-editor of the Series *AngloSophia. Studies in English Literature and Culture* (Mimesis) and a member of several international networks of gender and sexuality studies. She has recently co-edited an issue of the journal *de genere* on "Transnational Subjects and Intercultural Identities: the Global South" (2021) and is currently writing on Cultural Discourses on Desire between Women: A Queer Comparative Analysis (with C.E. Ross).

Lorenzo Buonvivere is a PhD candidate in Foreign Languages, Literatures and Cultures at "Roma Tre" University of Rome. He is working on a doctoral project titled "The Language of Ecotourism: An Ecolinguistic Approach". His research interests include ecolinguistics, cognitive linguistics, and Critical Discourse Analysis; he is particularly concerned with the linguistic representation of nature in a variety of discourses. He has recently published on framings and Positive Discourse Analysis in the context of Aotearoa New Zealand, and ecolexicography. His articles have been featured in *Textus* (2023), the *International Journal of English Linguistics* (2023), and the *Journal of World Languages* (2024).

Emanuela Ettorre is Associate Professor of English at "G. d'Annunzio" University of Chieti-Pescara. She has published extensively on Thomas Hardy, George Gissing, Anthony Trollope, Mary Kingsely, Charles Darwin, animal studies, women travel writing and the relationship between science and literature. She has translated three volumes of Victorian short stories and edited the works of Hubert Crackanthorpe with William Greenslade (MHRA, 2020). With Paola Partenza and Özlem Karadag she has coedited the volume *Different Voices. Gender and Posthumanism* (V&R, 2022). She is currently translating George Gissing's *Denzil Quarrier* (Marsilio 2024), and working on an ecolinguistic approach to Victorian voices of resistance.

Elisa Gugliotta obtained her Ph.D. in Arabic Studies in May 2022, with a thesis on *Tunisian Arabizi: Linguistic Analyses and Corpus Building using Natural Language Processing* at Sapienza University of Rome and the University of Grenoble Alpes. In 2023, the French National University Council conferred her the qualification to apply as *maître de conférences* in Arabic Studies and Linguistics. She is an affiliated member of the LIDILEM laboratory of Grenoble (Research axis 1: *Description et modélisation linguistique, corpus, TAL – apprentissage profond et annotation de corpus*). She completed two post-doctoral research projects, one at the Grenoble Informatics Laboratory and the other at the Istituto di Linguistica Computazionale of the CNR in Pisa. Currently, she is engaged in the ANR CLASS project at the LNPL laboratory (*Université Toulouse Jean Jaurès*), exploring the impact of Syrian Arabic as L1 on French language acquisition.

Antonio Gurrieri is Senior Researcher of French Language and Translation at "G. D'Annunzio" University of Chieti-Pescara. His research focuses on the linguistic and literary features of the French-speaking Caribbean. He is also interested in the analysis of contemporary translation and in the Critical Discourse Analysis applied to tourism and literature. His most recent publications include the volume: *Lingua e Parola: La poetica d'Édouard Glissant*, Aracne, Roma 2020; and the essays: "Le métissage linguistique en traduction: Ravines du devant-jour de Raphaël Confiant", *Synergies Italie*, 19, 2023, "La traduction de la créolité dans le roman La Rue Cases-Nègres de Joseph Zobel", *Le Forme e la Storia*, XIV, 2022, "Villa Amalia de Pascal Quignard. Lexiculture et "paramètre pro-drop" en traduction", *Testi e Linguaggi*, XV, 2021, "Langue de spécialité et dimension lexiculturelle: décrire et traduire la terminologie du patrimoine gastronomique sicilien", *FAEM* XXX, 50, 2020.

Lorella Martinelli is Full Professor of French Language and Translation at "G. d'Annunzio" University of Chieti-Pescara. She is the author of the volumes: *Tristan Corbière. Il linguaggio del disdegnoso e altri saggi di letteratura estrema* (Napoli, ESI, 2001); *Gli amori gialli. Canone in versi e identità poetica in Tristan Corbière: selezione di liriche con testo a fronte* (Pescara, Tracce, 2012). She has edited a French edition of Tristan Corbière's *Amours jaunes* (Paris, L'Harmattan, 2007), and translated the first Italian edition of *Il Negriero* by Édouard Corbière (Massa, Transeuropa, 2014). In the theoretical perspective of French Discourse Analysis, she has published the volume *Retorica e argomentazione nelle Amours jaunes di Tristan Corbière* (Roma, Carocci, 2017), and translated Sophie Moirand's work, *I discorsi della stampa quotidiana. Osservare, analizzare, comprendere* (Roma, Carocci, 2020).

Carlo Martinez is Full Professor of American Literature at "Sapienza", University of Rome, after teaching for twenty-five years at "G. d'Annunzio" University of Chieti-Pescara. He is the author of a book on Henry James's *Prefaces* (*L'arte della critica. Ideologia estetica e forma narrativa nelle Prefazioni di Henry James*, Roma 2001) and two books on Edgar Allan Poe (Liguori 1998; Marsilio 2014). His articles have appeared in *The Edgar Allan Poe Review*, *Arizona Quarterly*, *The Review of International American Studies*, *Ácoma*, and various other journals. His latest publication is a translation and critical edition of a short-story by Edmund Wilson set in the "Abruzzi" at the end of WWII (*Attraverso gli Abruzzi con Mattie e Harriet*, Ianieri edizioni, Pescara, 2024).

Giuliano Mion is Full Professor of Arabic Language and Literature at the University of Cagliari. He is specialised in linguistics and dialectology and is author of many publications dealing with Standard Arabic, Middle

Arabic, Arabic phonetics, Jordanian sociolinguistics, Tunisian dialects, and popular culture. He is currently working on the concept of time and temporality in the Arab classical culture and other Semitic cultures. He is a member of the scientific board of the PhD programme on Civilizations of Asia and Africa at Sapienza University of Rome, and he is the supervisor of several theses dealing with Arabic dialectology.

Paola Partenza is Associate Professor of English Literature at "G. d'Annunzio" University of Chieti-Pescara. She has published a volume on Tennyson's poetry, on women writings and on Jane Austen. She is author of essays in collections and journals. She is Editor-in-Chief of the book series *Passages – Transitions – Intersections* (Göttingen: Vandenhoeck & Ruprecht); she edited *Dynamics of Desacralization. Disenchanted Literary Talents* (2015) and *Sin's Multifaceted Aspects in Literary Texts* (2018). She has published on the concept of *Ecotopia* in Sylvia Townsend Warner (2019), and on the idea of *empathy* and the *unsaid* in Kazuo Ishiguro's *A Pale View Hills* (2019). With Emanuela Ettorre and Özlem Karadag she has edited the volume *Different Voices. Gender and Posthumanism* (V&R, 2022).

Adrian Tait, Ph.D., is an independent scholar and environmental critic. He has published widely in scholarly journals such as *Green Letters: Studies in Ecocriticism, Ecozon@*, and the *European Journal of English Studies*, and contributed to essay collections such as *Gendered Ecologies: New Materialist Interpretations of Women Writers in the Long Nineteenth Century* (Clemson University Press, 2020), *Apocalyptic Visions in the Anthropocene and the Rise of Climate Fiction* (Cambridge Scholars Publishing, 2021), and *Animals in Detective Fiction* (Palgrave Macmillan, 2022). His first monograph, *Environmental Justice in Early Victorian Literature*, was published by Routledge in 2023.

Moving Texts / Testi Mobili

Edited By Natalie Dupré – Monica Jansen – Inge Lanslots – Ugo Perolino – Mara Santi – Dieter Vermandere

Moving Texts/Testi mobili questions Italian memory and identity from the perspective of literary and media studies, providing a forum for discussions on major research topics, including migration and mobility studies, cultural studies, cultural memory studies, film studies, translation studies and studies on linguistic attitudes and sociolinguistic changes.

Moving Texts/Testi mobili is open to research conducted within established and emerging fields of investigation. It specifically promotes multi-perspective, multi-disciplinary and inter-medial approaches. The series uses double-blind peer review and is supported by an international advisory board. Proposals in Italian, French or English are welcome.

Potential contributors are invited to submit a book proposal consisting of an outline, a sample chapter and a CV. Only complete manuscripts following the series guidelines are accepted for peer review.

For further information or proposals, please contact one of the series editors:

Natalie Dupré (KU Leuven – natalie.dupre@kuleuven.be), Monica Jansen (Universiteit Utrecht – m.m.jansen@uu.nl), Inge Lanslots (KU Leuven – inge.lanslots@kuleuven.be), Ugo Perolino (Università degli Studi "G. D'Annunzio", Chieti-Pescara – ugo.perolino@unich.it), Mara Santi (Universiteit Gent, mara.santi@ugent.be), Dieter Vermandere (Universiteit Antwerpen – dieter.vermandere@uantwerpen.be).

Ultimi Volumi Pubblicati

Vol. 1 – GIAN PAOLO GIUDICETTI, *Mandricardo e la melanconia. Discorsi diretti e sproloqui nell' "Orlando Furioso";*